The Man in the Pulpit
DER MANN AUF DER KANZEL
Questions for a Father
FRAGEN AN EINEN VATER

University of Nebraska Press: Lincoln and London

Publication of
this translation was
assisted by a grant
from Inter Nationes.
© 1979 Carl Hanser
Verlag, München·
Wien. Translation
copyright © 1997
by the University of
Nebraska Press.
All rights reserved.
Manufactured in
the United States of
America.

⊛ The paper in
this book meets the
minimum require-
ments of American
National Standard
for Information Sci-
ences – Permanence
of Paper for Printed
Library Materials,
ANSI Z39.48-1984.

Library of Congress Cataloging in Publication Data: Rehmann, Ruth.
[Mann auf der Kanzel. English] The man in the pulpit: questions for a
father / Ruth Rehmann: translated by Christoph Lohmann and Pamela
Lohmann. p. cm. – (European women writers series) Includes biblio-
graphical references. ISBN 0-8032-3917-3 (cloth: alkaline paper). –
ISBN 0-8032-8960-X (paperback: alkaline paper) 1. Rehmann, Ruth –
Biography. 2. Authors, German – 20th century – Biography. I. Title.
II. Series. PT2678.E32Z46613 1997 833'.914–dc20 96-13097 CIP

The Man in the Pulpit

Ruth Rehmann

Translated by Christoph Lohmann and Pamela Lohmann

Contents

The publication of my third book, *Der Mann auf der Kanzel*, in the late 1970s caused curiously conflicting reactions. Older people, mostly belonging to the educated German bourgeoisie, which was then already in the process of disintegration, were filled with indignation about the "irreverence" of a daughter who presumed to "expose" her father in his different roles in life—as a father, a minister, a citizen of the Third Reich. The emotional level at which the accusations were made revealed that these people felt personally attacked. Christians and church officials resented any critical examination of various attitudes within the church toward the Nazi regime. Apparently my approach violated the tacit agreement that the churches, even if not engaged in active resistance, had been a stronghold of spiritual and intellectual integrity resisting demonic temptation. They pointed to resistance fighters and political martyrs within the church without considering that their church rarely gave them support but often treated them with resentment and isolation instead. For these representatives of the church, the truly upsetting aspect of my work appears to have been the "illegitimate interlacing" of personal remembrance with a scholarly, source-based inquiry into political and social conditions.

By the same reasoning but with exactly opposite assumptions, the younger readers of the radical movement of '68 raised their objections. They accused me of being much too gentle, too emotional, too considerate in treating a father who both in his pastoral office and by virtue of the fateful connection between kindness and incorrigible blindness contributed to the continued existence of an unjust political system.

These intense controversies reflected the hopelessly strife-torn German efforts at "coming to terms with the past"—a process that was once again called into question by the younger generation's attack on their parents' collective silence.

The loud noise of the debate drowned out the questions and insights of my book as well as the voices of those who were moved and liberated by it. I heard from them only in numerous letters and conversations.

The central question of the book is not Why have our parents done or failed to do this or that? but Why didn't they see what was happening? It relates to the formulaic phrase with which occupation forces and returning emigrants were met in all quarters after the war: "I didn't know anything, hear anything, see anything—no concentration camps, murder of Jews, horrors of war, etc." I myself, born in 1922, never used this formula, not because of a concern for its subjective truth but out of shame for having grown up among crimes and not retaining the least little part of them in my memory. That is unforgivable. Where, for heaven's sake, was I looking with my eyes?

In the effort to reconstruct my own thoughts and feelings of that time I had to return to my parents and the home that for me had always been particularly identified with my father, whose aura defined my life and my thinking far beyond the years of childhood—a father who abhorred lies and never lied himself, yet most likely would have used this dreadful formula had he lived through the end of the war.

Did my father lie? Did we all lie? What could have made us say these things?

I entered his life by way of my own memories, accompanied by written and oral testimony stored up by my family. But already in the description of my father's study—which I used as a sort of introductory exposition—I felt compelled not only to tell his personal story but also to examine the relevant contexts and influences in the light of my question. Hence the inevitable need to focus on the church and its contradictory actions and their consequences.

Reading through piles of contemporary writings, lectures, sermons, and church publications, I found that my father's inability to see was indicative of a widespread "fogginess" that prevented especially his tradition-bound social class from recognizing the signs of the times and taking a Christian stance toward them. Seeing, as well as thinking and acting, is of course a selective process, largely conditioned by a matrix of tradition, upbringing, and social context, by which certain things are defined as essential and others disappear from view as being unessential. This commonplace acquired a culpable significance against the background of a time of murder and terror — a significance from which I could not distance myself, because I myself had lived during that time but had seen nothing. But I learned that there had been people of the same social class and sphere of influence who had freed themselves from the matrix with its blind spots and fogginess in order to achieve a new perspective and a readiness for action. So it was possible — even then.

But such breakthroughs in perception never resulted from isolated thought, private faith, or scriptural reading but through conversations with others who saw more and saw differently and communicated their transformed view of the world in their attitudes and actions. That is why toward the end of the book I draw the conclusion that the cause of my father's inability to see was his isolation, which he assumed in conformance with the traditional concept of the pastoral office and which his congregation expected of him. In the last few pages I have tried to describe this isolation, which I know all too well from personal memory.

I wrote this book a long time ago. As I was reading it again for the first time, now in its English translation, I was struck by the fear that today we might also be surrounded by a fogginess that obscures our view of the world and inhibits our actions. It would now be differently constituted and situated than in those years. Swept along by streams of information, we are likely to see too much rather than too little, yet we see things in a way that produces surfeit and a sense of powerlessness because the basic causes and coherences drown in the plethora of propagandistically presented details.

The fogginess of our own time seems to lie between seeing and acting, and it seems to consist of the complexity, ambivalence, and anonymity of the social structures within which we live, as well as the loneliness of the individual. Used and abused by competition and consumption, the isolated individual does not bother to understand what he or she sees and refuses to act in concert with others, drawing on their knowledge and goodwill. Blindly tapping around in the fog, we may miss the opportunity to affect the course of politics and timidly withdraw into the safe ark of fundamentalism to listen again to the pious words preached by my lonely father: doing good in the small and humble place to which God has assigned us, leaving the rest to Him, for He shall provide.

But He doesn't provide—He certainly didn't in Germany in 1933. . . .

Ruth Rehmann's *The Man in the Pulpit: Questions for a Father*, first published in German as *Der Mann auf der Kanzel: Fragen an einen Vater* in 1979, is a book of many genres: partly biography and partly autobiography, in some ways fiction but in large part history, it is also a book of social and political analysis. She herself once called it a *Selbstfindungsbuch* — a book of self-discovery. That word certainly pinpoints one of her central concerns and perhaps even more if one understands the process of discovering the self not only in individual, psychological terms but also in terms of a larger context: a discovery of the self in the context of family and community, region, class, gender, and political, social, and cultural institutions.

Central to this book is not only the question Who am I, Ruth Rehmann, daughter of a Protestant pastor,[1] born in 1922, mother of a son and two daughters, who are asking me in the mid-1970s about my childhood and my parents? There is also the larger, infinitely more complicated set of questions: Who are we, the Germans who became adults after World War II? How do we view and relate to the generation of our parents, to their moral and political guilt or blindness? How do we understand them and render them for ourselves and for our children without either rushing to swift and thoughtless judgment or making excuses for them out of misplaced sympathy, affection, or equally thoughtless love?

The art and substance of Rehmann's (auto)biography lie in the movements that connect personal experience, specific observation, and vignettes of family and community life with the historical events that swept over Germany in the half-century leading up to its destruction in 1945. But these movements do not just establish more or less mechanical connections between the personal and historical. Rather, Rehmann weaves a fabric whose texture and pattern emerge from a skillful intertwining of the two strands. Thus, personal experiences, family anecdotes, house furnishings, the texts of sermons and letters, dreams, songs, books, conversations and arguments, jokes, festivities, acts of friendship and animosity—all take on larger dimensions in the historical context. By the same token, the Kaiser, World War I, the Weimar Republic, political and class conflicts, the rise of Nazism, the manipulations and brutalities of Hitler's henchmen, and the political and theological rifts within the Protestant church take on a palpable reality as they are rendered through lived and felt experience.

The thread that holds it all together is the subtle and penetrating, loving and critical analysis of the relationship between daughter and father. Rehmann did not begin this project until thirty years after her father's death, but in pursuing it she reaches far back into his childhood and youth during the last two decades of the nineteenth century, to his years as a volunteer army chaplain during World War I, and to his early experiences as a young minister. The occasion for beginning this exploration is a question from her son—a student of history, a young Marxist of the radical student generation of the 1970s—during a trip that takes the family to the small town of Auel, where Rehmann grew up. With the pointed skepticism typical of his generation, he asks how a man of legendary piety and probity of conscience like his grandfather managed to get through the Nazi period without either compromising his integrity or ending up in a concentration camp.

During the author's first visit to Auel since her childhood, she seeks out the old schoolteacher, Herr Limbach, a man of incisive intelligence and political awareness, who was in many ways her father's political opponent, yet a close acquaintance, almost a friend. He was the "Red" (Socialist) village schoolteacher who had worked his way out of the working class without quite reaching the status of the educated, "academic" bourgeoisie of the minister's family, for whom the German nation and its Kaiser were the manifestations of God's order on earth. In three long and memorable sessions—one during her first visit to Auel and the last one just before the schoolteacher's death—the author gains crucial and penetrating insights into her father's personality and ideology, his profound religious faith, and his role as a strong and effective, but also stubbornly otherworldly and politically naive, pastor of his flock. The schoolteacher helps the author understand how and why a man like her father, with all his intelligence and personal warmth, with all his insistence on constantly probing his conscience in the light of his faith, was ultimately capable of remaining blind to the political devastations taking place in his beloved church and in the country at large.

Rehmann's account moves from the early stages of the child's adoring love for her father to the young woman of eighteen who, now preoccupied with her interest in young men, does not know how to relate to a dying, lonely old man. At first we see them hop-skipping hand in hand, singing and chanting in unison ("The two of us. . . . nothing in the world was ever going to drive us apart"), jumping over puddles, laughing, as the child accompanies her father on his visits to his parishioners. In the end, they sit forlornly on a bench by the Rhine River, she impatient to get away to meet her date, he trying to hold her, trying to reach out to her for comfort and companionship as the loneliness of approaching death threatens to isolate him from everybody, even his closest family. The evolving relationship that ties these two scenes together is subtly drawn in its complex twists and turns, always seen from the perspective of the mature consciousness of the author in her mid-fifties, whose intellectual, social, and political commitments provide her with a sure sense of differentiation both from her earlier self and from her father.

At the time of its first publication, *The Man in the Pulpit* heralded the appearance of what in retrospect has been identified as a spate of *Vaterbücher* or *Väterliteratur*—books or literature about fathers—by a generation of younger Germans who, both psychologically and politically, were calling to account the generation that had participated in the rise of Nazism, World War II, and the horrors of the Holocaust. Among the authors and titles belonging to this group are Heinrich Wiesner's *Der Riese am Tisch* (1979), Jutta Schutting's *Der Vater* (1980), Peter Härtling's *Nachgetragene Liebe* (1980), Brigitte Schwaiger's *Lange Abwesenheit* (1983), and Ludwig Harig's *Ordnung ist das ganze Leben* (1985). These books are often confrontational in tone and substance, with the authors, in a manner of speaking, setting themselves up as judges—almost executioners—of their fathers. In the words of a recent critic, "As most of these narratives reveal, an investigation of Germany's fascist past entails a confrontation with the father. The father, as active or passive participant in the Third Reich (in gesture, or by default, if not in spirit), is placed on the witness stand and retried. . . . The literature of the fathers thus lends valuable insight into the intersection of history and the private sphere."[2]

However, contrary to many other "father books," anger and hostility are noticeably absent from Rehmann's book: she does not so much accuse as pose "questions for a father." Yet she consistently maintains a sharp and uncompromising definition of political and philosophical differences between herself and her father, while conveying a strong sense of her deep affection for a man who obviously exerted a powerful influence on her emotional and intellectual development. By tracing and articulating the nuances of this personal relationship, Rehmann manages to give a new resonance to her larger, historical project, which is to define the situation of the modern, socially and politically engaged German woman in relation not only to "the father" (that is, her own father) but to "the fathers"—the patriarchs who hover over the history of German Protestantism and nationalism: Luther, Bismarck, the Kaiser, Hitler.

This connection between the project of exploring her relationship to her personal past and the larger historical-cultural project is subtly underscored in the German original by Rehmann's insistent reference to her own family as "the family," to her father as "the father," and to herself as "the child," a practice that is well within common and idiomatic usage in German. It is part of her strategy to see herself, her childhood, and her family as though she—the mature author—were a dispassionate outside observer, a different identity, someone removed in time, age, political circumstance, and ideology, someone who looks at "a family" or "the family" as a sociologist or a social historian rather than as a daughter. However, even at the risk of injecting a somewhat more personal note that tends to diminish the author's strategy of distancing, the English translation could not retain this persistent stylistic device without becoming unidiomatic. Hence, most of these references to the father, the mother, and other family members had to be rendered as "Father" and "Mother," "my father," "my mother," or "her father" and "her mother." Yet it was important to keep the author's original references to her earlier self as "the child" (in later chapters as "the daughter"), but even in this case the translation loses some of the stylistic subtlety of the original. Because in German "Kind" is a neuter noun, "it" connotes an object of retrospective analysis, a being that appears to be in a still ungendered stage of life, almost an impersonal thing. The English usage of "she" or "her" in reference to the child weakens that objectification because it emphasizes the child's gendered humanity.

It is only at the very end, just before the scene of father and daughter sitting on a bench by the river, that Rehmann reveals how deliberately she has maintained all along her authorial distance from the autobiographical persona of the child (now the young woman): "I see the two figures approaching out of the darkness under the bridge ramp," she writes in reference to herself and her father, "but not so close that I could (or would want to) begin to say 'I' to the girl dressed in a pleated skirt." If the reader has somehow missed noticing the persistent strategy of distancing, this sentence drives home Rehmann's refusal to merge her earlier and later identities; it highlights her consistent omission of a name for "the child" throughout the book; it brings into focus her grammatically appropriate designation of the child as a neutralized thing, an object of historical study.

The problem of deciding how to deal with the definite article in connection with father, mother, and child and the elision of the neuter gender in reference to the child suggest only two of the many difficulties encountered in translating this text into English. Another, far greater, difficulty was to render for the English-speaking reader the abundance of allusions and references to German culture, history, politics, and the institutions of both the Protestant church and the Nazi regime. Even with the closest attention to detail and the greatest fidelity to the German original, many evocative nuances are inevitably lost in translation. For example, German readers of Rehmann's generation will hear in their minds not only the specific melodies but the historically or culturally significant associations every time she mentions a song—and her book is full of references to folk songs, children's songs, art songs (lieder), hymns, and political songs of all kinds. Similarly, the mystique of the Rhine as Germany's river evokes both a strong aura of romantic feelings and equally strong patriotic sentiments—or derision of such romantic-patriotic bombast, if the reader is of a different generation and mind-set. Both the romantic and the patriotic responses derive from familiarity with an abundance of poems, fairy tales, folklore, political propaganda, and popular songs that have shaped German cultural consciousness on virtually all social levels. Rehmann plays on these feelings and associations, often satirizing them in subtle and witty ways to convey multiple meanings.

Yet much of the thickness of the cultural tapestry Rehmann presents can still be seen and felt in translation even without a large number of explanatory notes, which would be more distracting than helpful. On a few occasions explanatory notes seemed unavoidable, irresistible, or simply useful to the non-German reader. However, even well-educated Germans who were born a decade or more after the end of World War II are likely to have difficulties with a good many of Rehmann's references and allusions. As for references to persons, many of the historical, political, theological, or cultural figures mentioned by the author can easily be identified by consulting any standard desk encyclopedia and therefore need no explanatory notes. Yet we wanted to underscore the importance throughout this text of several important Protestant theologians, such as Harnack, Schlatter, Niemöller, Barth, and Tillich, by providing notes for them. Several other, more obscure persons are sufficiently defined by the context and need no further explanation.

As translators, we hope that *The Man in the Pulpit* will contribute to a deeper, more complex understanding, among English-speaking readers, of the course of German history during the twentieth century. That is a large subject, and Rehmann's exploration of a very small part of it—her own middle-class, nationalist, Protestant family and the struggle between church and state under Hitler—cannot possibly do it all. But it is precisely the sharp focus on the specific and the personal—on the feelings and beliefs, on the psychological and ideological dimensions of people she knew and loved and disagreed with—that penetrates deeply beneath familiar generalizations about German society and politics. What remains the most remarkable quality of this book is the honesty with which Ruth Rehmann looks at herself, her origins, and her responsibilities as a writer; how she—through both her acceptance of her father and her resistance to him—defines her identity in her own struggle with the glories and the horrors, the achievements and the crimes of Germany's history and the patriarchal figures who shaped that history.

ACKNOWLEDGMENTS

We are very fortunate to have had the author's counsel during the process of translating her book: Ruth Rehmann's excellent knowledge of English, her willingness to help us understand some of the more difficult passages and references in her text, and the friendship she extended to us made our work much easier as well as personally gratifying. Our thanks also go to friends and colleagues at Indiana University, especially Patrick Brantlinger, Paul John Eakin, and Alvin Rosenfeld of the Department of English, who took an early interest in this translation project and urged us to continue with it.

The Man in the Pulpit

For my children

Virtue became the servant of vice, reason the servant of madness, humility the servant of arrogance, loyalty the servant of duplicity, conscientiousness the servant of baseness. Hence that terrible alliance between those who were honorable and those who were dishonorable: it was the secret of Germany's—albeit transitory—power.

Friedrich Wilhelm Foerster

Whenever we walked together, my father and I, we used to chant the refrain, "The two of us." It expressed a special bond between him and me, the oldest and the youngest in the family, and meant that nothing in the world was ever going to drive us apart. Starting on the left foot, we would hit the ground hard with the right foot at the word "two." Whispering and stamping our feet, we would walk through the streets of Auel, where my father was the Protestant pastor. He told me that his father, who had also been a minister, had walked with him, who was also the youngest, just that way through the streets of St. Goar and along the Rhine promenade, greeting, waving, discussing boats and water levels with the river pilots, and getting freshly baked buns from the baker; and all the children, even those who were Catholic, had come running to jump over his father's, my grandfather's, walking stick. . . .

I rarely return to Auel. While we were on vacation last year it wasn't my idea to spend the night there. I would have stayed on the autobahn and driven on all the way to Holland, even late at night. Thomas, the oldest, could have spelled me at the wheel from time to time. It was the girls, Johanna and Elisabeth, who, just as it was getting dark, wanted to visit Auel, the town where I had spent my childhood. The discussion began as we reached the Siebengebirge,[1] a drawn-out and contentious argument so typical of this family lacking a father, lacking the voice of authority. That is how we missed the first exit and had to take the second one farther north; and as soon as we turned into the forest at Lohmar I was caught up in a current that pulled me away from my children. It was impossible to tell them that we were entering the town by the back road, the bad, forbidden way through the woods, where girls were not allowed to walk by themselves; that we approached the cemetery from its ugly side, passing its portal with a guilty conscience (When did you last visit Hanneli's grave?), and proceeded down the dreary Auelgasse, the alley of funereal Sunday afternoon excursions: father, mother, and four children on their way to their dead sister, pressed tightly together by the burden of mourning under Mother's large, black umbrella braced sideways against the driving rain: Do not despair, o little flock. . . .

Then, at the corner of Kaiserstraße, the sudden entrance into the warm paternal ambience: holding his hand, "visiting the congregation," being recognized and greeted with beaming benevolence. How the child has grown! Her hair is like Hanneli's! She's going to be another Hanneli!

"She's growing," the father says with modest pride. "She's a real joy and pleasure."

A warm, dry hand reaching down from above. The soft inside of the fingers between the joints. The pressure of the wedding ring. Stepping in unison despite the difference in size. He takes short steps with his long legs; the child, with her short legs, tries to keep up. Holding hands, we swing our arms sometimes high enough to make a full circle, quickly changing our grasp at the top, but never letting go. Fancy footwork: hop-skipping, kicking a stone or a chestnut, jumping over puddles, stomping into puddles, wiping off splashes with his handkerchief. Large, white father-handkerchief with a drop of cologne. Hiking songs: The chimneysweep went for a walk . . . When the soldiers go marching through the town . . . Go forth my heart, be merry.

"Up there," I say, pointing through the car window at the dark house that we called our own even though it never belonged to us but to the congregation, which in the meantime has sold it to the gravestone company next door. "Up there, behind the last window on the left, I saw my father sitting underneath the portrait of his father when I came home from school. I would stop at the garden gate and whistle our special signal but not enter until he waved to me. But when I had a guilty conscience I would take the back way, over the wall topped with pieces of broken glass, through the basement door, and up the back stairway."

"Were you afraid of him?" asks Elisabeth, who knows nothing about being afraid of fathers.

"I was afraid I might cause him sorrow," I reply. Sorrow: what an old-fashioned word.

The daughters would like to have known him, a really old-fashioned pastor in a black frock coat and stand-up collar. The ministers they know are of the briskly modern type. They dress like normal people and refer to yesterday's TV program in class. Rather than speaking of the Heavenly Father, they talk about divine essence; instead of brotherly love, it is social commitment.

My father was different.

The things he left us are somehow part of, yet separate from, our household: inkwell, blotter, pen case made of Lebanese cedar, silver letter scale, long pipes with porcelain bowls, Grandfather's illustrated Bible ("To our pastor with gratitude and love from his congregation. St. Goar, 19 September 1885"), two-piece desk with an upright cabinet that once had been chock-full of theology but is now used by Thomas to store his Marx, Engels, and Lenin, the drawers still retaining a whiff of pipe-tobacco smoke. Letters, photographs, and bundles of sermons are stored in three wooden boxes.

How did he ever learn to write this tiny hand, thin and fragile like a spider's web? A twenty-minute Sunday sermon fills but half a page. The old German script with pointed ascenders and descenders; abbreviations nobody can understand: G.b.w.—what's that supposed to mean?

It means: God be willing. They think that's cool. Did he really believe in that?

Johanna wants to use the inkwell—a crystal cube with rounded silver lid (sterling?)—as a stand for burning incense. That would look neat! Can you still smoke those long pipes with their porcelain bowls? Everything is transformed by nostalgia: the pipes, the inkwell, the Christian faith.

It must have been really terrific to have a father who smoked long pipes and dipped his pen, a steel nib held in a wooden holder, into a silver inkwell. A father who believed—in God and all that.

I do not want to talk about my father that way! They don't understand: how else would you talk about him?

Thomas, a second-year history student, would like to know how my father, who lived from 1875 to 1940, behaved under the Nazis. He thinks that preachers played an extremely dubious role, except for Niemöller,[2] who is taking the right stand even today. What was your father's attitude toward Niemöller?

"He was an apolitical person," I say. "He acted according to his conscience."

"And, if one may ask, how did he manage to do that?"

By accepting every morning the command of the Bible and the daily devotion of the Moravian Brethren of Herrnhut.[3]

By practicing thorough self-scrutiny every night before going to bed, just as it had been recommended to the children:

Examine your conscience! Reflect upon the events of the day in the light of God's demands—not only upon words and deeds but upon the consequences of words and deeds: thoughts, feelings, desires, attitudes. . . .

Make up for failures, correct errors and lies, and make amends for your mistakes. Whatever you cannot undo, submit in penitent prayer to Him and to those against whom you have trespassed.

Confess your wrongdoings, ask for forgiveness, accept punishment with gratitude. For whom the Lord loveth He chasteneth.

Thomas does not understand how such a superconscience could get through the period of the brownshirts without ending in a concentration camp.

We have always communicated well with each other, Thomas and I, even when we argue about my "bourgeois consciousness," his "party-line mind," my "basic trust in the system" (which, he believes, really needs to be thoroughly questioned), his "scientific" view of history (which I call his "ersatz religion"). But we have never been able to talk about my father.

"Preachers," he snorts, releasing the inner pressure of pent-up anger through narrow lips. Then he gets over it and carries on with the discussion calmly and rationally, as he learned to do in political student groups at the university. But that doesn't fool me. I know that tone of repressed anger. There was a time when I heard and feared it. And then I remember when it was and who did it. It was my father angrily spitting out the word: proletarians!

We stayed overnight at the Hotel zum Goldenen Stern, which I never set foot in as a child because it was not considered proper for the minister's family to be seen in the local beer joints, particularly if the proprietor was a Catholic.

At breakfast, Johanna insisted that I had talked in my sleep, in an unnaturally high-pitched, complaining voice: "I can't do it . . . I'm asleep . . . can't you see that I'm asleep?"

"They surrounded me," I explained, overcome in the middle of our breakfast chat with the fear and paralysis of my dream.

"They stood around my bed as I lay naked and asleep, looking down at me out of their clever little faces with stealthy glances. They thought I was retarded the way I was babbling in my dreams without making sense. I tried like crazy to gain some kind of rational control. But it didn't work. I couldn't wake up. . . ."

"Let's leave," I said. "This tepid Rhineland air really makes me ill." On the way to the car an elderly lady walked up to us. "Isn't this a familiar face?" As she spoke, she did not look at me but at Thomas, who the older members of the family say is, among all the grandchildren, most like Grandfather in both looks and personality: in Grandfather's case they called it his "human warmth" and in Thomas's his "natural charm." Both have an "easy way" with people, the "Rhenish temperament," the gift of quickly gaining other people's hearts, and a "winsome" eloquence, which the minister used in his sermons and spiritual counseling and which the grandson . . . oh well, the family isn't supposed to know about that.

"The spitting image," said the old lady, whom I had in the meantime recognized as one of the "faithful parishioners," while she spotted me as "the Reverend's youngest." Now, of course, we absolutely had to come with her to her apartment, her "cozy little nest." She had something to show us: a photograph of the festivities in 1925, when the Reverend consecrated the church bells at Auel and gave a memorable address, in which he explained that the new bells had been tuned to harmonize with those of St. Servatius so that the sounds of praise coming from both denominations would fall sweetly on the Lord's ear. That was just like him, she said: a man of understanding and harmony, a peacemaker blessed by God. As long as he had been minister at Auel, Catholics and Protestants had not quarreled, and there had been no conflict between the church and the state either. He had held his flock together by the sheer power of his heart and soul, and when they later scattered in all directions it broke his heart. She knew very well whose fault that was, but she didn't want to mention names. But the name had come to me already. I knew it as soon as she said "fault": Limbach! The "Red" schoolteacher Limbach, who by now must be close to a hundred years old.

"Ninety-two," the lady said. "He is now living with his daughter."

She did not know any further details, nor did she want to know them. She would not have anything to do with "Reds"—atheists, anarchists, and terrorists. "Your father would have been better off if he had done likewise, but then he was always such a generous man . . . without guile, like the doves."

As we said good-bye in the hallway, she recalled yet another fond memory. She could still see, as if it had happened yesterday, the Reverend standing next to his Catholic colleague and the mayor, a storm trooper, on the platform, which was festively decorated with swastika flags. In moving words he thanked the Lord of all history for the happy turn of events—the very picture of the unity of the patriotic church and the Christian state. If she had a photograph of the event, she would place it next to that of Hitler shaking hands with Hindenburg at Potsdam[4]—another symbolic image.

She waved at us from the second-floor window as we left: her rosy-powdered face behind glass, framed by little white curls and faded pink curtains—incorrigible, indestructible, immovable, that generation!

"Sometime you should have a talk with that Red schoolteacher about your father, but I guess you don't really want to," Thomas said on the way back to the car, less in anger than in resignation, a verbal kind of shrug. My reaction was inappropriately harsh, even hostile: "What is that supposed to mean?" They looked at me rather shocked: What's the matter with her?

Whispering to each other like doctors at a patient's bedside,

12

they waited outside the phone booth while I checked the directory under L, dialed the number, and made an appointment with the teacher's daughter for that afternoon: "Yes, my father is at home; he is available, he'll be glad." Only Thomas understood that I was serious when I asked him to take the car and go on ahead with the girls and leave me in Auel for a day or two.

They dropped me off at the garden gate of the schoolteacher's house; they waved, so did I. Tears, but that's nothing special. In this family we all cry and laugh easily and copiously. It is our legacy from St. Goar, from Auel.

As I walked up to the house, rosebushes on either side of me, the children had already dropped out of my mind, leaving an empty space in which the schoolteacher Limbach could now freely appear: hands clasped behind his back, wandering across the yard of the Protestant elementary school on Humperdinckstraße, gaunt frame, his shoulders already slightly stooped, lank limbs, shiny, black hair that always hung in strands over his deep-set eyes. You can tell from his looks, Mother says: the fanatic, the radical, the Red Socialist! That dark, shifty, devious look. Can't look you straight in the eye. Can't give you a decent handshake.

"Foe," she calls him. "The evil spirit of our Christian community."

He unfolded himself out of his armchair, even lankier, more desiccated than I had remembered him. Still thick and tousled, his hair had turned white, and there was no trace of flesh on his sharply protruding cheekbones, nothing but brown-spotted, leathery skin. I shook his hand and saw—hardly believing my eyes—actually saw for the first time that his eyes, instead of being dark, flickering, secretive as we had always described them, were actually a deep and quiet gray.

Did he have different eyes in those days? Did we see him with different eyes?

That there are people in Auel who still speak of him as the "Red schoolteacher" elicited a dry cackle from him, which

gradually changed into a cough. After all, he had been appointed principal after 1945, and he had never truly been
"Red"; rather what today one would call a radical democrat.
A member of the rapidly diminishing German Democratic
party before 1933, he quit after the last five legislative representatives had thrown in their ridiculous yes votes in favor
of the Enabling Act.[5] After that, no more party membership,
only the Confessing church ("If you are old enough to know
what that was"). The Reverend decided differently. Yet they
continued to work well together, and after the minister retired, he, the Red schoolteacher, was among the few, and in
the end the only one, who visited him at his sickbed in Bonn.
You surely remember that much. But, no, I didn't. Even
Mother had never spoken of it. And if she had spoken of it,
I had forgotten. The teacher said that it was really interesting
to track down the workings of a family's memory, what it
transmits and what it doesn't, and to ask yourself why.

"The family's memory is no longer functioning," I told him.
"It suffers from interference in the transmission line: Nazi period, war, total collapse and chaos. How do you talk about
fathers who were neither Nazi criminals nor resistance fighters? How do you maintain their living individuality in the
process of grinding them through the mill of generalizations
and sweeping judgments? How do you protect them against
being distorted by images of horror or wishful thinking? How
do you explain the difference between the actual experience
and a retrospection of the past without falling into that sick-
eningly apologetic tone, that tone of I-was-too-young, I-never-
saw-anything, I-had-no-part-in-it?"

The teacher made talking easy for me. Ensconced in his
armchair, his eyes turned to the window overlooking the garden, he listened quietly and attentively, nodding every now
and then, helping me along with short interjections, and giving me the feeling that my monologue was actually a conversation, the first one after all those broken-off, derailed attempts, choked in misunderstanding, of the past few years.

Do you know what I mean, Herr Limbach: the distance

14

between generations as soon as one attempts to give a historical account? The change in language itself that comes with the effort to make oneself understood across the distance? The wrong notes produced by that effort? As if something had to be hidden—dark blemishes, dirty little secrets. . . . Do you know the disgust at hearing those wrong notes in your own voice as it wrestles with the truth, and the macabre desire to find the dark secret, the hidden dirt, so as to get over it once and for all: that's what he was like; that's what he did, and now he is dead?

"Dirt," the teacher said. He had gotten up, gone to the wall cabinet, and was rummaging in one of the shelves. He pulled out a large yellow envelope, which he weighed in his open palm. "You're not likely to find any dirt." And the way he pronounced "dirt" and left the word "find" hanging in midair sounded as if a "but" was going to follow, or some word suggesting that something just as bad or much worse than dirt could be found here. That would have been the moment to ask some very precise questions: What is there instead of dirt? What does it look like? Where can it be found in such a life of transparent kindness? But I did not ask. His manner of balancing the envelope in his hand as if its weight were important to the continuation of our conversation, of reluctantly opening it and partly pulling out its content without looking at the few sheets and newspaper clippings held together by a paper clip, all gave me the ominous feeling that something abhorrent or even dangerous was approaching me for which I was unprepared. He too seemed to be dejected, still reluctant to proceed, and breathed a sigh of relief when his daughter appeared at the door to remind him of the doctor's imminent arrival. "There is an expression by Hegel that has always seemed to me very fitting for a certain German state of mind," he said as he put the envelope back in its place and carefully locked the cabinet. "He called it 'mushy soulfulness.' "

It wasn't until I got to the door that I asked him whether I might come back. I told him I was thinking of writing about my father, since it was so difficult to talk about him. "We'll have to be quick about it," he said with a smile, which I returned until I realized that he had been speaking of his death.

He insisted on accompanying me all the way to the garden gate. Snipping a few wilted leaves and blossoms from his rosebushes, he told me about my father's study and how it had appeared to him when he came for appointments. Sometimes he had to wait for the minister to finish writing a paragraph, and he would look around the room, very slowly along the walls, finding my father in every object, every picture, every piece of furniture, reading his entire life and character, past and present, as in a book. "The past loomed large," he said. "Your father had three fathers: his biological father, the Heavenly Father, and the old Emperor and King of Prussia. They were all assembled in that room, and among them the tiny child that was you. She stood behind her father's back on a little footstool by the window; three or four years old, apparently quite a lively child, but in that room she kept as quiet as a mouse. 'She doesn't bother me,' your father would say full of praise. 'One hardly knows she's there.' When I saw her standing there, looking so quietly and contentedly down into the street, I thought that it must be difficult or nearly impossible for such a child to leave a room so replete with paternal aura."

"I'm grown up," I told him. "That room doesn't exist anymore."

"Are you so sure?" he asked, as he carefully closed the garden gate between us.

Father's study is large and deep, the ceiling is high, with an oval stucco wreath; four arched windows, arranged in two pairs, one facing east, the other the street.

Like a stage, on which the scenery and props for the entire play are always in view but are highlighted only in essential parts for each act, the study is arranged into three temporally rather than spatially defined areas: the "morning study," the "noonday study," and the "evening study." Each has its own light and center, around which the furnishings arrange themselves in shifting accents.

Warmed and brightened by the sun, the colors of the morning study range from a dusty pink to shades of violet and to reddish brown in the corners farthest from the windows. Wafting light blue layers of tobacco smoke make the sunshine appear like slanting beams of dancing dust specks. Dust softens the edges of the old but undistinguished furniture, mellows the glare of the polished linoleum, and lends to the surfaces of the furniture the dry matte of pastels.

When Mother complains about the layer of dust on top of his desk, Father pulls out his large, white handkerchief and fans the surface. "All gone!" he says with a twinkle. She cannot help smiling, and both dust and Father remain the victors—at least in this room and at this desk. Like no other part of the house, it is his realm, his mysteriously ordered world that appears chaotic to everyone else: a world of papers, writings, books, calendars, ashtrays, pipe cleaners and tampers, penholders, pencil cases, inkwell, blotter, tea glass, and such curiosities as have come to him as gifts or bequests like the paper weight of Parian marble, a small cross made from the wood of an olive tree in the Garden of Gethsemane, a letter opener shaped like an officer's saber.

The center of the morning study is the desk in the southeast corner, which receives its light from the window at the left. Sexton, vicar, and deaconess direct their steps toward it for their daily reports but never quite reach it; they are blocked by a waist-high shelf filled with government gazettes and church journals that forms a barrier between the desk and the rest of the room. Here they place whatever they were asked to bring and pick up whatever he gives them to take along. There is no place to sit down.

The desk is made of the cheapest spruce, cobbled together to make a crude box with a space in the middle. It supports a bookcase containing Hebrew, Greek, and Latin dictionaries, the Old and New Testament in their original languages, commentaries, compendiums, liturgies, and theological texts for everyday use. At the very top stands a sturdy crucifix made of white marble. It partly covers a portrait of Grandfather, the upper edge of which touches the ceiling—not a painting but a much enlarged half-length photograph: a large, friendly face, just a hint of a smile in the corners of the mouth, white, shoulder-length hair, black preacher's robe. Pipes with stems as long as an arm, flexible mouthpieces, and porcelain bowls hang from a board decorated with pyrographic designs; above it, in a black frame, a woodcut of Martin Luther with his round, coarse head, penetrating eyes, and defiant mouth, which, though firmly closed, seems to be constantly saying: Here I stand, I cannot do otherwise, God help me, Amen!

Above a chest with torn leather upholstery hangs a child-like painting of the small Hunsrück[1] town of Simmern, where Father had his first pastoral assignment. Next to it, in the corner between the long and the transverse walls, on a black pedestal, stands a statue of Christ by Thorwaldsen—white, smooth, not particularly welcoming in spite of the engraved inscription. Suffer the Little Children to Come unto Me.

A portrait of Kaiser Wilhelm II has been carefully placed in the best light opposite the window, above the gas heater with its black cylindrical openings: eagle-crowned helmet on his head, his chest heavily hung with medals, his atrophied arm—"his tragic affliction"—hidden behind his back. His posture calls to mind Lohengrin in the prow of the rowboat. His glance darts like an arrow diagonally upward, penetrating the wall at a point just above the curtain rail.

For a short while a small bust of Hitler, made of reddish clay, appears on top of the gas heater. It was brought in by the deaconess in a furtive effort to bring together her two dearest favorites—her pastor and her Führer. Every morning she checks with a suspicious glance whether the little head is still in its place and takes it as a personal insult when it is gone one day. Father has no idea what has become of it. He has never taken any particular notice of "that thing." Much later Mother confesses that she personally beheaded it with an ax on the chopping block in the furnace room.

There are no pictures on the rest of the long wall, only the office cabinet, a heavy piece of furniture with three sturdy doors holding the church books and the tools of the pastoral office. The pouch containing the communion cup, decanter, and paten must not be opened; the content is not to be touched. It is sacred. Next to the double doors that open into the hallway hangs a photograph, "Grandfather's House," in an art nouveau frame; underneath is a poem of many stanzas with the title "The Parsonage on the Rhine." The high slate roof with its turrets and gables extends into the wooded hillside—Rhenish Schiefergebirge,[2] middle section—which rises precipitously directly behind the house. The pretty side of the house, with its terraces, large windows, and half-timbered porch, faces the river. Many small figures stand behind the parapet of the terrace and in the open windows.

"Where am I?" asks the child.

You weren't born yet is what Father should say but doesn't quite have the heart to say. Not without a slight pang of conscience, he points to a flyspeck above the parapet: that could be the child, still too small to look over the top, but Grandfather can see her from the second-floor window on the left.

A pyrographic inscription on a wooden plaque above the door of the daughters' bedroom reads,

Eternity,
Shine thy light
Into time.
Let us see as small what's small
And perceive the great in all.

"What does that mean?" the child asks. Her father explains that God's concept of what is essential differs from mankind's, that we must strive to find out what in God's view is truly great and essential and not be caught up in mere superficialities.

When he is in the morning study, Father sits at his desk. Bent forward over the green blotter, he rests on his arms, which are inside the threadbare sleeves of his robe. He writes with the thinnest, most sharply pointed steel nib on small sheets that have been carefully cut from old official communications. He can read his own minuscule handwriting only when he adds a magnifying glass to his spectacles and pince-nez. Now and then he turns around and blows smoke rings toward the child, who stands on a footstool behind him, poking a finger into the center of the wafting circles. He slides a chocolate with cream filling toward her along the windowsill that he has taken from the upper left drawer, where he also keeps raspberry drops and alphabet cookies. Father and child eat only those with white or pink filling. If they bite into one and find that it is brown, they save it for Mother, assuming that she is especially fond of chocolates with brown filling.

These morning hours are so quiet that the child can hear the pen gliding over the smooth paper and the sound of her father's lips as he inhales and exhales the smoke. These sounds—together with the warmth of the room, the dusty sunlight, the smoke from the pipe, the bent back covered by a morning robe—make up the child's nest, in which she sits securely and, peeking out over the windowsill, looks at the world from above: the milkman, the vegetable cart, housewives with baskets and shopping bags, cats on their secret missions, sparrows in the lilac bushes in the front yard.

On the cobblestone street below, the town's only streetcar passes every half-hour on its winding tracks. Father looks up from his work as the rattling and rumbling old cars approach from the direction of the market place. He waits behind the window until he can see the Little Man on the front platform of the second car. Then he raises his hand, and the Little Man, who was his orderly during World War I, waves back. For twenty years, until the Little Man retired, Father waved at him when he rode toward the railroad station and again when he returned to the market. "That is true loyalty," Mother says.

The sound of the gong announcing the mid-day meal ends the time of the morning study. Silence gives way to the noises of getting ready for dinner. The pipe must be emptied and cleaned. The child jumps down from her footstool. Father tears open the window: fresh air! Holding hands, they leave the morning study, which rearranges itself silently while they are eating.

When they return, laughing and out of breath from their daily race up the stairs, the desk has slid off to the edge, standing there with everything on it as if deserted. Released from their earlier purposes, from their order and hierarchy, the furnishings lapse into a tired, relaxed neighborliness. The reds and yellows of the morning sunlight have long since disappeared behind the windowless southern wall. An afterglow still clings to the vines that crowd the corner formed by the windows, but the color of the room is now defined by the huge, gray old post office across the street.

Father and child have their assigned roles in the game played around the couch: he must lie down, the child has to cover him; but he prevents that by catching the blue blanket with his foot and tossing it to the floor. Finally he lets himself be wrapped up and is already asleep as the child hauls the Bible from the Martin Luther stand over to the sofa. She lies down with the Bible; sleeping is not required, just being quiet. "If you're not quiet, you have to get out," Mother has told her.

With a dampened finger she lifts the pages and lets them float softly to the other side. She looks at the woodcuts made from drawings by Julius Schnorr von Carolsfeld; nods off as she is breathing in the dry smell made up of cinnamon, dust, and marzipan; wakes up with a start, looks at the hands of the clock on the wall, which sometimes jump ahead and sometimes creep slowly forward; peers across the table at her father, who is lying flat on his back, his profile pointing to the ceiling, deeply set eyes, curved nose, and receding chin—like a corpse. Terrified, she turns away her eyes and hides under the fringed blanket. Ham was cursed when he looked at his sleeping father. His brothers walked backward and averted their eyes as they covered Noah's nakedness.

The Children of Israel wander through the sands of the desert and among the rocks of the mountains: muscle-bound bodies; wide, flowing, pleated gowns; wild and mild beards; grand, sweeping gestures as they dance around the Golden Calf. Moses smashes the tables of the law. Thou shalt not make unto thee any graven image, or any likeness of any thing that is in heaven above. Holy, holy, holy is the Lord of Hosts. All-knowing, almighty, ever present. He brings on the cloud and the column of fire, the rain of blood, manna, and the angels of mighty wings, who carry neither harps nor cymbals like those at Bethlehem, but swords.

Doesn't Isaac see the knife Abraham is holding in his right hand as he gently supports his son's neck with his left? Turn around, Abraham! The ram is already hanging in the thicket. Why doesn't God tell Abraham that He is only tempting him?

"Then it wouldn't be tempting him," Father has told her.

Why is there no picture of Isaac and his father going home together, away from the fire, with the smoke rising toward heaven to please God? Just like the smoke from Abel's fire, while Cain's fire is crushed to the ground by an evil wind. Poor Cain: he also wanted to be good, but God would not let him.

The evil brothers sell Joseph for money because he has dreams and a coat of many colors. The dreams aren't his fault. And the coat isn't his fault either; it was a present from his father.

The child spits on the evil brothers and scratches their faces. You are mean, mean, mean! And what happened with Potiphar's wife?

"Don't be so curious," Father said. "Children don't need to know everything."

22

Now they are even taking from Jacob his son Benjamin, his youngest, his darling. Please don't do him any harm, Joseph! It's not his fault. He wasn't even born yet.

With the tip of her tongue, the child touches the tear of joy that Joseph sheds as he jumps from his throne, his coat billowing behind, clutching Benjamin to him with his right hand, holding up his left against the brothers, who are pressing up the stairs toward him. Trust in Him, He will be righteous! But not with Cain, not with Absalom, not with Judas . . .

At the stroke of half past two, Father throws off the blanket and swings his feet to the floor directly into his shoes. He scurries around the room with quick, small steps, gathering up his things: newsletters, the daily devotion of the Moravian Brethren of Herrnhut, the New Testament, and the hymnal. That's the end of the noonday study. From three o'clock on it will be deserted while he is "visiting the congregation": visits to the hospital, house calls, and confirmation classes. The study is not locked. It could be used—for reading or for homework—but that wouldn't occur to anyone. There are no witnesses as the light fades, dusk creeps out of the corners, and the room rearranges itself to become the evening study.

After supper the family moves in. The lamp, hanging from the ceiling with its shade of green fabric, makes a new center, a bright inner circle, which encloses part of the table with the fringed tablecloth and the darning basket; the shiny straight line parting Mother's hair in the middle; her bony hands resolutely pulling a strand of darning wool through stocking heels; Father's long, outstretched legs, his head with his gray-blond, cropped hair, and the book from which he is reading aloud.

The heat rising from the stove plays with the fringes of the lamp shade, and their moving shadows fall on the table, the floor, the couch, on which the child makes herself inconspicuous, trying to put off her bedtime. In the green twilight outside the circle of light, on the sofa with the ornate back, the two middle children, Dorothea and Herbert, act bored. They would much rather "see the sights" downtown or take in a movie—at least *Frederick the Great, Queen Louise,* or *Red Dawn*—but at night children belong in the house. The oldest, Gerhard, rocks in the creaky rocking chair while Father is reading from some religious or patriotic text: Luther's table talk, the sermons of Court Chaplain Keßler, Bismarck's letters, or the memoirs of Lettow-Vorbeck and Oldenburg-Januschau.[3]

Sometimes Mother reads aloud from Fritz Reuter's *Ut mine Stromtid*.[4] Stories from Mecklenburg, Father points out, should be familiar to her, since she comes from the Lower Rhine. She disagrees: the dialect of the Ruhr area is completely different from that of the Baltic Coast. For him there is no difference—it's all "northern Germany," far away, even though not quite so far as "East Elbia," where the Mongols live.

The reading matter for these family evenings is selected from the shelves behind the rocking chair that house the "heavy fare." That is where the German classics are kept, the lyric poetry of Gerok, Rückert, Arndt, Uhland, Lenau, Liliencron, Freiligrath; the prose of Seidel, Grimm, Flex, Freitag, Wilhelm Schäfer; biographies, memoirs, letters, books on the Kaiser and on war (*Invincible on Land, Invincible at Sea, Invincible in the Air*); art books on Dürer, Spitzweg, Richter, and Roman art; and the bottom shelf is stuffed with Baedekers and old issues of *Kladderadatsch*.[5] Nothing by Thomas or Heinrich Mann, no Hauptmann, Shaw, Ibsen, Strindberg, Döblin, Werfel, Tucholsky, or Brecht—not even Carossa or Jünger—and nothing by or about Freud, Kierkegaard, Klages, or Einstein. No art book on the impressionists or expressionists, and in the entire house not a trace of the Bauhaus or the Blaue Reiter movement. Art seems to have stopped with Caspar David Friedrich (*Mountain Cross*). In this house so filled with music one cannot hear a single note by Bruckner, Mahler, Pfitzner, Strauss, Ravel, Debussy, or Hindemith. Even Hugo Wolf and Reger are considered "extreme," Tchaikovsky and Chopin are "low-brow," Brahms "rather pompous," Mozart—like "Papa" Haydn—"cute," and Bach a bit "hard to digest" but very suitable for church services. This is true also for Handel, but they like him better because he is "easier to take," especially the Largo from the opera *Xerxes*, which the child, confident of the family's applause, has learned to scratch out on the violin.

To console her for having to turn in earlier than the "big ones," Father sits down on the edge of her bed for a short game of sixty-six. Then Mother comes in to pray with her. The door to the study remains open just a crack. As long as the bent ray of light runs across the ceiling, her fear remains under control, under the bed, in the dark corner behind the closet. . . .

Every now and then things suddenly get noisy next door. The child raises her head from the pillow. What they are doing over there is usually referred to by the family as "talking things out": they drill and dig with words and stir up the old family muck. Usually it concerns the two middle children, who are not quite as God would like them to be. Dorothea has boys on her mind, and Herbert does not value the essential things in life. He does not read books and isn't interested in anything, though everything has been tried, even Brehm's illustrated volumes about animal life. The friends he chooses are all good-for-nothings, and he takes up every fad that comes along, wearing skimpy jackets, berets, and bright scarves inside his collar. Instead of getting himself a decent haircut at the barber's, he comes home with a headful of curls and pomade. He longs for cheap entertainment and superficial pleasures. He flirts with married women. In church, he refuses to sing with the rest. He wants to have what everyone has and do what everyone does. He simply doesn't understand that what everyone has and does is no measure for "our kind."

He remains silent for long stretches. Then he suddenly screams at them. Good heavens, he even dares to argue! In the end, he breaks down, crying.

"Why are you crying?" Mother asks. "You had better pray to the Lord that He may help you to change."

In comparison to the middle children, the "child" is a very good child, and Gerhard, the oldest, a good, obedient son. It's the middle ones who step out of bounds. A line will simply have to be drawn.

After the words "I'll never do it again! I'm going to be good!" have finally been spoken, the storm passes, rumbling off into the distance. Pleasant chitchat, yawning, shuffling of chairs. Father's shoes drop to the floor with a thud. Mother indulges in one of her rare attempts at being playful: "Our dear father is ready to go beddy-bye."

With "Good night" and "God bless you" the daytime hours of the study come to an end. Doors creak, water flows into wash basins, bed frames groan. With a low growl, the Evil One announces himself.

It is always in her father's study where evil nightmares haunt the child. The body snatchers drag her by her hair across the linoleum floor with the worn floral pattern. She has to unlock the office cabinet with the stolen key, hand over the sacred implements, and betray the Lord, just like Peter, just like Judas.

Lying under this blue cover, Father does not fend off the flashing metal blade as it descends and cuts his head into thin slices, which one by one float softly to the side.

Squatting on this threshold, the boogieman's cats stare with red-glowing eyes, big as saucers.

The child sleeps restlessly, talks in her dreams, sleepwalks. The family doctor prescribes valerian and lemon balm. The child has her own prescription, which she keeps a secret: after saying her prayers and kissing her mother good night, she stealthily climbs out of her crib, looks under it, makes the sign of the cross, feels sinful because only Catholics cross themselves, kneels in front of her crib like a Catholic, and prays to the Catholic God and the Virgin Mary to keep the bad dreams away. Sometimes it works, sometimes it doesn't.

The next morning she avoids her father so that he will not detect the sin in her eyes.

But the Lord looketh on the heart. . . .

Every year the family travels to St. Goar where they spend their summer vacation. As soon as they stand on the platform of the railroad station at Auel, Father becomes "a new man." Swinging his cane, he circles his flock, full of the anticipation of "going home." Though he is the only one in the family who as a small child was at home in St. Goar, everyone is expected to be caught up in the excitement. The family will stay in a hotel just like tourists, but that doesn't matter — they are going home!

On this day he is wearing neither a hat nor his starched wing collar but a gray suit and a light blue shirt with a casual, soft collar. Casting quick glances toward the station house, he makes sure that there is no one he knows or — heaven help us! — any member of his congregation who might ask him for pastoral counsel. That is all behind him now. He wants to get away; nothing is to interfere with that. Flipping open his pocket watch, he grumbles about the possibility that the train may not be on time and, as if to begin the journey on foot, strides to the end of the platform, where the pavement turns to gravel. Already exhausted before things have fairly started, Mother tells Gerhard to follow him: Can't we all stay together? No, he can't. Sighing, she shoos the children away from the edge of the platform. Oh, this family, what a headache! When the train pulls in, they keep searching for the right compartment until the very last minute. They open and close one door after another. It's got to be a nonsmoking compartment for Mother's sake; third-class, of course, but — if you please — one of the newer ones that are clean and not so smelly. Above all, there must not be any other passengers sitting in it. They want to be by themselves.

The whole family gets swept up in that grand, communal Rhine feeling shortly after they pass through Koblenz, where the mountains begin to crowd in on both sides, forcing the river, the road, and the railroad tracks into a narrowly winding course. The first castles come into view, and the family rehearses their names. Who can tell the legend of this one? Little Rhenish towns nestle in the smoky mist at the bottom of the valley and scramble up into the adjoining valleys. The slate roofs, tightly stacked at odd angles, give the family a feeling of home, comfort, familiarity. Vineyards appear sometimes on the right, sometimes on the left—to allow for optimal exposure to the sun, the children are told. They also learn why the ground underneath the vines is covered with slate. Everybody now wants to look out the window to decipher the names of the passing steamboats and to count the barges. A barge dog is yapping at the river bank. Children are waving. Oh, to go just once on a barge all the way to Rotterdam!

A stately white excursion side-wheeler paddles its way upriver. Proud as a swan, Mother says, her voice full of longing. Father doesn't approve of the flag at the stern: black-red-mustard! He is even more annoyed at the blue-white-red and all those other international colors flying on "our river." That will simply have to change! They are not going to get our own, our free German Rhine! Germany's river, not Germany's border.[1] The child sticks out her tongue at a Belgian ship, but no one can see her from that distance. Yet she is reprimanded: That's not how we do it!

Overcome by holiday happiness and patriotic feelings, the child sticks her head out the window (in spite of repeated warnings that an oncoming train might cut it clear off) and is exhilarated by the clanging of the wheels and the hellish noise of the train as it shoots through the tunnels.

After passing through Boppard, they heave down the luggage. The sun is just breaking through the clouds. The mist above the river dissolves in shreds. Window panes flash.

"Is there any place in the world prettier than this?" Father asks. No answer is required. Of course not.

At the station the bags are taken care of. Everybody here knows that Father does not like to carry them himself. At the stairs leading up to the hotel the manager receives him with a bow and a handshake: So, you have come back home again! The rooms smell a bit musty; the parents have a large double room with a balcony facing the Rhine; next to it is a long and narrow chamber for the two girls, and for the boys a room across the hall looking out over the kitchen. Mother tears open all the windows and the door to the balcony. Still wearing her hat and coat, she starts unpacking. Father is not present; he has met some old friends and is drinking his first glass of wine on the terrace.

After supper the family walks on the tree-lined promenade down to the harbor and back again, greeted by townspeople who still remember Grandfather and Father when he was barely knee-high. The river pilots are particularly pleased with the family's loyalty to their old hometown. Grandfather used to report to them the number and names of the ships going downriver whenever he returned from attending a synod in Koblenz. The largest wreath at his funeral was donated by a family of river pilots, the Goederts: "For our pastor, in faithful memory...."

Mother refers to these walks as "running the gauntlet" or "being on display."

When they get to the end of the town, things quiet down. The parents now stroll arm in arm; the child is holding on to her father's hand, the oldest walks next to Mother, and the two middle children are slowly hanging back — a fact that is noticed with some displeasure. They stop in front of Grandfather's house at the northern end of town and have to crowd against the railing of the embankment to see all of it. Father points to the little turret window where his room used to be. The child thinks it is an elegant house, with its terraces, stairs, porch, and turret, built right into the hillside — almost a mansion. But her father dislikes the word: "A minister doesn't live in a mansion."

If the current occupants show themselves at a window or on the terrace, the family quickly moves on. The child thinks of the new people as vulgar, rich showoffs with lots of money but no class.

They walk to the farthest point of the bend in the river, across from the rock of the Lorelei. In Grandfather's time, at large family gatherings, it would echo the trumpeter's sounds:

"The Rhine is my home, the Rhine is my life; the Rhine, my native river. . . ." Leaning over the railing, they wait until the lanterns on the riverboats light up.

Although the child has never been inside her grandfather's house, she knows what it looks like. Words spoken by long-forgotten voices on occasions she cannot remember—bed-time talk, summer conversations, family reunions with their orgies of shared memories—have created rooms and pictures in her mind that get mixed up with her own recollections. Sometimes she confuses the stories she has heard with actual experience, and her brothers and sisters make fun of her: "You've never been there! You weren't even born yet!"

"Yes, yes, yes, I was there!" she shouts. "I was there! I was born, but you weren't."

The rooms in Grandfather's house are bigger and darker than those in Auel. It is hard to make out their furnishings. Many people with blurred features and old-fashioned clothes come and go. In Auel, Father is always called either "Father" or "Reverend"; at Grandfather's house they call him "Rein-hold" or even "the little one." During family dinners he sits at the foot of the large table, and Grandfather—his father—sits at the head. In between, there is much noise and talk: nine children and an endless number of guests. The boys in-vite their friends from school or university and the girls their classmates from boarding school. As the years go by, fiancées and in-laws begin to appear, finally Elisabeth, Reinhold's fi-ancée, who regularly loses her appetite, what with all the hubbub. "At my house we didn't talk at the dinner table," she says when she tells her children about those earlier times.

She keeps a straight posture, her elbows tucked in. With impeccable manners she pokes around in the simple family fare and speaks only when spoken to, softly and haltingly. She is always a little slow, taking things in with her shy, green eyes and a mind that wants to comprehend things thoroughly and deliberately. It is a difficult spot to be in: a girl from the smokestacks of the Ruhr among the "true" vintage of the

Rhineland, an artisan's daughter among the academic middle class.

The children talk a lot, loud and fast. They shout across the table, poke each other in the ribs, and laugh with their mouths open and their heads thrown back. When a quick thought or judgment is too tempting to resist, their barbs can sting. Letting fly a few pointed remarks or indiscretions doesn't bother them too much — just as long as it snaps and crackles. Afterward they are just as quick to apologize and to press a wet kiss on the victim's cheek. No offense intended. They clear up misunderstandings in heated arguments — and create new ones. Grandfather makes sure that everybody adheres to the rules of the game: spare the young and the weak. He has a certain way of clearing his throat or looking you straight in the eye that nips any impertinent remark in the bud. No one dares to disobey him. Occasionally he winks at Reinhold's bride: Don't worry, I'll stick by you.

"He has always been fond of me," Mother says. One can hear in her voice how much she used to depend on it.

When Reinhold tells the "young folks" at the lower end of the table one of his witty stories and gets them all to laugh, his father leans forward over his plate, cupping his deaf ear, and shouts, "Be quiet! I want to hear what Reinhold has to say." Then Reinhold repeats his story, and when he is finished, his father falls back in his chair and laughs till the tears come to his eyes, all the while looking up and down the table and at each person as if to say, Isn't he something, the little one? Doesn't he just make you feel proud of him?

Reinhold is the quickest and nimblest in the family, always ready to move when something needs to be done. He gets things, goes to the store, runs after whatever has been left behind, shows their guests around, and accompanies his father on his rounds and on hikes into the countryside. He is not really athletic but has a way of doing things that always keeps him on the move. When it comes to swimming or skating he leaves them all behind. Perhaps he might have become an excellent dancer, if he had been allowed to dance. He is not very strong; neither his arms nor his legs are muscular. Military service doesn't do anything to broaden his shoulders. No matter how old, he looks younger than his age. Just as soon as he can, he grows a mustache.

He is no good at physical labor. Though willing and eager enough, he is all thumbs when it comes to handling objects and tools. One can tell by his fingers that they are not made for shaping, gripping, or holding things. And he never improves because there are always people nearby who can't stand watching him struggle. "Why don't you let me do it," they say, as if to suggest that's the way they like him: nimble on his feet, brainy, not very practical, "destined for higher things."

When he was little, he wanted to be a mailman. Later he decided to go into the ministry. All of his brothers are ministers, all of his sisters marry ministers—just as they were expected to.

He is generally seen as "bright" or even "brilliant." He has a quick mind, and his speech is trenchant, precise, witty. He never hurts people's feelings, has a soft heart, is easily moved to tears. When he is in high spirits, the entire family abandons itself to unrestrained silliness. When he is blue, he retreats to his room in the little round turret and locks the door. There, sitting at his desk, he recites the poetry of Uhland, Rückert, Lenau, or Freiligrath, addressing the river, the ships, the barges. He copies their verses into a leather-bound scrapbook and sometimes composes some of his own and presses flowers and leaves between the pages. Laboriously, with his two left hands, he weaves tiny book marks for Christmas and his father's birthday. He writes long, tender letters to absent members of the family. One of his favorite words is "heartfelt."

When in town, he is met everywhere with kindness and respect. In school, he earns the affection of his fellow students by his witticisms and practical jokes. A life without warm feelings and affection will always be unimaginable for him. Like his brothers, he is sent to a boarding school in Westphalia for his secondary education.[2] There are no records of those years, except for the lyrics of "On a little Swabian railroad" rendered in Westphalian dialect.

A minister's children—as the old ditty goes—are like the miller's cows, which rarely or never turn out well. Everyone knows that millers should have donkeys, not cattle.

A minister's child can never say, "My father is a pastor," without eliciting a certain kind of smile, which in predominantly Catholic regions seems to have something to do with housekeepers and secret sins. Hastily, the minister's child explains by adding "Protestant." Whereupon people will say, "Oh, I see," but they keep smiling. Ministers' children just have to get used to it—the child's father in St. Goar as well as the child in Auel.

They never seem to really belong. True, having an academic degree, their father is part of the "elite," but the children are required to conduct themselves with humility, to make nothing of their social position, to befriend the "lowly," to help and care for the sick and the infirm, to share with the poor and to act as their spiritual guides.

Laughing at others, scolding or making fun of them, lying to them or fighting with them are out of the question. Teachers have high expectations of them and a direct line to their father. What would be a practical joke with others is a serious transgression with them; fudging is deception; a little white lie, dishonesty. Throwing cherry bombs or stink bombs or sticking matches in door bells are considered downright mean. Think of the poor old lady having to answer the door.

They are dressed plainly, kept on a tight budget, and are expected to frown upon current fashions. They do not indulge in "superficial" pleasures.

They are given only good books and are expected to admire only serious music and true art.

They are easily duped and therefore have to tolerate a good deal of mockery, but they are supposed to grin and bear it.

They are never to be a nuisance, always an example.

They feel themselves misunderstood, yet somehow as being among the chosen few. To avoid the appearance of being moral cowards, they aspire to something special — a special cheekiness, a special wit, a special talent.

As everyone knows, parsonages have brought forth outstanding individuals; also terrorists and untold psychopaths, but nobody talks about them.

A minister's children have many privileges they are not supposed to brag about. They are permitted to take flowers and apples from the garden of the parsonage to sick parishioners and play the part of the angel in the Christmas pageant. If they have any musical talent, they are allowed at an early age to play their recorders and scratch the strings of their violins before church audiences. They distribute small presents and religious tracts in the hospital. To those who are approaching death they are one of the final pleasures of this life. In church they are allowed to light the candles, spread the altar cloths, and arrange fruits and ears of grain on the altar steps for Thanksgiving. On Sundays they are permitted to enter the vestry and help the Black Man, their father, tie his clerical bands. During the service they and their mother sit in one of the front pews, a team assisting their father in directing the congregation's hymns with a sense of personal responsibility. On the way out, they wink at the minister as he shakes hands with his parishioners. An hour later he will sit down with them for the midday meal.

These privileges are not apt to elicit either respect or envy from their peers and do not result in tangible advantages. Not even the house in which they live belongs to them. For in this world, says the Lord, they have no continuing city; and the one to come, the one they are to seek, is invisible. They are told that the values they have are, because of their very immateriality, superior to all material values. This possession of hidden values gives rise to a sense of superiority and self-righteousness that is easily and seamlessly joined to the required attitude of humility. No one, not even they themselves, can take that away from them. In everything they do or fail to do they are accountable both to their earthly parents and to the ever present Father above, whom they cannot offend without paying for it with a guilty conscience. It is much less painful to submit—to be good and obedient. In these parsonages, one does not speak of "love" but of "caring" and "being good." Thus they blunt the arrow of the heathen god and forge it into a wedding band, into a family circle. The dangerous heat is put to use in the family hearth. Those who have warmed themselves in its glow will always feel cold anywhere else in this world.

Grandfather's letters to his youngest, who was then at the university and in his vicarage year, form perfect rectangles of minute black lines, placed with a sure sense of order and propriety on small sheets folded in half. The smooth, heavy paper handles well, the old German script flows easily, yet each letter is fully shaped, and the letters of the signature are no larger than those of the text. Everything in "the little one's" life, from the smoking kerosene lamp to the difficulties of preaching the gospel, is taken up with paternal care and affection. And the Heavenly Father is just as tenderly concerned about each detail. Grandfather can still refer to God in phrases that today can no longer be used without reservation: His eternal will; His boundless love; His steadfast paternal heart; His infinite mercy. The use of supporting adjectives reveals the inflation of pious phrases. Soon this kind of talk will sound like lies.

He reports in detail about his congregation, giving specific names: our dear so-and-so, our faithful such-and-such; he asks his son to think with him about these people and recommends prayer. Nothing in these letters to the student at Tübingen and Halle refers to contemporary political or social issues.

Just once, shortly after graduating from the gymnasium, Reinhold escaped from under his father's watchful eye. Without asking permission, he takes a "frivolous trip" to Italy, but his father's letter calls him back: "I hope you see how wrong it was of you to decide on your own to take this long trip. You are too easily distracted, my dear son. I wish you would sit down quietly in your room and think about your life and yourself, what it was before graduation and what it has become since. That is all I will say today, except to express my hope that these words of affection will strike the right note of cheerful obedience in your heart."

Grandfather's death is documented in a letter by his widow. While preaching in his pulpit, he is overcome by unspecified pain. He finishes his sermon. After the benediction he lets himself be taken to the hospital. For some time now he has spoken to the Lord about his feeling that "his time has come." The doctors confirm it after he has assured them that death holds no terror for him. "Now I shall see my Savior," he says.

During his last hours he asks his wife to convey messages and greetings to all his "loved ones"—a long litany that is interrupted by lapses into unconsciousness. He expresses his gratitude for the many "loving kindnesses" that they have bestowed on him and apologizes to those he believes he has offended or neglected. He speaks of his hope that the "greater love" he is experiencing during these hours may find its way from his sickbed into their lives. He wishes his pastoral colleagues and his successor "a rich harvest in the Lord's vineyard." When he reaches the goal toward which he is traveling he will ask that they be blessed. He dies "with a clear vision of the Heavenly City before him."

It is February, a mild day in the early spring of 1906. Reinhold is thirty-one years old. He has just received the news that after hearing his trial sermon, a small congregation in the Hunsrück mountains has unanimously elected him as their pastor. But somehow "joy refuses to blossom. I cannot grasp the fact that Father will not be there to install me in office."

Reinhold and Elisabeth did not meet on a street, at a restaurant, on a train, or while visiting friends, the way most of us meet people, but at an entirely irreproachable, even pious, occasion: at the Young Ladies' Afternoon Circle, which meets once a week at the parsonage.

4

The young ladies, mostly of the upper middle class, bring along their little baskets with embroidery and crochet work. As they busily ply their needles, the minister's wife reads to them from pious books. On warm days they sit outside on the garden terrace among berry bushes and fruit trees. They wear ankle-length, tightly buttoned dresses that require a certain formality and dignity of demeanor. Above the waist their dresses are richly decorated with pleats, broderie anglaise, flounces, jabots, and lace collars. Some still use corsets, but those who are more progressive permit themselves the freedom of "reform dresses" that flow loosely over waist and hips.

The minister's wife is always dressed in black — heavy, stiff fabrics that rustle when she walks and enclose her voluminous chest like steel armor. She is fond of conducting pious conversations after her reading. Sometimes it is not easy to "maintain the proper level." As soon as her sons appear, the girls start acting silly. Then she flashes warning looks and breathes a sigh of relief when the minister appears for his closing words.

The new girl, Elisabeth, the stranger who recently moved here from the Lower Rhine with her somber and sickly father, is shy, does not make friends easily, and is too serious for her age and not outgoing. Unlike the other young ladies, who return to town by taking the road running along the river, she takes the footpath that climbs from the garden half-way up the hill and continues along the hillside to the other end of town. As long as she is within sight of the house she steps demurely. Beyond the second terrace she gathers up her skirts and starts running. She works her needle with skill but little patience. Occasionally her thread breaks because she pulls it too hard.

Rarely does she join in the conversation. If a remark happens to escape her lips, she blushes and shuts her mouth more firmly. One of the older sons, who already has an eye for women—more than his parents consider proper—finds the new maiden rather striking: her black hair and high cheekbones are almost exotic. A classy figure! His sisters find the shape of her eyes not bad, except for the unfortunate green color of the iris. Their eyes are like Reinhold's: small, gray blue gimlet eyes under heavy lids. Green eyes are cats' eyes, they say. At this point father intervenes. Looks are not essential, he says. Man looketh on outward appearance, but the Lord looketh on the heart.

One evening, as a thunderstorm threatens, Reinhold accompanies the young ladies back to town. Near the end, he and Elisabeth walk alone. He tries to make conversation but cannot think of anything to talk about. He has no experience with the ladies: "still wet behind the ears" is what his brothers and sisters say about him. His father calls him pure and innocent.

On the hill above the town, at a place overlooking the river, he asks her if she, too, loves poetry. He mentions that he owns a leather-bound scrapbook into which he copies the most beautiful poems he comes across in his reading. It also contains a few of his own—nothing important. Blushing, she reveals that she has one just like it, with poems and dates. On rereading them later, she can relive exactly her thoughts and feelings on such and such a day though not a single word is her own. Her sentences come rushing out as if they had been pent up behind her lips. How beautiful! he says, feeling as if she had made him a gift. He asks if they might not exchange their scrapbooks. She does not answer and is suddenly in a great hurry, almost running the rest of the way. Before he can say good-bye she has disappeared inside the house.

He is late for supper that evening and fails to excuse himself, silently spooning his dish of sour milk. The older brother, the one who made the remark about the classy figure, clears his throat and says, "Well, well!"

During the remaining weeks of his vacation, Reinhold arranges things so that toward the end of the young ladies' afternoon meeting he is walking somewhere near the footpath on the hillside. There is a small ledge—he later points it out to his children—with a flat slab of slate to sit on, well screened from his sisters' eyes by blackberry vines.

There he sits waiting, holding a book from which he wants to read to her, straining his ear toward the house below. It is springtime, the break between winter and summer semesters at the university. Whenever a train enters the tunnel, a tremor goes through the hill under his feet. Every now and then he looks up from his book at the scenery, experiencing nature's response to his own feelings of love and expectation. "In every purple leaflet—Adelaïda," he sings, joining the song of the finch and the buzz of the bumblebee. His desire to tell Elisabeth about all this beauty lends to each detail depth and significance. He prepares the right choice of words, finds them wanting, searches for others, more profound, loftier, preferably rhymed. So intently does he concentrate on the scenery and on the words that he misses the end of the maidens' gathering on the lawn below. Only the sound of Elisabeth's feet rouses him. He follows her quietly, then announces himself by clearing his throat or calling out to her. He does not tell her that he has been waiting for her, nor does she let on that she knows. They do not talk about love but about nature and poetry, about music, about last Sunday's sermon, about books. Everything they say is heavy with unspoken feelings. From time to time they have to sigh, as if straining under an invisible burden.

Toward the end of spring vacation he takes her to an outdoor concert in one of the courtyards in the ruins of Rheinfels Castle. They are accompanied by his sisters, otherwise Elisabeth's father would not have permitted her to go. They are sitting on garden chairs in a recess of the wall while the music stands and chairs for the musicians are being set up so as to achieve optimal acoustics. Candlelight lanterns shine on the sheet music, replacing the waning daylight. Bats are on the wing and fireflies blink in the bushes that cling to the window sills and the crests of the walls.

Two of the musicians are ladies. They appear in flowing gowns and wear their hair in curls that are tied back from their foreheads in the ancient Greek manner. Like actors in a classical tragedy, they step solemnly forward from the backdrop of ruins. Then they seat themselves and begin the discordant tuning of their violins. Reinhold's sisters poke him in the ribs and wink at him. He is about to start one of his mocking routines, but a look at Elisabeth checks him. She has the posture and the distant, longing look of Anselm Feuerbach's Iphigenia—he is her favorite painter. Reinhold prefers Spitzweg and Richter, but he sympathizes because he is in love. Looking at his sisters, he gives them to understand that giggling and mockery are out of place.

Naturally, *Eine kleine Nachtmusik* is part of the program. Some people in the audience cover their faces with their hands, others lean back and gaze at the stars rising above the battlements, a few lean against the castle wall, dreamily looking across the river. During intermission they tell each other how exalted and moved they feel and that this is a rare, magic hour.

Colored goblets filled with Rhine wine are passed around. A gentleman with a white beard offers a toast to His Majesty. As the final piece, the musicians play Haydn's String Quartet opus 76, no. 3, in C Major. As Reinhold hears the melody of the German national anthem in the second movement, his eyes fill with tears. He takes Elisabeth's hand: frightened, the hand pulls away, but then returns. From then on they are engaged—for seven years.

Much later, when they were already married, Reinhold told his wife that she had been the cause of one of those terribly loud and vociferous family scenes that from time to time shook the parsonage on the Rhine like an earthquake. Visi-

40

tors always reacted in panic, but the participants felt rather refreshed because in the quiet recesses of their minds, which remained untouched by these thunderous eruptions, they were absolutely certain that no harm would come from any of this. None of those heart-rending rows had ever wrought permanent damage.

It began rather quietly with a slight draft between the door and the window of the room in the turret. Wilhelm, the oldest of the siblings, entered — even then a dignified gentleman with a full beard and the beginnings of a paunch, a fully invested minister and civil servant, married and thoroughly conscious of his authority as the first-born during this short visit back home.

He apologized for the late hour, sat down noisily in one of the wobbly wicker chairs, and asked a few perfunctory questions about Reinhold's state of health without listening to the answers. Then he went straight *in medias res*, as he liked to call it. Of course, he was happy that his little brother had finally — perhaps a bit belatedly — started on the road to adulthood. Love was an important step that every true man must sooner or later take. However, it could easily lead astray unless reason stepped in, guiding and pointing the way. At this point he lit a cigar, which he had brought with him in the pocket of his evening robe. Reinhold, still a nonsmoker at the time, ran to fetch an ashtray.

However, love and marriage, Wilhelm continued, noisily puffing on his cigar, were two entirely different things, and only someone who had already successfully steered this capricious emotion into the harbor of marriage could be a trustworthy judge in such a matter. Before braving the storm, he must think carefully about the likelihood of a successful and safe arrival in port.

His brother had selected a charming and certainly virtuous creature as the object of his affections, but that in itself was not enough in the light of possible future advancement, which could certainly be expected in this family.

41

Reinhold interrupted: he had not thought about any of this, and even if he had, he didn't want to talk about it.

Nodding and slowly exhaling the smoke of his cigar, Wilhelm acknowledged this comment, and Reinhold hoped against hope that this would end the conversation. He still had some work to do, he said, leafing through the papers on his desk, but nothing could stop Wilhelm at this point.

He intimated that—without of course in any way wishing to meddle—he had felt compelled by fraternal affection and a sense of responsibility to gather a little information about the young lady, who fortunately came from the same region as his, Wilhelm's, dear wife.

Elisabeth's father, Reinhold interrupted with irritation, was a manufacturer, if that's what he was hinting at. Her family had as much social standing as that of his sister-in-law, who was the daughter of a textile manufacturer.

On this point he decidedly begged to differ, said Wilhelm, raising his voice with the obvious intention of staying in control of the conversation. His dear wife's family had for generations owned a major industrial enterprise. They had had ample time as well as ample means to elevate themselves from the base pursuit of money to the realms of intellect and culture. The young lady's father, on the other hand, had begun as a mere rope maker and worked his way up only in recent years—unarguably with much hard work—to start his own small business, which one could call a factory only with the utmost good will.

Given this background, it was quite understandable—and no one was in the least blaming the good man—that art and culture had not yet had time to find a home within his family. As to one's own family, on the other hand, it had been anchored in the realm of the intellect by a long chain of academics. Hence one had good reasons to doubt that a natural harmony—a prerequisite for a minister to have a successful marriage—would result from such an alliance.

Perhaps private individuals could afford such facile disregard for perfectly reasonable and time-honored class distinctions—an attitude that nowadays seemed to dominate in less respectable circles—but not a minister, whose preeminent position in the community could be maintained only through the respect of all social groups and classes.

He delivered this sermon with sonorous deliberation, yet without providing the least pause for disagreement. Reinhold, who sensed a delicious anger rising within him, made several attempts to speak but could not get a word in, so he had ample time to let his wrath grow and to sort out and sharpen the weapons of his argument. While Wilhelm took another slow puff on his cigar, he asked softly and pointedly whether his older brother considered his position to conform to Christian principles. What did that have to do with anything, Wilhelm grumbled.

For a Christian there was nothing in this world that did not relate to Christ, Reinhold told him sternly. Contemptuously he swept aside Wilhelm's lame objection that Jesus had, after all, never been married. It was simply a matter of attitude. Whoever wished to follow Jesus must follow Him in spirit, and—as his brother well knew—it was the spirit of humility as well as freedom that Jesus represented. Anything less amounted to a betrayal of the Lord, just as Peter betrayed Him at the crowing of the cock.

At this, Wilhelm flared up, denying the validity of the comparison. Smiling perfidiously, Reinhold asked whether he really felt insulted by being compared to the most prominent disciple.

Meanwhile, their voices had grown loud. The door to the hallway had opened a crack, revealing the sisters' shiny, white nightgowns.

Wilhelm returned to his point about the order of society and pointed out that even Jesus had accepted it by saying: Render therefore unto Caesar the things which are Caesar's . . . , and so on.

Reinhold quickly countered that what had led up to this answer was a trick question by the Pharisees, which Jesus had deftly parried with his reply. But the Bible also commanded us to obey God rather than men and said that whosoever shall exalt himself shall be abased.

While Wilhelm was searching for counterarguments, Reinhold sank his teeth into the Pharisees, who supplied him with a wealth of biblical ammunition. Striding up and down in his room, he declaimed: "Beware the Pharisees! All their works they do for to be seen of men: they make broad their phylacteries, and enlarge the borders of their garments, and love the uppermost rooms at feasts, and the chief seats in the synagogues, and greetings in the markets.

"Ye are like unto whited sepulchers, which indeed appear beautiful outward, but are within full of dead men's bones, and of all uncleanness. . . ."

But, Wilhelm interjected vehemently, Jesus also said that He had not come to abolish the law of the scribes and Pharisees, but to fulfill it.

"But what was He going to fulfill it with?" Reinhold shouted, raising his hand toward the ceiling as if to pluck the answer from above. Then he himself came up with it: "With love!"

That was the cue for the sisters to slip at long last into the room. Wilhelm's marriage surely had less to do with love than with the filthy lucre that had come to his dear wife via the textile manufacturing business, Johanna needled her oldest brother as she passed by.

He objected to those disgusting insinuations, Wilhelm screamed at her. Anyway, this was men's talk, and the girls had better make themselves scarce.

Of course they didn't, jumping instead on Reinhold's untouched bed and wrapping their feet in his blanket because they had grown cold from standing in the hallway so long. "Carry on," Johanna said. But the two combatants had lost the thread of their argument and did not get going again until Maria said, "But the Kaiser . . ."

"What about the Kaiser?" asked Wilhelm.

"The Kaiser rules by the grace of God. Doesn't that mean that the order of society is part of God's will?"

44

"Exactly!" said Wilhelm.

"The Kaiser," Reinhold said, straightening himself, "the young Kaiser would have long since swept away the barriers that bar the people from his heart if they would only let him."

"That's where you are dead wrong," shouted Wilhelm. "His Majesty would order his guardsmen to shoot at the rebellious rabble if . . ."

Without noticing it, they had suddenly moved far away from the subject of their quarrel to the field of politics, where both were tapping around in the dark. That did not stop them from fighting the more vigorously about what the young Kaiser would have done or might still do if a clique of courtiers, secret counselors, the "Gray Eminence,"[1] and a senile chancellor did not stand in his way.

It was Wilhelm, of course, who brought up the Reds—a favorite gambit even then. He used them the same way Reinhold had used the Pharisees a moment ago, except that he did not base his arguments on the Bible but on the conversations his father-in-law, the textile manufacturer, was wont to conduct in business circles.

Under this barrage, an unsuspected little revolutionary raised his head in Reinhold's breast; fed by anger, he now shot to his full height. Even in the conservative town of Halle, where he was studying at the time, it was possible on occasion to meet a Christian socialist. Not that he was personally acquainted with any of them. He had, so to speak, taken in their slogans with the air he breathed, and even though he knew little or nothing about his background or any other details, he quickly decided in favor of Naumann because that would force Wilhelm, if anything, to take the side of Court Chaplain Stoecker. He railed against the ultraconservatives of the *Kreuzzeitung* party and demanded, with appropriately dramatic gestures, a "popular and progressive empire" in which "the Social Democrats would be part of the political process."[2]

At the mention of Social Democrats the sisters flinched as if he had used an indecent expression. He relished their horror and began to expound effusively on liberty, equality, and fraternity. Then he thought of Beethoven's Ninth Symphony: Love, toward countless millions swelling, wafts one kiss to all the world! Brothers, 'neath yon stars unfurl'd, some kind father has his dwelling. . . .

Relishing the sound of his own voice, he fervently wished that Elisabeth were there to listen, instead of a gaggle of silly sisters. Cautiously, so that no one would notice, he reached behind his back and opened the window, hoping that now, at this very instant, she would be taking her evening stroll on the Rhine promenade and, halting her step, would turn her ear to listen.

"Oh, if only my Elisabeth were the daughter of a tannery worker," he shouted louder than necessary, "then I could prove to you all . . ."

"You are out of your head," Wilhelm screamed, and Father, who had for some time been standing unnoticed in the doorway, cleared his throat and said, "All right, now, that's all!"

Reluctantly, like runners who are stopped before reaching the finish line, the two opponents turned around.

"It's about Elisabeth," said Johanna. "Wilhelm thinks . . ."

Father did not want to hear about Wilhelm's opinions.

"I think our little one has made a good choice," he said.

They wrote each other every day during the seven years of their engagement. He usually sent picture postcards covered with tiny, scraggly letters and every now and then a weighty epistle written in installments. She wrote to him every night. Impatiently, with forceful ascenders and descenders, the old German script of her writing rushes forward, toward him. . . .

In 1906 they were married and traveled to Capri for their honeymoon, presumably with a heavy conscience because both their fathers had recently died. They had waited, contemplated, anticipated, and written to each other for so long that now they could not wait another day. A sepia-colored

46

photograph shows them standing in a kind of bower between ancient columns and bushes of oleander. He is dressed in dark colors, except for a white button-on collar and tennis shoes. He stands in a somewhat awkward pose. One can see he is knock-kneed. A bushy mustache covers up his lips. He holds her hand behind his back. She seems to have just stepped up to him. Her long skirt still swings out to the side, the bow at her neck is slightly askew. She looks younger and livelier than in any of the earlier photographs. Her cheek-bones are less prominent, her lips are more relaxed. She carries her head more freely, almost charmingly, as if she needed no longer pull herself together.

5

When they speak of the Kaiser in the parsonage at Auel they mean both the old and the young emperor. The young emperor is meanwhile also so old that in the child's imagination the two figures blur into an aged "twinity"—almost as distant as the Father in Heaven and just as beloved and honored.

Every January Father writes a birthday letter to His Majesty the German Emperor in Doorn.[1] He prepares several drafts, which he reads to his wife for her comments. They ponder and choose carefully, thinking about what impression this or that phrase might make on His Majesty. The general tone is to be reverential, yet the wording must appeal to the heart.

Once they have decided on the final text, Father makes a fair copy in his fine, black, "etched" handwriting on the very best handmade paper, specially purchased for the occasion. He personally carries the envelope to the post office.

On 27 January the family gathers around the black piano in the parlor. Mother plays the accompaniment by striking hymnal chords, which she sets down side by side like monoliths. Sometimes they come a little late because she is searching for the right note; that in turn causes the others to slow down so that she will not get upset and confused. They sing the family's birthday song, "Praise ye the Lord, the Almighty, the king of creation," and after that "Father, give Thy blessing to the emperor and his house."

Father announces that this is a day of happiness because the Kaiser has been given the gift of another year of life, but it is also a day of sorrow, since he cannot celebrate it among his own, beloved people. He concludes with the Lord's Prayer.

The child makes an effort to "participate with all her heart," tightly shutting her eyes and thinking of something sad. Sometimes she succeeds in "seeing" the Kaiser. Dressed in his helmet and uniform, he sits by the window of a gray palace by the sea, turning his sorrowful eagle's eye toward his distant Germany, which has disowned him. The Kaiser's birthday is one of those days on which the children are expected to conduct themselves with dignity even after the family service is over. That means no silliness, no light music, no laughing. If they forget themselves, a pained look suffices to awaken their conscience.

February is a time of great expectations: long hours of waiting whether this year perchance will bring a reply that is different from those received in all the previous years. But it turns out to be the same, after all: a white, unlined envelope with the return address: Berlin W 8, Unter den Linden 11 (formerly no. 26). Why not Doorn? Nobody asks. Some day H.M. will return to his palace Unter den Linden. Meanwhile he maintains an office there that takes care of whatever work needs to be done, such as replying to birthday wishes. "There are a great many of them," Father says as he carefully opens the envelope with his penknife, "literally mountains of good wishes, so that with the best will in the world H.M. could not answer all of them personally." He speaks these words hastily, as a precautionary measure, even before unfolding the sheet of paper, so as to provide an excuse for the meager, typed line that appears as the paper is unfolded:

SINCERE THANKS FOR THE GOOD WISHES ON
THE OCCASION OF MY BIRTHDAY

beneath an imposing letterhead with the eagle-headed coat of arms, from which is suspended the Order of Merit; below that it says, in pompously ornate letters:

MAILGRAM FROM HIS MAJESTY THE EMPEROR
AND KING.

But the envelope bears nothing more than a regular 12-Pfennig Hindenburg stamp. The IR appearing inside the third loop of the signature does not stand for "in retirement," the children are told, but for "Imperator Rex." At some length Father contemplates the paper that contains so little, then hands it to Mother, and the child knows exactly what is going through her head as she quickly glances at it, folds it, and returns it. She is thinking: just once, after all these years, His

Majesty could have written a personal reply; he could have spared that much time from chopping wood.

But she does not say it out loud. Nobody says anything, and Father carries the envelope up to his study. He sits down at his desk and examines the letter once more with utmost care, using his glasses, the pince-nez, and a magnifying glass, with a glimmer of hope in the back of his mind, like a child who keeps searching under the Christmas tree, after all gifts have been unwrapped, for the one present he had most passionately wanted but did not get—secretly, of course, so as not to hurt anyone.

Only once does he reveal a touch of disappointment. "The old Kaiser . . . ," he starts out; then he stops, raises his shoulders and drops them in a gesture of resignation: "Those were different times. . . ."

Reinhold had just turned thirteen when the old Kaiser died at the age of ninety-one. In this black month of March 1888, the boy writes in his scrapbook:

> *Kaiser Wilhelm went in peace*
> *Up into his fathers' realm,*
> *Closed his eyes and left his children*
> *Without guidance at the helm.*
> *In our hearts we shall retain him*
> *And remember those clear eyes*
> *Of a king who loved his people,*
> *Of a father good and wise.*

In some places the letters look smeared as if water had run over them. Perhaps he was crying as he wrote.

Grandfather is said to have referred to the old Kaiser as the king. It appears he would have preferred that Bismarck had let His Majesty remain King of Prussia and left the old order of things unchanged. The tears that Wilhelm I shed just before he was crowned emperor in the Hall of Mirrors at Versailles seem to have flowed straight into his heart. That is the way he loved his king: plain, modest, loyal, a man of "simple, upright spirit" (no more mention of the "grapeshot prince"[2]), a good father, a devoted husband, an attentive but thrifty host. Before uncorking a new bottle of champagne, he asks if any is left over from the day before. He says that he did not learn how to eat lobster at home; it was the Czar who finally had to teach him. He feels most comfortable in his dressing gown. Plain home cooking is what he likes best. Intrigues do not touch him. Like his grandfather, he is hard of hearing.

Warm family feelings go from the father of the household in St. Goar to the country's father in Berlin.

Those are the "old times" that remain behind when Reinhold begins his one-year stint of military service in the barracks at Diez on the Lahn River.

There is a photograph dating from the time he served as a soldier. The flat cap sits squarely on his head, the visor covering his forehead almost down to the bridge of his nose. His head looks flat, as if someone had hit him over the pate. A martial mustache, its tips carefully brushed upward, sprouts above an uneasy smile.

The half-length picture—gold-buttoned uniform coat, stand-up collar, epaulets and all—is framed by a horseshoe decorated with violets and anemones. Dramatic thunderclouds above, a tiny landscape with a tiny church and a tiny house in front of an Alpine backdrop. They would have hung that kind of poster on their walls, if posters had existed at that time.

Once, during the 1930s, parents and child traveled from St. Goar to Diez on the Lahn to see the town where Father had been a soldier in 1899.

It was a difficult but wonderful time, he says, as they ride the train up the valley of the Lahn—a time among men. Not just any group of men, but soldiers; and not just any soldiers, but one-year volunteers, officer candidates, the Kaiser's elite—they called him the "young Kaiser" although he was already forty-one years old. One could tell at a glance that today's young people had never served their country: they lacked self-possession, polish, and discipline as well as a sense of authority and obedience. Such qualities could not be acquired at the university, let alone at party headquarters. Not that he had exactly been a model recruit. Keeping order and doing "manual things" had always been problems for him. He often made himself conspicuous during roll call. Endurance had not been one of his strong points either. He had never been much of a blood-and-guts type. But he got along well with his superiors and his fellow soldiers and always performed with a double dose of enthusiasm.

While he looks with unseeing eyes at the lovely scenery that is passing by, he tries to relate how he felt when they marched through the narrow streets of Diez, their songs and marching steps echoing from the walls of the houses, and all the polished, shiny boots flying up in unison and coming down on the cobble stones with a single crack. He felt a thunderous rushing in his head, tears welling up in his eyes, a sense of exhilaration that he can describe only inadequately as feeling both small and grand at the same time: small, as a single entity submerged in a crowd of equals; grand, as part of the close formation marching behind the young emperor into the future.

He had almost pitied the civilians watching the parade from the side of the street: they seemed so small, a gray and somehow sorry lot.

His cheeks flush as he is talking. With an undertone of censure, as if to suggest that alcohol is involved, Mother finds him to be in "high spirits." The child also feels that he is strange, less loving, not quite her father. She throws herself across his lap but is pushed back impatiently: Go and sit up nice and straight!

It was here in the barracks at Diez, he says, not while studying at the universities of Halle, Tübingen, or Bonn, that he realized for the first time that he had outgrown his parents' home, that he was an adult. For all the love he felt for it, the parsonage on the Rhine and his aged parents with their distrust of the ambitious empire suddenly seemed to him to belong to the past. His Kaiser did not sit in a dressing gown at the family table but astride a stallion, medals gleaming on his uniform, saber pointing to the heavens: Onward! Follow me! Only after he had joined the young emperor's retinue did he become a true man—an experience women probably could not understand.

After they get off the train and are walking through the streets, he is mostly silent. There is probably not much left from those earlier days, or he does not think it worth his while to point out this or that because he may have noticed that his wife and daughter do not understand the essential point: the exhilarating feeling that makes the tears well up while marching through those narrow streets lined with wretched civilians.

The child finds the small town dreary and wants to return to St. Goar, where they have a swimming pool and a ping-pong table. But he wants to stay on, though he is unable to explain why. He lets the noon train depart and insists that they enter a tavern, where he drinks more than his usual quantity of the dangerous young wine. He sits facing the window and looks out through the filthy curtains as if he were expecting someone.

"Think of your stomach," Mother says, and the child asks: "When is the next train?" She senses his rejection and is angry with him for wanting to be rid of mother and daughter so that he can sit in the twilight with his private memories of men, soldiers, comrades in arms. She begrudges him these thoughts. Suddenly he relents. They arrive at the station an hour early, sit around, and have nothing to say to each other. On the way back he pretends to be asleep.

To please Father, the child invents a new game—"soldiers." She puts her father's black helmet with brass spike and brass eagle over her pigtails and makes the boy next door put on an army cap. She puts him through his drills with a BB gun: "Shoulder arms! Order arms! Preeesent arms!" In the back of the parsonage garden in Auel they dig a trench and fog themselves in against the enemy by burning wet leaves in a little potbellied stove. When it is time to sound taps, they stick a beanpole flying the black-red-white colors into the drainage hole under the kitchen window and shout three cheers for His Majesty.

"Go ahead and shout," says Gertrud, the servant girl, who wears her red hair fashionably bobbed. "He can't hear you back there in Holland. He's made his pile already."

Furious, the child storms into the kitchen, confronts her, and badgers her until she reveals in a whisper what she thinks of the Kaiser: He's a coward. First he started the war, and when it was lost he took off and left his people to take care of the mess.

For a moment the child remains dumbfounded, then she screams: "The Kaiser is not a coward! The Kaiser didn't take off! I'm going to tell Father!" She is beating Gertrud with her fists, but the servant catches her by the wrists and holds her firmly at a distance so that the child cannot reach her with her feet. The child is dancing in her grip, screaming and spitting, until her mother enters. Sobbing, she throws herself into her mother's arms and tells her what the girl has said to her. Mother's withering glance does not reach Gertrud because she is bending her flushed face over her embroidery: a tablecloth for her dowry—red flowers, brown stems, green leaves, cross-stitched hem. . . .

The child sits waiting in the playroom, poking holes into the little wooden school bench, while her parents are having a long talk in the study. Then Father comes down alone and takes her along on his way to the confirmation class.

For a while they walk in silence, without the usual fun of her jumping over his stick and race-walking him. He has placed his arm around the child's shoulders, holding her close. "Don't listen to any of it," he finally says. "They don't know what they are talking about. The very same people who are complaining today that he left them in the lurch sent him away in 1918."

"Can an emperor be sent away?" the child asks. "Does an emperor have to leave when he is sent away?"

"He doesn't have to," he says. "Only God, who anointed him, can release him from his task. God knows what these people don't understand: that his departure was a sacrifice, the last and the most trying sacrifice that he made for his people. Sacrifices, too, can be heroic deeds, but few are able to recognize actions that do not shine. One can always tell those who are truly loyal; they maintain their loyalty even in adversity—just as the song has it: "When all become disloyal, we never shall lose faith." Rats leave a sinking ship!"

"You are one of the loyal," the child says. "I want to be loyal, too."

On the way home the child asks what is going to become of Gertrud. Will she have to go, or is he at least going to give her a good dressing-down?

But he will have nothing to do with it. Handling the servants is Mother's business, he says. And nothing much is accomplished by talking. There are people who simply cannot fathom greatness and nobility because their lives have never been touched by what is great and noble. ("You should thank God that your parents have provided you with that experience.") One has to be a model of greatness and nobility for them, so that they will get some inkling. As for Gertrud, there isn't much hope. She is stirred up, exposed to a bad influence. Her boyfriend, who is taking her on motorcycle rides every Sunday, is Red—like most proletarians; and it was the Reds who betrayed the Kaiser.

In Auel, the Reds live "on the other side of the tracks," in a part of town called Zange.[3] The child is not allowed to play there, nor does she want to. She is afraid and walks through the underpass, where it smells like pee, only when she can hold her father's hand. On the other side, everything is more depressing: the light is grayer, the people are shabbier, the houses look less like homes.

Russia must look like that.

Reds are people who do unspeakable things to little girls. The unemployed man who sometimes helps with the yard chores pulls the child on his knee behind the compost bin and, quick as lightning, puts his hand between her legs. She runs away, does not mention it to anyone, but can never forget it: he must have been one of the Reds.

In elementary school there is a girl named Sonja. Her brother, one grade ahead, is called Dimitri. Their father is Red, a Russian peon, the minister's children say. They follow the two in the street and chant:

> *Sonja Sonja and Dimitriyevsky*
> *Live behind the post offe-e-ece.*

Their parents complain to the child's mother, and she reprimands her. "It is not the children's fault," she says.

The child knows about Russians from a picture book about the war. A wild, bearded oaf with slanted eyes, boozy-red nose, and a mouth full of fangs, the Russian tramps through the swamp. With one of his paws he holds open a bag, with the other he reaches for Willi, the brave little soldier:

> *The Russian, covered all with hair,*
> *Comes tromping like a grizzly bear.*
> *His snort one never can forget:*
> *Just wait, you runt, I'll catch you yet!*

In the next picture Willi fires his gun, and the monstrous fiend sinks roaring into the swamp, throwing back his head so that one can see into his mouth and hairy nose.

> *Quick, shoot the gun, straight at his head!*
> *Bang! Bang! the Russian fiend is dead.*
> *But Willi laughs and thinks forever,*
> *I'm mighty smart and pretty clever!*

56

Only once in his life, in a French village called Maure, has Father come "face to face" with his Kaiser. He points out the place on a torn military topo map, on which the name of the town has become illegible by repeated touching. Maure must be somewhere in the Champagne region, south of Vouziers, where Father began to serve as a volunteer chaplain in December 1914. "That's where it was," he says. "Suddenly I stood directly in front of him and didn't even recognize him."

It was Reinhold's first outing in the horse and wagon he had been issued for official business, because riding horseback was still something of a problem for him. Engrossed in preparing for a speech, he almost fell off his seat when the orderly sharply pulled on the reins in the middle of town and pointed to a group of officers by the roadside. Reinhold recognized and greeted his commander, who signaled him to come over.

Reluctant, because he was in a hurry, he climbed down from the wagon. Only after he had gotten quite close did the circle open and reveal the man at the center.

"I must have been a total blockhead," he tells the child, "completely blind, not to have known immediately before whom I was standing—the noble features of the Hohenzollern, the incomparable look. I was even annoyed about the delay until someone spoke the word 'Majesty.'" By that time it was all but over: handshake, mumbled words about unselfish devotion and gratitude of the fatherland, military salute. Reinhold, as speechless as a fish, actually did not feel anything at that moment, none of the honor, the immeasurable joy, only dizziness and nausea rising from his stomach. Perhaps it was too much, too grand, too brief. Already the gentlemen turned away and, with the Kaiser leading the way, walked toward the open military vehicle that was parked a short distance away in the church square. They got in, drove down the muddy village street, and the orderly cleared his throat behind him and said: "They sure have a way of gadding about, these gentlemen!"

He won't exactly say that he was disappointed, but it took a long time before he began to feel joy—not until he composed the telegram to the family. Among picture postcards and letters written in those years of the war, he searches for the yellowed form of the military postal service. It bears the date of 17 March 1915, and reads:

I HAVE MET MY EMPEROR. OVERJOYED. FATHER.

In the mid-twenties, when the Weimar Republic experienced its economic miracle, Reinhold and his two older brothers took a cruise through the fjords of Norway. They called it their "Northland voyage" and kept thinking of the Kaiser and his cruises aboard the H.M.S. *Hohenzollern.* "Along this miraculous coastline, which bestowed on H.M. such well-earned peace and relaxation after months of hard work on behalf of his beloved people," he writes on board the *Sierra Cordoba* to his family back home.

They also wanted to memorialize the only navy battle of the First World War and, at the beginning of the cruise, had arranged with the captain to hold a ceremony, for which Reinhold, the most military of the brothers, had prepared a speech.

When the ship reached the Straits of Skagerrak, the captain stopped the engines and assembled the crew. The passengers, properly dressed for the occasion, also appeared on deck. While Reinhold was barking his brief speech into the wind, he sorely missed his uniform. Only the small ribbons that came with the two Iron Crosses marked him as a war veteran. The atmosphere emanating from the rather mixed audience suggested to him that they were "moved." The only disturbing element was a group of young people who did not participate in the ceremony. Instead of having the decency of withdrawing to the rooms below, they sat and talked at the other end of the deck. They were not really loud, but during a pause between the final prayer and the trumpeter's rendition of "I once had a brave, young comrade" the wind carried over a woman's laughter, which deeply hurt not only Reinhold's feelings. A general murmur went through the audience regarding the lack of respectfulness of the young generation, while a wreath, which the brothers had jointly launched over the railing, was bobbing upon the waves.

The "sad experience" that Reinhold mentions in a letter mailed from Vansges happened a few days later during his stay at Sognefjord.

In the afternoon, the travelers had gone ashore to admire the enormous statue of Fritjof,[4] which H.M. had presented to the Norwegian people in 1913. They returned for supper on board, but later the brothers wanted to go back to Vansges to mingle with the "hardy people" who were "so dear to the heart of our Kaiser." But it was not to happen, at least not for Reinhold.

The sad experience began, at the start of supper, with gales of laughter at the next table. A certain "cynical tone" reached his ears and prevented him from continuing an informative conversation about the midnight sun. Whether he liked it or not, he had to listen to what a "young snotty fellow," allegedly on the basis of his intimate knowledge, reported about the daily routine aboard the H.M.S. *Hohenzollern*. It concerned the imperial morning exercise, for which H.M. assembled his companions at 9 A.M. Nobody was permitted to absent himself, no matter how heavy his stomach felt from indulging in too much food and drink the previous evening. Wearing an admiral's uniform, H.M. took the lead: Chest out! Suck in your gut! Down with your butt! And jump—one, two, three! And if one of the wobbly-kneed dignitaries held his creaky knee bend too long, H.M. would walk down the rows, kick him in the behind, and send him sprawling. And everybody would laugh, including the one lying flat—albeit with a sour face.

He wasn't telling any fairy tales, the snotty fellow asserted. His very own uncle, then in his sixties, had been a favorite object of these kicks. He had violently complained of such imperial highhandedness—or rather highfootedness—to his brother, the snotty fellow's father.

Already at this point Reinhold wanted to "intervene." What stopped him was the young man's appearance, which was not what he had expected: he was not puny, did not wear glasses, nor did he have the offensive features of a lout who had risen like scum from the yeast of the people, disadvantaged by nature, hence poisonous, treacherous, infamous, possibly Jewish. To the contrary, he was tall, slim, blond, evidently of good stock, and it was entirely plausible that he had an uncle in the emperor's retinue. Even his voice had that hard, ringing tone, the brisk diction of the imperial officers corps, which made what he said even more of a "slap in the face." Reinhold flushed in anger; each forkful of food "stuck in his throat," as the snotty fellow continued, mocking the religious services on board, in which H.M. played the role of the preacher, and by laughing at the festivities held on board with their dramatic presentations, which were on the level of a "school for the mentally retarded." Finally Reinhold could no longer square it with his conscience to listen to such disgraceful talk. He noisily dropped his spoon in his plate, stood up, stepped up to the snotty fellow, his knees shaking inside his pants because he loathed nothing more than making a public scene, and said: "Shame on you!"

All conversations stopped. Heads turned his way. The snotty fellow told the woman who was with him (though they were allegedly not married) to stop giggling under her breath, turned around, and studied Reinhold with a look that struck him as "brazen." The Kaiser had really not been a bad sort of fellow, he said casually—and Reinhold felt that he deserved to be smacked for "had been" and "fellow," but in spite of his towering rage he could not bring himself to do it. To hit someone, to actually inflict pain on a face or body with his hand, was something he could not bring himself to do, a physical impossibility, an insurmountable barrier that he considered a "weakness," a personal "defect." He felt like a "sissy" as he turned away with a barely audible expression of disgust and walked the long way to the door with all eyes focused on him, all the while afraid that his shaking knees would be visible to everyone. The brazen voice followed him and penetrated his ears despite the drumbeat of his racing heart throbbing in his temples: "You preached so beautifully at the Skagerrak ceremony, Reverend. Did you ever ask yourself whether the people may have paid too high a price for this imperial toy, the fleet, which was not allowed to fight at the right time and then was sent into battle at the wrong time only to be pulled back at the peak of the conflict, after having sustained totally pointless losses of sixty-one thousand tons and several thousand sailors?"

The words were still ringing in his ears as he threw himself on the bed in his cabin. When his brothers arrived, they immediately began talking to him: He had made a noble exit; everyone had taken his side and shown contempt for the shameless lot. They would have followed him at once—honestly!—had they not looked for another opportunity to lay into that ingrate. Unfortunately, it did not happen. As soon as they started to tell him off, he got up and walked out without a word.

What was going on inside him as he stalked the empty hallways of the ship—the others had meanwhile crossed over to Vansges—would have been impossible for him to explain to his brothers. Even the letter contains only hints about the suspicion that was growing within him like a tumor: that there might be some truth to what the snotty fellow said, "that modern, ice-cold kind of truth that is devoid of shame, reverence, and love." He had successfully fended off that truth for years, but now for the first time—perhaps because he was alone, without family, without congregation, without the elevating steps of altar and pulpit—it got under his skin; it spread like acid over the picture of the Kaiser as a shining hero riding in the vanguard, a picture he had carried steadfastly within him since Diez despite all the dirt that had been flung "from below."

He had suddenly felt old, he writes, "as old as I actually am—fifty." He had always been able to joke about his age—an old man is no spring chicken!—and had been amazed that aging did not bother him either mentally or physically: "When you are busy with your work, you have no time to think about getting old."

Now it was suddenly upon him, not just internally, with something like a cold shudder, a heaviness of the limbs that made it difficult to walk the hallways, but also externally, as if everything that the eye beheld were in the process of rapid decline: threadbare carpets, bleak passages, shabby stuffed chairs, tarnished fittings, stale air. Even the "grand northern night" shrunk before his eyes. No matter how deeply he breathed, he could not relieve the constriction in his breast.

When he finally returned to the salon, tired to the bone with a fatigue that he knew was not conducive to sleep, the ceiling light had already been extinguished; only the small reading lamps with their green silk shades were still burning.

He began a letter to the Kaiser on the ship's stationery, which had been set out in folders. Beneath the letterhead North German Lloyd, on board S.S. *Sierra Cordoba,* he wrote to H.M. how hard and lonely a life it was for his loyal followers in this new Germany, where people no longer aspired to the high, the true, and the beautiful but to the gutter, wallowing in dirt, throwing dirt, even creating so-called works of art out of dirt. . . . Then he read what he had written and tore it up: Who am I to presume to burden the emperor's heart with my troubles? Only the letter to his wife survived.

Later he once more went out on deck. Leaning against the railing, he stood for a long time and breathed his pain into the night, until he finally came up with an idea that compensated him for the anxieties he had experienced that night. This ship, he imagined, was not just any steamer on a pleasure cruise but his Kaiser's own vessel; and he who was standing exhausted at the railing was not just a tourist, but the last loyal follower, who silently took upon himself all adversities so that his sovereign could sleep peacefully. When one of the crew tiptoed past him, he awoke as from a dream, he writes. He quickly left and clambered down to his cabin, where his brothers were dissonantly snoring their way toward breakfast. He felt almost cheerful, "mysteriously comforted." The whole sad experience had, in the end, shown him a way to honor his Kaiser, not the shining hero riding in the vanguard, but the "young man of noble lineage," imperiled, helpless, in need of protection; someone for whom one has to assume an almost paternal responsibility, who must be defended even when the attacks against him contain a grain of truth.

"Impulsive" and "immature" he was able to call him in later years, without considering it a betrayal. "Too broadly gifted, hence somewhat volatile, undecided, often misunderstood and misguided, driven by a high enthusiasm for ideas and people, lonely, yet with a burning desire for friendship, a hotspur, a brilliant mind soaring beyond the petty business of politics, too easily taken in, too trusting, too frank and honest for this evil world that begrudges him his soaring flight." All the world's envy and the misfortunes of fate had forged an alliance to clip the eagle's wings: the misshapen arm, the scheming mother, the evil old Bismarck, his false friends, the greed and ambition of the courtiers, the envy of other nations, the internationalists, the disloyalty of the people, the Reds. . . . In the single letter to H.M., which he wrote and promptly mailed the next morning from Vansges, he writes: "Three brothers, pastors from the Rhineland, stood in front of the magnificent Fritjof memorial and thought of Your Majesty in steadfast love, vowing to follow Your Majesty's example loyally by devoting all their strength to tireless and total service on behalf of their beloved fatherland."

The answer arrived with a photograph and signature and a text that was somewhat longer than usual:

WE ARE PLEASED TO ACCEPT THE VOW OF
STEADFAST LOYALTY AND FIRMLY TRUST THAT,
IN ACCORDANCE WITH THE ENCLOSED GUIDE-
LINES, TIRELESS EFFORTS BE MADE FROM
ALTAR AND PULPIT FOR THE RECONSTRUCTION
OF OUR VANQUISHED FATHERLAND AND FOR
THE KAISER AND EMPIRE. . . .

The enclosed guidelines have unfortunately been lost.

Fourteen years later, shortly before the beginning of World War II, a major from northern Germany had been issued quarters at the Auel parsonage during maneuvers. In the evening he liked to sit with the family "because the atmosphere reminded him of his own home." He had insisted, already at the first introduction, that the pastor's face looked familiar; my father, in spite of his excellent memory for faces, did not remember him. One evening, as they got to talk about traveling and the pastor recalled his Northland voyage, the major jumped to his feet, seized him by the shoulders, and shouted: "You are the minister whom I offended so deeply at that time!"

He was delighted, he said, that he was finally given an opportunity to apologize for his earlier faux pas. Even while still on shipboard, he had tried to talk to the minister, but he had ignored him in a manner that made it impossible to establish any contact.

When the minister shrank back in annoyance, the major pulled up his chair and spoke with emotion of the change he had undergone in the meantime. He had not exactly become a monarchist—those times were probably gone forever—but in the course of the years and in view of the sorry spectacle presented by the Republic, he had realized ever more clearly that the German people had neither the inclination nor the talent for what is called democracy. Even Bismarck had said: "As for the Germans, their love of country requires a prince on whom they can focus their devotion." Only a ruler legitimized by God would be capable of bringing out the best qualities of the Germans. Now he was happy to be able to serve his Führer.

They must celebrate their reunion with champagne, he said, and since the cellar contained only wine—no sparkling wine, let alone champagne—his orderly would have to get up from his straw mattress in the attic and go in search of champagne.

The pastor let himself be persuaded to tell some of his war stories, and the major all but went into ecstasy. Life was such a stale and empty thing in times of peace, and people were so petty, narrow, and selfish. The great emotions—love of one's country, death-defying courage, manly friendships—could only blossom in the presence of death.

He envied the minister for having participated in the great World War. If he had been born only fifteen years earlier, he too would have been a part of it. Well, there was always hope for the future.

At some point, the minister left the room and was absent for quite a while.

The major began to talk of his childhood. He too had been brought up in such a decent, patriotic family but had parted from them in anger, thrown himself into the big-city bustle and cheap pleasures of Berlin, and forgotten the ideals of his childhood. Then his eyes had been opened at one of the Führer's speeches, and he had returned to the old, sacred values.

Even Mother was deeply moved by this account.

Suddenly the door opened and the minister was standing in the door, dressed in his old, green gray uniform: the short military jacket, the tight pants with violet stripes, the southwester trimmed with a violet ribbon on his head.[5]

The major burst into applause, roared bravo!, filled the glasses, and went up to the minister with his glass, trying to draw him into the room by the arm to toast the Kaiser and the Führer. But the pastor suddenly pulled back. Confused, as if waking from a dream, he stared at the glass and the hand on his arm. Then he shook the hand off and stepped back out into the hall.

The door had barely closed behind him when Mother got up and said: "Now it is time to go to bed."

As she said good night to the child, she explained that Father had not intended to have the kind of masquerade that the major made of it with his applause. The cause was far too sacred, the uniform too honorable.

Father did not come back. He had already gone to bed.

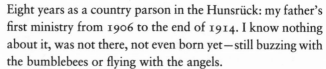

6 Eight years as a country parson in the Hunsrück: my father's first ministry from 1906 to the end of 1914. I know nothing about it, was not there, not even born yet—still buzzing with the bumblebees or flying with the angels.

Simmern belongs to my older siblings. I cannot share their memories. The invitations to come and visit the Hunsrück and the food packages from the country are not addressed to me; the names of friends mean nothing to me. There are no letters from that time. Mother never talks about it. A single surviving photograph shows her alone with the "four little ones" on the stairs of a country house. It must have been taken in the spring of 1915. Father had already gone off to the war. With a list of questions, not just about Simmern, I visit Gerhard, the older of my brothers, a country parson carrying on a family tradition that the others have more or less abandoned—especially the youngest, the one who is called "the child," "the kid," or "the brat" by her brothers and sisters. Gerhard has always said that she was treated with kid gloves and permitted to do what the others did not dare dream about, that the parents were "blinded by love" for their youngest and some day would "have a rude awakening."

Even though decades have gone by, the pattern of our old relationship clicks in with lightning speed as soon as I enter the parsonage, where all the relics of the paternal profession are stored: marble crucifix, Luther woodcut, Grandfather's portrait.

The flow of information runs unevenly: smoothly in regard to personal anecdotes, but slowly, even haltingly, in answer to more fundamental questions: What was Father's attitude toward the war, toward authority, toward the Republic, toward dialectical theology?

I have prepared myself for this conversation by reading a good bit of history and theology, with particular attention to those who were my father's teachers and models—Martin Kähler, Adolf Schlatter.[1]

Gerhard does not think much of my effort: I would hardly come to the right kind of understanding by reading books

66

because I do not share the basic assumptions on which these writings rest. He is referring to what in theological circles is called "prior knowledge," the essential foundation of their whole system of thought; namely, that God exists. What I am lacking, he assumes, is the "personal experience of God." I recognize the smile of the theologian on his lips. "With all due love," he pushes me aside, places me on "the bench where the scornful sit," puts me among those who lack the authority of faith. He treats me like the pushy beggar who, when he appeared at the door of the parsonage at Auel, never received a handout, in contrast to the "modest," "self-effacing," "grateful" one, who was richly rewarded. In his mind, I deserve the epithets that the family's vocabulary keeps in stock for such cases: "forward," "annoying," "presumptuous." I lack "modesty," "perspective," a "tactful disposition." I am a "snoop," "sticking my nose into things that are none of my business"; I "force things out of context" and "presume to make judgments." One would think that I myself would loathe my journalistic nosiness, he says, knowing full well that our likes and dislikes spring from the same source. Had I not been brought up in a different spirit of infinite love— more lasting, more tender, more indulgent—than my older siblings?

All of this is familiar to me from my childhood and evokes childish reactions in me and a sad feeling of futility that I cannot articulate. With jaunty arrogance I put my jeans-clad leg across the corner of his desk and read to him what I have culled from my readings of old church journals that I have looked up in the Institute for Protestant Theology. My brother turns away and steps up to the window. I see his back and his narrow, sloping shoulders that remind me of our father. Angrily I repress the childish desire to have him, just once, think well of me and praise me, as my father used to praise me. Of course, that doesn't occur to him. He nods, calls out, and raises his hand as he greets passing parishioners, demonstrating for me his success as a country parson, his experience—contrary to our father's—in the affairs of farm-

67

ers, craftsmen, laborers, and shop keepers. Whoever succeeds him in office will find it difficult to fill his shoes. It will be hard on him to see someone else laboring in his vineyard. Listening to me is also hard on him. I can tell by the tension in his neck. We know each other and cannot fool each other: neither am I fooled by him nor he by me. How old does one have to be to see the human qualities in a brother?

Deliberately cool and casual, I read to him some of the passages my father also must have read in the past (did he skim them? accept them? agree with them?): "As the church manifests itself in Christ, so the state manifests itself in the person of the ruler. . . ." "The Prussian monarchy is for us Protestants a thousand times more than a political issue—it is a matter of faith. . . ." "Democracy is rebellion against God's commandment. . . ." "Political parties are contrary to the spirit of the Protestant church. . . ." "Nothing can be more superficial than the guaranteed freedom to pursue social systems and institutions or political philosophies, rather than seek after a morality based on religion and a conscience honed by faith. . . ."

Would our father have agreed? Would those ideas have been confirmed by studying the Bible or by his personal experience of God? Did the break that occurred in Protestant theology with Karl Barth's interpretation of the Epistle to the Romans[2] have any consequences for him?

"You must have discussed these things," I say, "you, a student of theology since 1929, who attended Barth's lectures in Bonn, and your father, the minister." All Gerhard remembers is that our father once said that Barth, after all, was Swiss. His tone had been not so much derogatory as sad, as if referring not simply to a different nationality but to another—perhaps even enviable—relationship to nationality. It seemed to him less profoundly fateful, less emotionally satisfying, less of a weighty responsibility to be Swiss in the tradition of Calvin than to be German in the tradition of Luther and the sacred obligation that came with Luther's commitment to the divine purpose and function of the state, no matter how such a state came into being or what particular form it took.

Gerhard and his father had not discussed the political implications of Barth's theology. "Is it really all that important?" He sees something compulsive in this fixation on politics. At the time of the empire, the questions I now raise were not yet at issue. There was no conflict between following Christ and worshipping the Kaiser and the fatherland. The state is God's executive on earth. Every Christian owes obedience to the state as long as obedience does not hinder him in the exercise of his Christian duty. Such a conflict was not anticipated and did not occur. The king and emperor was an active member of the Protestant church.

"But there were people who felt deprived of their freedom," I interject. "For example, the younger Blumhardt."[3]

"He was one of the Reds," says Gerhard. "And with the Reds reconciliation was, of course, impossible."

"Why 'of course'? Is there a law against it?"

Gerhard believes that I have come under the influence of my son Thomas, who has been infected with Marxism. "Are you two still raking up the past? Aren't you getting sick and tired of it by now?" In case I am referring to a sense of guilt, there isn't a Christian without it, because we are all sinners.

"I did not mean it generally, but specifically, individually."

"No psychology, please!" He is suspicious of psychology, refers to it as "Freudian soul picking." A Christian has no need of it. He has his conscience, God's word, and the forgiveness of sins.

He finds my agitation amusing. Acting the older brother, he points out that a person of my age and family background should assume a posture of superiority. "If you only knew your proper place!" These young fanatics, caught up in outmoded theories, are completely estranged from life, both past and present. They are forever shut out from the most profound and most sublime experiences of a person of faith wrestling with moral scruples and his conscience.

"That's why I am here," I say, "to talk with you about moral scruples and wrestling with one's conscience."

"Talk," he snorts. "Nothing but words!"

We are unable to communicate. In the end, our discussion yields only personal affairs stored in the family memory, unrelated to the historical context, of which I have nothing but "irreverent" book knowledge, from the "German fleet fiasco" to the "war that was to prove the survival of the fittest." All of that is irrelevant, has "finally nothing to do" with our father. Apparently he passed through it completely untouched—just like the children of Israel, who "went into the sea upon the dry land, and the waters were a wall unto them on their right hand, and on their left." The family memory refers to those years in the Hunsrück as "a hard but happy time," and to the town of Simmern as "a cozy nest," quite different from Auel, which was never a cozy nest in the same sense.

He says that our father was popular from the start because of his "friendly, warm, unpretentious ways." Short sermons, accessible even to the "simpler minds," without literary and philosophical "excrescences." Concrete and practical images that stick in the mind: wine and grain, ox and ass, sower, shepherd, fisherman. Personal involvement with "young and old, rich and poor"; "cheerful with those who are full of cheer, sad with those who grieve"; neither "taking on airs" nor hiding behind his desk. During those early years in the ministry, he has not yet established a steady work routine and still has to learn that a minister must maintain distance so as to "treat all alike." He is constantly doing his rounds within the parish tending his flock. One can see him riding his bicycle through the countryside on his way to neighboring villages and outlying farms. He loves his work, the "children" of his parish. There is no division between his work and his private life. They are a single entity cast from the same mold. He will have none of the conventional hobbies of a country parson—bees and roses. He is devoted to people, to individuals, to the essential being within each individual, to what God means when He says: "I have called thee by thy name, thou art mine." Of physical labor, farming, or handicrafts he knows nothing. But that does not diminish his popularity. On the contrary, Gerhard stresses, people have taken him to their hearts for his lack of practical know-how, his unawareness of greed, ambition, wrangling over inherited property, hatred among neighbors. He is a stranger to the evils of this world, always assumes the best in everybody, forgets failures and setbacks with his undaunted confidence in the "new man," who, with God's help, can be reached at any moment: turn around, grasp His hand, follow Him, and ascend with eagles' wings. His flock wants to oblige him. They like him. Their affection is his tool. Even if they don't exactly change their lives, they desire goodness for his sake and want to prove it to him personally. Soon they will get their opportunity.

After the birth of the second child, the young wife contracts tuberculosis. For months, she fights in hospitals and sanatoriums against losing the third child, who is born while she is delirious. Friends within the congregation take in the older children, prepare meats on slaughtering days and cakes on holidays for the minister; they help out in house and garden. From head to toe he now becomes their very own pastor, and his children become their children. It is love, Gerhard says, his love, their love, nourished by God's inexhaustible love, that is the secret of his success as a minister to their souls; and if I now insist on starting in again on my number one topic, it is a sure sign of my spitefulness, my negative attitude, my compulsive fixation.

Did the men from Simmern have any choice but to go and fight in the war? Wasn't it a matter of love and duty to explain to them the war as a necessity, a sensible course of action that was pleasing to God? To make dying easier for them and the loss to their families less intolerable? Would it not have been unnecessarily cruel to speak to them of death as dirty and of their sacrifices as futile? And what would it have wrought but despair and wretchedness? Perhaps that a fellow here and there would drop his gun or refuse to see the enemy as an enemy? That would have violated our father's deepest convictions.

"That's just what I mean," I say. "This dangerous mingling of faith and patriotism at the 'innermost' core, which in my view has nothing to do with the Christian faith."

"You of all people presume to tell me what is Christian!"

It is a cool parting, in spite of the embrace between brother and sister, which for the first time strikes me as something of a farce. There is an aftereffect from that functional, loving family home, which prevents both quarrels and mutual understanding: too much "consideration," insufficient courage to call a spade a spade, a need for harmony that covers up differences and lets hostilities and their hidden causes smolder in the dark.

On the way home I force myself to think about my father. What went on in his head when he heard about the war, which in some of his church journals was referred to as "necessary," as a "savior appointed by God," a "reformer of terrible mien," an "educator of the people by God's grace"? Did he think of his childhood and celebrations of the anniversary of Sedan[4] —ringing bells, thundering cannons, heroic deeds far from the sacred soil of the fatherland? Lofty emotions that move the young and the old to tears when watching the parade through the streets of Diez? Did he share in his heart the sentiments that a Herr von Heymel put into verse in 1910:

The gift of quiet peace is like a deadly pall.
We do not know reluctant obligation,
We desperately long, we scream for war.

Did he feel like "a people without space"? Did he long for "a place in the sun"? Did he want to get his "slice of the big cake"? How did he deal with the Fifth Commandment and with the admonition: "Put up thy sword into the sheath"?

How did he differentiate between "direct" biblical commands (Let every soul be subject unto the higher powers) and those that were considered to have merely figurative meaning (Go and sell what thou hast, and give to the poor)?

Did it trouble him that Christians on both sides invoked "God with us"?

When war finally breaks out in August 1914 and a sense of "God-given national unity" sweeps all political factions (Catholics, Protestants, and Socialists) into one "German brotherhood," he reads the name of his much-admired teacher, Adolf Schlatter, among those who have signed the "Manifesto of Intellectuals." When Karl Barth read the same list of names (Harnack!)[5] he was so shocked that the rift between him and his teachers was never repaired. It appears that my father was not shocked.

He enlists in the army, and in early December 1914 — "under horrendous weather conditions" — is put on a train at Koblenz, heading west.

7

Sunday afternoons smell like boxwood, pachysandra, and rotting flower stems. Striding down the center walk of the cemetery in Auel, the family approaches the statue of *Faith, Hope, and Charity*: three white female figures, two of them in various stages of swooning, the third lifting them up; Charity is the tallest among them. Just before they reach the statue, they turn off to the right and walk uphill through the rows of graves to Hanneli's grave. The weight of mourning slows their steps, muffles their voices. The dead do not like it if the living act too lively.

After they have finished weeding, removing the wilted flowers, and watering the fresh ones, they stand for a long time at the grave, heads bowed and hands folded, shivering in the wind that blows over the hill. The child makes an effort to shed tears. She would like to have her mother think: Such a dear child! She weeps for the sister whom she didn't know!

The return is easier. They separate, taking different routes. The child remains with her father, who lets her jump and chatter as soon as they turn the corner. While the others are heading for the center walk, they walk across the military cemetery.

The square of regularly spaced gray headstones is separated by a lattice fence from the civilian graves. It allows glimpses of brightness that gradually change as one walks past. They step between the rows, read names and dates, calculate ages. Father talks about the war — the Champagne, Verdun, Galicia. . . .

As Mother airs the winter clothes, she shows the child a carefully darned hole in Father's overcoat, which has been handed down to his sons. It was caused by a bullet that lodged between the cloth and the fur. Our father was never one of those "goldbricks," she says, but always out in front where the bullets were whistling. He did not heed his own life, but the Lord stood by him.

In one of his letters from the front, which she has kept in her air raid bag throughout the Second World War, he writes: "I am so busy I have no time to think whether I might be shot.

Moreover, we know that God's grace extends beyond death. For whether we live, we live unto the Lord; and whether we die, we die unto the Lord: whether we live therefore or die, we are the Lord's."

In order to find out more about his military career, I questioned both of my brothers. According to Gerhard, there was no such thing. As he had entered the war—without title or rank, as a "volunteer chaplain"—so he came out of it in the spring of 1918. He chose not to be promoted to division chaplain because he considered it more appropriate to move freely among the ranks and to talk to every man as an equal. Although he revered the military, he acted like a civilian— open, warm, friendly as was his wont—untouched by the conventions of military hierarchy, career concerns, or worries about jurisdictional boundaries. Whoever needed him, whether general or private, was treated like a brother. His comrades rewarded him with their love and confidence. They called him "the good spirit of the regiment."

Gerhard tends to play down the "personal courage" that is mentioned in the extant letters written by some of his fellow soldiers. Our father certainly was no hero (despite his Iron Cross First and Second Class); he just didn't think about danger. Gerhard compares him to the nurse's aid in the typhoid station who is so busy tending the sick it does not occur to him that he might catch the disease, and so he never does. Neither before nor after the war did our father ever have such a strong sense of being needed. He simply could not allow himself to fall down on the job. He was the official comforter.

Herbert (two years younger) remembers things differently. He believes that our father was rapidly promoted. His relations with the officers, "well up into the highest ranks," were particularly close and friendly. Toward the end of the war he was recommended for the position of court chaplain. Unfortunately that did not come to pass.

Herbert attaches much value to the "rank of officer." On this particular point he feels closer to his father than Gerhard, who is rather indifferent to military matters. He secretly wishes that Father could watch him from heaven as he, the only one out of four, upholds and honors the officer's tradition within the family. According to Gerhard, there never was such a thing.

I ask no further questions but continue to read the letters.

Shortly after his arrival in Aure on 16 December 1914 (the date of his letter)—he has not yet unpacked his box nor contacted his commanding officer—the chaplain is asked to attend to a wounded soldier who apparently has asked for spiritual assistance. The nurse takes him through an endless row of beds to a man who looks "in the pink of health": round cheeks, no trace of a beard even though he is already nineteen; a baker's journeyman from Kreuznach.[1] A piece of shrapnel is lodged in his body. "He won't last much longer," the nurse says so loudly that the startled chaplain puts his finger to his lips.

Because the wounded man has his eyes closed, he assumes that he is asleep, but as he bends over him he suddenly feels that he is being grabbed by the chain he carries around his neck to hold the cross; he is pulled down close to the other face, whose swollen lips begin to talk at a crazy speed, whispering indistinct words, of which he understands nothing. It takes him an agonizingly long time before he realizes that the man is complaining about the doctors and the nurses. They didn't do a thing for him. They were simply letting him croak. The piece of shrapnel was still inside him. He could feel it with every breath. The pain was driving him mad. He had to get out of here, or it would be all over for him.

While he is whispering, his eyes follow the nurse, who is busy at some of the beds in the rear. The horrified, suspicious look reminds Reinhold of the horses' looks in the freight car where he spent the night.

Discreetly he tries to unclasp the fingers from the chain, all the while speaking softly to the wounded soldier: He is in good hands here; doctors and nurses are doing their best.

Would he be willing to make a leap of faith and place his confidence in him, the chaplain?

The wounded man has not been listening. He wants something, and he won't let go of the chaplain until he understands and is willing to promise. He wants him to write a letter to his mother—urgently, instantly. She should come and get her son out of here. At home he can get well. Here he will surely die.

Finally he lets go of the chain, but the horrified, suspicious eyes remain fixed on the chaplain, on his hands searching in his pocket for paper and pencil, placing the Bible on his knees for support, spreading the paper on it, and setting the pencil to paper: Dear Mother . . .

Until this moment the soldier has been steadying his trembling lower lip with his teeth, but now he resumes his hasty, indistinct whispering. Reinhold repeatedly pleads with him to speak more slowly and clearly, but he is unable to do so. Mortal fear drives him; there is little time.

Someone named Karl, brother or friend, is mentioned. Under no circumstances should he enlist. Mother should talk him out of it. Everything is so different.

He tries to say what it is that is different, but there is no sound, only whispers and burbling breath. Reinhold has long since lost the thread and would like to get on with it: to prayer, to those grand, good, quiet feelings of faith, trust, and peace in God. Several times he tries to interrupt, but the look in the man's eyes is more compelling and drives his hand across the paper, line after line of nonsense words, just to show him that he is writing. Because he cannot think of anything else, Reinhold writes down the Lord's Prayer, which he would really like to speak; he keeps writing line after line, just like a letter, and after he finishes, he starts again from the beginning: Our Father . . . At some point the whispering stops.

"He is done for," says the man with the amputated arm in the bed next to him.

At this bedside he realized that he still has much to learn before he can be a "good comforter," Reinhold writes in his letter. It is not enough to mourn with those who are grieving and to fear with those who are afraid. One has to muster enough strength to rise above misery and to reveal the power that inheres even in the weak. They that wait upon the Lord shall renew their strength; they shall mount up with wings as eagles—that is not just something to talk about; the weak must see and feel it to be truly comforted. It is a matter of being and of being perceived as the lowliest servant and, at the same time, the worthy executor of the mightiest Lord. That is his problem. While he manages the part of the servant rather well, he apparently does not reveal much in the way of the Lord's power. That will have to change.

The doctor, who is just returning from having dinner, catches him on the stairs of the villa that has been converted to a military hospital. The table has already been cleared, he says, but they are saving a portion for the chaplain. When he tries to withdraw, explaining that he doesn't feel like eating anything, the doctor says: "If we were to stop eating every time someone bites the dust around here, we would soon lie down next to them."

Reinhold touches only reluctantly on the subsequent events of that evening. He appears to have been shocked at the generally "jocular" tone. He misses an attitude of seriousness and dignity, a high sense of courage in the face of death, but immediately adds that he is convinced that these "brave men" are giving their best in fulfilling their heavy responsibilities. Moreover, everyone is expecting that the French will attempt to penetrate the German lines at Christmas; they almost long for it, just to break up the stalemate and get the front moving again.

From the eastern front one hears an amazing rumor: the Russian army has been destroyed—two hundred thousand prisoners (God grant us that this is true). The Russians are said to have asked for a truce.

"We are speculating that if Russia has been eliminated, things on this side cannot continue much longer. One of the doctors expressed his hope that he will be back home among his loved ones by Easter."

At this, they all raise their glasses. The chaplain takes this opportunity to say good night. On his way out, he asks what would be the best time for him to introduce himself to the commander; he is ready to take up his work. The gentlemen are amused at his eagerness. Tomorrow would not be the most opportune day for the introduction. A hunting party has been arranged. His Excellency will be up and gone early in the morning.

It bothers him that his quarters are so far from the front lines. When nobody shows any interest in taking him "to my people in the line of fire," he goes it alone, riding his "crazy nag," accompanied by his orderly, who considers this kind of extracurricular expedition unnecessary.

"Last night there was some activity at the front," he writes. "Surely there were casualties, both dead and wounded. The general atmosphere there is supposed to be more serious and dignified than behind the lines. That's where I want to be, with my new congregation. . . ."

Looking through a periscope from a captain's observation post, he gets his first view of "the battlefield that has soaked up so much blood of our Hunsrück people. A deathly silence, not a person in sight, not even the tip of a helmet; nothing but artillery pieces and clouds of smoke and dust. Is that what war looks like?"

The captain suggests that he turn back. As long as he has his eye on them, they ride in the direction he indicated, but "every step went against my feelings, which urged me to go forward. It seemed to me all but unbearable to return to Aure and wait yet another day for the introduction. But I did feel sorry for the orderly, who could have spent the day comfortably in quarters if he had not followed me so faithfully. Several times I was on the verge of asking him to turn around and let me ride on alone, when a sudden burst of enemy fire made a decision unnecessary. At the first explosion I lost control of my horse; it took off in a crazed gallop. All I could do was try to stay in the saddle, which to my astonishment I actually managed to do."

As they ride on—"soaked by the drizzle, splattered with mud up to our stomachs"—they reach the village that has just been fired on. A gaping shell crater yawns in the main street; next to it is a puddle of blood. A ladder leans against a nearby house. Soldiers are busy on top of the roof. One of them picks up an object and shows it to the others: a severed human hand.

"Three guardsmen from Dortmund were standing in the village street to light their pipes when the shooting started. One of them was seriously wounded, the other two were literally blown to bits."

He rides behind the tarpaulin containing the body fragments to the village cemetery. Half an hour later the grave is ready.

"I thanked God that he gave me the strength to speak words of comfort even though tears were streaming down my face. Some of the other men also turned away their faces to hide their tears. I had them give me the addresses of the dead so that I could send a word of comfort to their wives. When I shook their hands to say good-bye, my heart was as heavy as if I were parting from brothers. This very evening they are to be sent to the front."

Then they continue their ride toward the front lines.

After several exhausting miles along the muddy road, a patrol stops them and asks for their papers. The orderly, of course, carries his with him, the chaplain does not ("typical"). In that case he will have to arrest him, says the MP.

The chaplain thinks this is ridiculous, absurd; he points to his cross, which does not impress the MP, and begins to turn his pockets inside out for something resembling an ID card; first his overcoat, then he unbuttons it with stiff fingers, searches the pockets of his jacket, and unbuttons it to reach into the shirt pocket. His rain gear constantly gets in his way; besides he has to hold fast because the "crazy nag" is getting nervous. "Not the picture of dignity," he confesses; and just at that moment a vehicle has to appear out of the dusk, an open military car without lights, evidently carrying high-ranking officers, because the MP jumps out of the way as if something had stung him and freezes in a military salute.

The orderly also ambles out of the way; only the crazy nag stays put right in the middle of the road "like a statue" and will not budge no matter how much he jerks the reins or kicks his rump with his heels. Car and horse stand nose to nose, the foam from the horse's nostrils dripping on the muddy hood.

"What's going on here?" one of the officers shouts from the car, then notices the cross, stifles a curse, and gets out.

"What are *you* doing here, Reverend?" he asks, snapping his fingers at the orderly to lead the horse out of the way.

After a short palaver they order him to go back. They tell me that up ahead preparations are underway to counter an attack by the Frogs. There is no place for a chaplain there, he will only be in the way. At any rate, the dead and wounded are being moved behind the lines. Whatever ministering to the troops is to be done takes place in quarters, not in the trenches. There is a lot of work for him at Aure, and they have been expecting him for a while: Christmas services in three different locations will have to be organized and working arrangements be made with his Catholic colleague (a Jesuit, not easy to deal with!). Frontline services are also being planned, if contrary to expectations things remain quiet: services in the trenches, but, of course, only with an official escort. "Riding around by yourself, Reverend! You better get rid of that idea right away." He will be issued a horse and wagon. Still seems to have some problems staying in the saddle.

They are not angry anymore and in the end become pretty friendly—considerate, helpful, a bit patronizing. They are old war horses, he nothing but a greenhorn ("which I am likely always to remain in some things").

The conversation ends with an invitation to dinner with the staff scheduled to be given after the hunt. If he wants to get there in time he should join them in the car. The orderly can return the horse.

"It was an inviting offer because I was soaking wet, but for the sake of the boy I declined."

Toward midnight they arrive back in Aure "totally beat." He goes to bed immediately but cannot sleep. "The distress kept me from quieting down." He gets up again, tries to blow the embers in the potbellied stove back to life, does not succeed ("what would I do without the boy, who is so much my superior in all the practical aspects of life"), stands for a while next to his bed listening to him snore ("couldn't get myself to wake him from his well-earned rest"), slips into his fur coat, lights a candle ("again, no electricity"), and writes a letter to his wife, ending with these words: "Thus the good Lord has brought me, this impractical man, if not to my goal, then at least back to my quarters. I will serve wherever He places me and act according to His holy will, not my own wishes and vanities."

The letters continue through March 1915. After that, there are only postcards containing little information other than pictures of various towns, dates, "faith in final victory," and "the love that unites us." He has no time for narrative details; perhaps later, "when we are all gathered around the family table again."

One of his responsibilities is to send death notices to the families back home. Judging from the answers, he notified them by writing long, hand-written letters, which give the impression that he was a close acquaintance of the dead man. Almost all of the families express the wish to get to know him personally "on his next furlough" or "after the victory." They would like to hear more details about their son or husband, his last words, the exact location of his grave (if possible, with a sketch), a copy of the funeral sermon, "if it isn't too much trouble." Mothers write: "Only for brief moments am I able to grasp what happened, and in those moments I cling to the words you dedicated to our dear Curt and to us as a farewell and as a comfort. I take from them the strength to bear the unimaginable."

"Many thanx for your 2 comforting letters, yes it was a comfort: that you could visit with my dear boy and burried him and prayed for me. Keep me in your prayers I am glad: that you also sent me the 2 comforting hyms and text of yr. sermon. Oh: how happy my dear child would of been to still be conscience when you visited him he was always glad when you did the field service. Thats what he always wrote me: our Rev. chaplin preached and it made him feel he was back home: He prepared himself for his death, you can tell from his letters and my wish and prayer for my child: Saved just Saved that is my only comfort now that he is saved thru Christ's blood. Like you wrote he was my youngest son aged . . ."

"It is a precious thing," he says at the open graves.

"Greater love hath no man than this, that a man lay down his life for his friends."

"Be thou faithful unto death, and I will give thee a crown of life."

"The lines are fallen unto him in pleasant places."

"The greater the gaps that death tears open in our ranks and the heavier the burdens and duties that war places on us here and at home, the more urgently we must dedicate ourselves to the fatherland and put our souls into the service we render. This happens when we recognize and understand that doing the most demanding duty is our highest privilege. He who made Paul glad and strong, rich and free is the same today, is your and my Savior, ready to reveal His glory unto each of us. Our people need Him. We all need Him. May we all dedicate ourselves to Him. Amen."

Not far away, near Verdun, another chaplain was doing his work. He too was the son of a minister, had studied in Tübingen and Halle, and had volunteered for frontline service. After having spent one night under constant fire among the dying, he woke up with the thought: "This is the end of the idealistic part of my thinking!" An abyss had opened before him, Paul Tillich[2] writes, "an abyss into which only the most courageous dare to look—the abyss of the absence of all meaning."

Did my father ever experience the absence of all meaning?

"How did he take it," I asked my mother, "defeat, collapse, the flight of the Kaiser?"

"We did not talk about it," she says. "It was too painful for him."

The new congregation is, so to speak, a legacy of the war. One of his army buddies, an officer in the reserve, has pleaded with Reinhold that he is the right man to shape up this run-down lot. He is a businessman in Auel and an important citizen. Perhaps it is because a conservative pastor suits his purpose in the chess game of local politics. Nothing of the sort is mentioned.

Reinhold feels that it is God's call. During a brief home leave in January 1918 he presents his trial sermon. He is not the only one. Another businessman, the owner of the largest contracting firm in town, has already submitted another candidate, whose selection is all but final. Now this other one comes along, probably dressed in uniform, the two Iron Crosses pinned to his chest, the look of frontline spirit in his eyes, though not particularly military in demeanor—outgoing, warm, modest—in short, a likable fellow. Toward the end of the meeting it turns out that all of the church elders have "caved in." Suddenly they want this one and no one else. Grumbling under his breath, the contractor is the last to sign the list.

In April, Reinhold returns from the front "with a heavy heart; as far as I was concerned, not without tears." Farewell, until we meet again after the victory! His family has already completed its move to Auel. When he appears in his uniform, five-year-old Dorothea takes to her heels and hides in the coal cellar.

He starts his work with zest, a man who loves to take on new tasks, a genuine morning person. Mornings are his best time: no dozing, no hesitating, no lingering over breakfast. After having communed with God and read the daily devotion of the Herrnhut Moravian Brethren, he sets up his work schedule for the day: desk work in the morning, parish work in the afternoon. A short, refreshing nap in between. After supper he "fades out." No burning of the midnight oil. A gradual winding down. At ten o'clock he is ready for bed.

The pace of his daily routine dispels any feelings of distress. They crowd in on him during breaks. Then he suffers. But the breaks are short. At night he sleeps soundly; no problems in that regard. He can be "inexpressibly sad," but not for long. "All things work together for good to them that love God." The center of his work is the sermon. On Thursdays he selects the Bible text, works on it in the original, then consults compendiums, and reads up on the historical and geographical contexts. He knows his way around the Holy Land better than around his own Rhenish province. Fridays he writes out a draft, word by word. The length is fixed (a minister may preach on any subject, but no more than twenty minutes). He reads aloud what he has written to his wife for her comments and criticism. Then he commits it to memory, as he paces his study murmuring to himself.

Evenings are taken up with Bible readings, women's groups, council meetings with the elders, preparations for children's services. On Mondays he takes a holiday, like a barber.

During his first year he has walked the length and breadth of his parish, knocked on the door of every person listed in the register, and introduced himself as the one who will henceforth take up a particular place in this particular person's life. Later on he establishes a regular round of visits: once every week at the hospital and once with a group of those most in need, the old and the sick. Time permitting, he continues his general schedule of visitations. He expects to "cover" the entire parish in the course of one year. New parishioners get squeezed into the regular schedule as soon as they appear in the register.

He gradually gets his people used to telling him not only about their spiritual but also about their physical and material troubles. As he listens, he divides them into troubles that have to be borne with patience and humility and those that can be "tackled." With the former, he resorts to prayer, asking God's help in bearing the cross; with the latter, he goes to work: pleads, negotiates, appeals to the conscience, uses his connections, sometimes even leans on people: he usually starts softly, but if need be he "pulls no punches" and "talks turkey."

He never forgets anything he considers essential and is familiar with the landscape of the souls that are under his care. There is no one, no matter how high or low in the social hierarchy, on whom he does not have some kind of "leverage": old promises; good intentions; a debt of gratitude; points of vulnerability: a pious mother who would be hurt, a wife who deserves her husband's consideration, children whose father wants to set a good example for them, fellow citizens whose esteem is valued.

I'll talk to him (her), the minister says when he is told about squabbles or complaints, leaving behind relief and hope and earning gratitude that on occasion can be used as a lever for a good purpose. He never makes appointments for his missions of advocacy, intercession, supplication. Smiling and greeting everyone cheerfully, he strides into fenced and barred factory grounds, executive suites, and villas surrounded by protective walls, so confident that his visit is a delight to everyone that his targets have no other choice but to feign delight. To him, no place is out of bounds. This is his parish, his vineyard. Without preliminaries, except for showing his famous "warmth," he buttonholes his customers. Government bureaucracies are approached in the same personal way. He despises official procedures, refuses to wait, has no use for wasting his precious time. Filling out forms "offends him to the core." Financial matters are taken care of by the church accountant.

It would never occur to him to fight against general social conditions. They belong to the first category of afflictions, those that are to be humbly borne.

His reputation as a comforter, counselor, and peacemaker has survived his active ministry for decades. Even today his name evokes warm feelings. They say that he had a special gift for dealing with people. Many a tough nut never knew how the minister managed to crack him.

"You just have to approach people," he says, "and go straight *in medias res*. The good Lord will see to the rest."

Trust with a faith untiring
In thine Omniscient King,
And thou shalt see admiring
What He to light shall bring.[1]

It was the time when proletarians used to write on church doors: GOD IS DEAD! GIVE US BUTTER FOR OUR BREAD! One day a man who called himself Schmitz Gustav, one of the Reds, of course, came to the house—loud, obnoxious, drunk. Stuck his foot in the door before Mother could close it on him ("the Reverend is busy right now"), and shouted wildly in the lower hallway, waving his arms, which were covered with dirty bandages up to his elbows. Mother was about to call the sexton, who was in the cellar filling wine into bottles from the little St. Goar cask, when Father shouted from above: "Let him come upstairs!"

She was not at all happy about that, Mother says. Our gentle father was no match for that sort. Worried, she listened from the stairs, something she had never done because it was beneath her dignity.

Quite calm at first, Schmitz Gustav complained about his dismissal from the paint factory, apparently because he had developed an eczema as a result of the poisonous work ("most likely there were other reasons," Mother says).

"That's how they treat us," he said (using the local dialect, which she cannot imitate and wouldn't want to because she considers it too vulgar). "First they ruin us, then they kick us out into the street just like a . . . just like a . . ." He could not think of the comparison, and Father used the pause to say a few encouraging words ("much too nice; these people are used to another kind of language").

He will look into the matter. If what Herr Schmitz says is correct, he will see what he can do. He can't promise anything right now, but the boss is really not a bad sort of man; he probably just isn't aware. . . .

Suddenly the man raised his voice again: not a bad sort? He is a bloodsucker, a cutthroat. Everybody knows it, except for the Reverend! It wasn't just him, Schmitz Gustav, who was being squeezed and kicked out just like a . . . just like a . . . This sort of thing should be shouted from the church steeple; it was time for the minister to prick that boil. As the man continued to rant, he moved in on the minister with his alcoholic breath, waving his arms, from which the torn bandages were coming loose ("perhaps he just wanted to show me his eczema," Father demurs when Mother starts talking about physical assault).

The minister took cover behind a table, mumbling all the while: "Please calm down, dear Herr Schmitz, please calm down!" But the man kept following him until the minister's retreat was blocked by his desk. Suddenly Schmitz Gustav turned around: "Oh, you . . . you!" he shouted and ran out of the room and down the stairs. Mother just barely managed to duck into the toilet on the landing, as the man drunkenly tromped down the last few steps, stumbled, and fell flat on his face in the lower hallway.

He must have hurt his ankle when he fell because when he tried to get up to continue his flight he could not get up but remained in an awkward crouch on the ground, groaning.

Mother and the maid dragged him to the couch in the dining room and treated his hugely swelling foot with a cool compress. They also put a fresh bandage on his eczema, while Father was standing there and kept saying: "Please, do calm down!" even though Schmitz Gustav was lying quietly with closed eyes, softly gnashing his teeth. At some point, after they had left him alone ("let him sleep off his inebriation," Mother said, though she worried about the new cover), he must have skipped out through the garden gate without so much as a word of thanks or excuse. Nor did he afterward ever make an appearance in church, even though Father actually managed to get him reinstated in his job.

"That's how ungrateful those people are. You offer them an inch and they take an ell."

From then on, Mother refused to let anyone of that ilk near him, but insisted on getting their address right at the door, promising that "the minister would stop by within a day or so."

"And that's what he did," she says. "Always on the move, our dear father, always on the jump to help people; his entire life he was on the road for the sake of others—and you, his little darling, followed him everywhere just as soon as you were able to walk."

The child walks on his right. In his left hand he holds his walking stick, every now and then stealthily tapping her with it from behind. The child rebukes him with feigned annoyance. He pretends he has no clue, looks around in all innocence: Who do you suppose did that?

The horseplay stops when they reach the entrance to a house. Silently they enter hallways and climb stairs. Occasionally a door opens before they ring the bell. Father has been expected. He is a man of punctual habits. One cannot exactly set one's watch by him, but he never fails anyone.

He does not stand around very long in sickrooms, parlors, or kitchens. At a glance he discovers the proper seat—his seat—sits down, feels at home, even gives the appearance of feeling at home. No fuss, please! He is not the type who notices dust or disorder. What lovely flowers you have! Who crocheted this beautiful blanket? Is this a picture of your son? A handsome fellow. You should be proud of him. That is how he creates "his ambiance."

The child has been hustled into a corner with a glass of juice and a piece of last Sunday's cake. A cat or a doll is put in her lap. She has to be quiet now; there is no point in talking to him. His mind is now completely focused on this man or this woman; everything else is forgotten, including his own child. Uneasy and determined not to let herself get nauseated, she sits in her corner, sniffing the smells of illness and of food from the kitchen. Jesus washed other people's dirty feet, and the grave of Lazarus couldn't have smelled like a bed of roses. Inasmuch as ye have done it unto one of the least of these my brethren, ye have done it unto me.

At first she listens, but after a while the voices pass by her ear. Endless stories of illnesses, complaints about children, relatives, landlords, government offices, and employers, and tears. Father pulls out a tiny, leatherbound pocket calendar and takes down some notes. He will see to it.

His posture suggests that he is listening and taking things in. Leaning comfortably back in his chair, his legs crossed, his hands placed on the arm rests or in his lap, he receives and absorbs. When reluctance halts the flow of speech, he helps it along with questions or comments that suggest he is quite familiar with this particular problem and perhaps even knows it from personal experience. But he does not get into anecdotes. Although he gives the impression of having all the time in the world, he never stays long. The conversation comes to an appropriate end. Everything he has heard is formed into a prayer that expresses a commonality of concerns: "We," he says, "we ask You to ease the pain. Do not lay upon us heavier burdens than we can bear. Never let us forget that You provide well for us." Before beginning the Lord's Prayer he looks at the child. She may now reappear and join in the prayer. Now and then people want to sing a hymn: Lead me by the hand . . . Jesus, be my guide on the path of life. . . . The child is embarrassed. She finds the sound of voices without accompaniment dreary. Should she bring her violin or accordion on the next visit? she asks her father. He thinks the violin sounds shrill and the accordion is not appropriate.

Father does not raise his hands during the final benediction as in church and changes the words from "you": "May the Lord bless you and keep you" to "us": "May the Lord look upon us and give us peace."

He likes the "simple people," especially if they are modest, friendly, patient, and loyal. The pushy, obstinate, impertinent ones he is less fond of. Although he starts food and clothes drives even for them, tries to find them jobs, and remonstrates against their dismissals, the shy ones are closer to his heart; their suffering would remain unknown were it not for the Ladies Aid, which he organized to find out hidden needs. Just as the simple people are to be modest and grateful, so the well-to-do are to be kind, caring, and equally modest. If they flaunt their wealth, he calls them "snobs" or "show-offs"; the women are "stuck-up geese" or "made-up mummies," the children "spoiled brats who ought to have their ears boxed." He grumbles about special requests like a separate cup at communion ("hygienic fussiness") or home baptisms, home weddings, and home funeral services with flower arrange-ments and chamber music: "frills and frippery!" And all that clamoring for culture! More music in church! "I'm not a con-cert agency!" "Balderdash," "intellectual twaddle," "culture vultures!" "Higher standards? I don't give a hoot! Just be-cause they make a donation, they think the minister has to dance to their tune. Well, I have news for them: the Lord is not impressed and neither am I!" He takes no part in the town's social life and accepts invitations from the leading citizens only if he can pursue one of his missions: give counsel, dispense comfort, raise money, plead a cause, lodge a com-plaint.

On the way to "the show-offs," riding in a chauffeur-driven Maibach limousine with the glass partition open be-tween passengers and driver, he jokes about people putting on airs at their host's dinner table: "I hope you've got some-thing to eat at home so we don't have to go to bed hungry!" he says to his wife, who is already anxious: visitors should always adapt themselves to the "host's style."

He disagrees. Like Bismarck, he is of the opinion that "Wherever I sit is the head of the table."

During the solemn, silent dinner he manages to elicit a smile from the servant, who is wearing white gloves: What might that be (artichokes)? Can you eat that? If so, with which of the four forks? — of which at least three, in his opinion, are superfluous. He responds with the brightest of smiles to his wife's horrified look: "Don't you agree, Mother?" "You are embarrassing the poor man," she whispers in the dark corridor between the dining room and the "hall," where coffee is being served.

The child cannot resist asking why she is not allowed to behave like her father. Before he answers, she already knows what he will say: "Quod licet Jovi, non licet bovi!" — with the child, of course, being the bovine, and the father Jove.

If she were to do or to say what her father does and says, she would be out of line; he, on the other hand, "is above those things" or "transcends" them.

He considers the moderately modern paintings, which they view as they pass from room to room, "contrived"; Mother remains painfully silent because she can think of nothing appropriate to say. He does not care much about art. In so far as he likes paintings, they have to make sense: Ludwig Richter, Spitzweg, Moritz von Schwind, a man by the name of Rudolf Schäfer, who illustrates bibles, and *Mountain Cross* by Caspar David Friedrich.

Most of all, he would like a good cigar now.

At the "opportune moment" he takes up his charitable mission. As they stroll through the English garden, he kidnaps the hostess and steers her to Happy Home or *Mon Repos,* where garden chairs have been arranged to relax and enjoy the scenic view. When they return, deep in conversation — which they break off as they come closer — the lady's cheeks have taken on a rosy flush. Someone who does not know him might think he has held her hand. Mother and child know better. He has made it possible for her to do a good deed, and that stimulates the heart and circulation. Now he takes his wife's arm and his child's hand. With his return, the dull party comes back to life.

When he enters a store while making his rounds of the parish, he does not spend much time in front of the counter. Summoned to the front of the store, the owner appears and urges father and child to step into the back room, which regular customers never get to see. Miraculously, a cup of tea appears, or a glass of vermouth: "Please, only half a glass; that's all I can take during the day."

Lowering his voice, the owner complains about his employees. When he has to leave the room for a moment, the employees sneak in to complain about the owner. The minister promises to put in a good word. There is always a problem when it comes to paying for the merchandise that is brought to the back room. A donation for the poor box is silently slipped in with the change.

He buys only a few things, though always the same: lozenges for his strained throat, boric acid for his tired eyes, a certain brand of tiny bandaids for razor cuts, and cologne; at the baker's he gets croissants and alphabet cookies, chocolate biscuits, and cream-filled chocolates for the child; scissors for clipping his mustache and fingernails are obtained from old man Peters. He already has a drawer full of them, but he always buys new ones just to please the old man.

Visiting old Peters, an invalid who has been in a wheelchair for sixteen years, is a "comfort and joy" even to the minister, who is healthy: just to see how happy he is to hear the pastor's voice. Laughter spreads over his pale, hairless face "as if the sun were rising." He has been waiting for hours even though the minister always steps into the cutlery store at the same hour, waves at Mrs. Peters behind the counter, and proceeds to the back room.

Carefully, first the father and then the child take the hand resting on the brightly colored blanket—bent, bony fingers, the skin soft and fragile to the touch like the membrane inside an egg. The minister asks if he had been able to sleep during the night and whether the pain was bearable. He finds that Herr Peters looks rather well today.

The back room, with its high ceiling, is small and square and always dim. Herr Peters never gets to see the sun. Just a narrow band of daylight falls through the open door that leads to the store. Gray cartons are piled on shelves all the way to the ceiling.

After Herr Peters has finished complaining about the past week's woes in his high-pitched child's voice, intermittently shedding silent tears—the child watches with fascination as the tears gather in his eyes, overflow at the corners, and slowly drip down along his nose and between temple and cheek—after they have prayed together, after Herr Peters has for the hundredth time made the minister promise he would bury him no matter where he was when his time would come—after all this is over, he asks his question: "Is there anything you need?" The minister pretends to give it a thought, then his eyes light up with the answer: a pair of fabric shears for his wife because the old ones have lost their edge (as if he had ever known anything about the condition of her scissors and knives).

For several happy minutes Herr Peters has been relieved of his suffering. His face twitches under the pressure of activity, which cannot find any other outlet. As he tries to call out— come here, Mother!—his voice breaks into falsetto.

"I'm in no hurry," says the minister, but the wife appears instantly even if there are customers in the store.

"Third row from the top, seventh carton from the left," Herr Peters says. His wife sets up the ladder, laboriously climbs it, muddles the numbers in her old head, and takes the sixth or eighth. He immediately notices it, corrects her in a whiny voice, keeps his eyes on her until she finally pulls out the right carton, climbs down with it, places it on his blanket, and raises the lid.

Sure enough, there are the fabric shears he chose, genuine Solingen steel, the best article currently on the market, "with best regards to your esteemed wife."

The minister is astonished. It is simply unbelievable, bor- dering on the fantastic, how Herr Peters remembers where everything is among all these identical-looking boxes—better than the minister knows the back of his own hand. What would your wife do without you? What would become of the store? The best hired help could not replace Herr Peters' unfailing accuracy.

Completely exhausted, Herr Peters smiles but does not permit himself to close his eyes. The wrangling about payment is still to come. His wife would not be disinclined to accept the money, but he watches her like a hawk.

"Stop," he hisses, when the minister tries to slip some bills into her apron pocket. "Don't you dare accept money from our pastor!"

Out in the store, she sometimes does take it, regardless. She does not dare to say thank you; he hears everything.

"Next Thursday at half past three," the minister shouts in the direction of the back room.

At home, Mother takes the shears with a barely suppressed sigh and stores them in a box of presents that are waiting for next Christmas at the bottom of her linen closet.

On Sundays the family goes off to church together. Sleeping late and staying at home are completely out of the question. Even a hint of reluctance triggers the much-feared "sorrowful look" on Mother's face. Guests who refuse to come along are considered tactless. When they come within hearing of "our church bells" at the corner of Tierbungert, they feel uplifted and supported by the kindness of the Heavenly Father, almost intoxicated by the booming sound of the bells, the rhythm of the family's marching step, and the respectful greetings the members of the congregation offer them at the church door: the minister's family is approaching!

I and those who are mine will serve the Lord! Father's steps proclaim on the pavement.

As they tromp across the gravel of the front yard, he separates from the family group and walks on ahead. The children wait in the cellarlike shade next to the side stairs leading to the vestry. Mother, and occasionally the child, are allowed to enter.

He is already dressed in his robe; only the bands are missing. Mother ties them on, hiding the starched ribbons under the turned-down collar. No one is permitted to speak to him now. His thoughts are "elsewhere." The robe gives him an air of remoteness even before he ascends the steps to the altar.

He arranges the black books, tells the sexton the number of each hymn, and gives him a written note for the organist.

The parting is ceremonial, with a kiss on the forehead: "God be with you!"

As organ music takes over from the ringing church bells, the family—now fatherless—enters the church through the main entrance. Merely suggesting greetings here and there (their thoughts are now also to be "elsewhere"), they walk single file, Mother at the head, down the right aisle to one of the front pews (but never the very first one). The children remain standing, their heads bowed, until Mother sits down. Then they also seat themselves. They open the hymnal to the first hymn. One beat ahead of the rest of the congregation they start singing. Only Herbert does not open his mouth. He claims to have lost his voice.

"You just don't feel like it," Mother says.

"Why didn't you sing?" I recently asked Herbert. "I just can't," he says. "Nothing comes out."

I don't buy that. I am convinced that somewhere in Herbert there is a singing voice. Sometimes, after he has had something to drink, I think I can hear it humming in his throat. I take out my guitar and try to coax it out by playing some chords. But nothing comes out. As if Herbert were gagged.

I imagine that some day when the pressure within gets too strong the gag will pop like a cork out of a champagne bottle. Then you will hear my brother Herbert sing. . . .

"Were they happily married?" my daughters ask.

"I believe so," I say.

9 "You ought to know!"

"We never asked that question," I say. They don't understand. When we talked about married couples, we said: they live and work well together; they are a good match; they carry each other's burden; they stand by each other in fair weather and foul, in joy and in sorrow, in good and in bad times. No one spoke of being "happy," not in this context. It was generally said that Father had a "happy disposition," whereas Mother "took everything too hard." My brothers and sisters remember that there was "something somber" about her, perhaps because of a difficult childhood or because she could not get over the death of her first daughter. Why would God have inflicted that on her?

Hanneli died when she was sixteen. Shortly afterwards I was born.

"You were supposed to be a comfort to her," Gerhard says pointedly, leaving open whether I lived up to that expectation.

They christened me Auguste for the last empress and Ruth for the Moabite woman who was a comfort to Naomi: "Whither thou goest, I will go; and where thou lodgest, I will lodge; thy people shall be my people, and where thou diest, will I die, and there will I be buried."

"A new child, and thus renewed hope! We may be glad again," Father said at my baptism. Was Mother glad, too? Did she ever laugh, free and uninhibited, with open mouth and chortling throat? We do not remember.

At night she bends over the crib in which the child is lying deep down like Moses in the bulrushes. In whispers she speaks of the one who died and is now an angel: beating of wings in the darkness; light that fades as one looks at it.

How charming she was, she says, how soft her hair, how pure her being, how clear her intelligence. Her absence is unfathomable.

She ends her evening prayer pleading that God may grant a reunion in heaven. "I wish we were there already," the child says. "Why don't you ask Him to call us home soon?"

Mother turns away.

When the child's father comes to her bedside, she asks the same question: "Why don't you ask Him?"

"Nonsense," he says. "Isn't God's world beautiful? Aren't we glad to be alive?"

They walked well together even though they had very different ways of walking: she with her quick, tight step, reaching energetically forward from a straight back; his rather casual, almost leisurely. One became aware of his fast pace only when trying to keep up with him. Both of them had endurance, except that at the end of holiday outings she was more exhausted than he.

After he died, her swift manner of walking became something of a compulsive habit. She raced ahead of her children as if she couldn't wait to join him in heaven.

But they also walked slowly, even arm in arm, though only during vacations or on summer evenings as they strolled through the garden. Then she moved more gently and appeared smaller and softer because she walked with her back slightly inclined toward him. It actually looked as if he were leading her, even though the garden was "her domain." They looked like characters from Goethe's *Wahlverwandtschaften* or Stifter's *Rosenhaus*,[1] bending over the flowers planted along the cinder path: columbine, peonies, bleeding heart, bachelor's buttons (Queen Luise's favorite flower), roses, and, later in the season, wallflowers and asters. She would never have allowed herself to spend her time in such leisure, except to please him.

Both are musical and have trained voices: he is a baritone, she an alto. In order to be able to accompany him, she has learned to play the piano. The children also are musical, even Herbert, who they thought really did not have it in him. Out of sheer anger, because he does not get to take music lessons like his brother and sisters, he has taught himself to play "The

99

Happy Farmer," "To Elise," and Brahms's waltz. "Pretty good, but too much pedal," Mother says.

Occasionally they play music together at home. The vicar scratches out a tune on his violin. With an expression of strained resignation Father suffers through it: "The poor fellow tries hard; unfortunately he has no talent whatsoever."

After the vicar is done with his scratching, they can finally start singing together; until now it has been "rather a trial" for Father. The family crowds around Mother at the piano, singing Schubert, Schumann, Löwe, and Brahms lieder; only one piece by Beethoven: "Knowst thou the Land. . . ." Father dramatically builds up the tension leading up to "The rock descends and water floods it all . . . ," and Mother pours out her secret longings in "Gone, gone . . ." only to gather them up again and contain them within herself in the soft lament of the final "gone."

During the weeks of Advent and the Christmas season they turn to the Christmas songs of Peter Cornelius.[2]

Father always starts the Simeon canticle in too fast a tempo: "After eight days the child was taken to the temple in Jerusalem. . . ." He catches himself when he gets to the words, "Forth steps an aged man . . . ," slows down mightily at "Prophetic words he speaks . . . , and, after a dramatic pause, pours his whole heart into Simeon's words: "Now lettest thou, O Lord, your humble servant go. . . ." And so it goes until he arrives at the stumbling block of "Provide a torch of light . . . ," at which point, due to harmonic complications, his rapture turns into annoyance at wrong notes. It is not until he gets to the last line that he recovers himself and returns to the cheerful tempo of the beginning: "And then they carry the wondrous child away."

In "The Kings" he tries to maintain the underlying choral melody of "How brightly shines the morning star," but it usually goes awry. Mother sighs. He tries again, looking about him in triumph if they succeed to stay together until "O human child." From there on it is clear sailing and their voices blend. "Not so loud, Father," Mother reminds him, "not so fast!" But he can no longer be stopped and pushes on with crescendos and accelerandos because the words demand forward movement: "Keep pace with the kings as they wander afar!" The accompaniment is falling behind, and when it finally catches up, he is already into a ritardando with a lovingly rendered flourish at the words "Give your whole heart to the sweet, blessed child." And then another ritardando, diminuendo, smorzando to the very last breath pumped up from the remotest corners of his lungs: "Give him your heart. . . ."

When it comes to folksongs, she prefers the simple ones, he such tragic ones as "Red of Dawn," "Little Sister," and "A knight and his squire went ariding. . . ."

Before the children are sent to bed and the adults sit down to a glass of wine, they conclude with something vigorous and martial: "A roaring call like a thunder clap . . . ," "Our God who made hard iron grow . . . ," and "On your horses, comrades, on your horses, friends! Let us ride into battle, to freedom. . . ."

The girls, Dorothea and Ruth, continue to sing in bed: "Victoriously we (mustn't say), dying like a brave hero-oh-oh. . . ."[3]

During the day the parents are rarely seen together. The center of Mother's activities is the nursery, where she has arranged a wicker chair on a raised platform by the window as well as her sewing table and her sewing machine. This is where the threads of the household run together. Did she enjoy being a homemaker? Later, after he died, when she lived by herself in a three-room apartment, she would, on a sunny day, leave the dishes unwashed, sit on the balcony, read, and watch the tomatoes ripen. "My tomatoes," she would say, "my afternoons on my balcony." In the parsonage at Auel she never called anything "mine." The room that was supposed to be hers—the room with the desk and the books that she had brought into the marriage (Storm, Raabe, Gottfried Keller, Fritz Reuter, Conrad Ferdinand Meyer)—was made into a "reception room" as the years went by.

The general understanding within the family was that she did not care to have a room of her own.

His center is the study. It is the only room with which he is really familiar. As thoroughly as he knows the topography of each soul in his care, his concept of the house in which he is living is rather nebulous.

When the children want to have some fun with him they ask him trick questions: How many rooms are on the top floor? Which way do the windows face? They make him guess whether the cubbyhole for the garden tools is on the left, on the right, or straight ahead when entering the cellar. "Don't pester him," Mother says, "why should he know those things?" He pretends to have no doubts: of course he knows; after all, he lives here. But they never get a precise answer. They have known it all along: he doesn't have a clue.

Actually, except for his study, he barely makes use of the rest of the house. He never plays the "master." He does not notice the orderliness, which primarily serves his work, his relaxation, his well-being. He never complains, and he praises when praise is expected, but without understanding. The way his things are arranged in closets and drawers remains a mystery to him for decades. It is a waste of time to ask him to look for a tie or his underwear. He has never grasped the system.

He never goes up to the attic. Of the different parts of the cellar he knows only the one with the wine racks. No matter how often he has been down there, he has never noticed that the first door to the right leads to the chicken coop and the second to the furnace room. He has no idea how the furnace works. If he were in charge of it, the family would always be sitting in the cold. In spite of all his goodwill, he is of no help to Mother, although he makes generous offers. Good intentions, but never mind, she says.

The children watch him from the sun porch as, spurred by grand plans, he starts turning the potato bed. He goes at it in a frenzy, driving the spade deep into the earth, and throwing the clods behind him. Soon his movements slow down, the thrusts of the spade get shallower. He stops at ever shorter intervals, mops his face, looks at what he has accomplished, and compares it to what still needs to be done; imperceptibly, his expected goal for the day keeps dwindling.

Tomorrow is another day.

He does not know what the children understand so well: that tomorrow he will be too busy. And the day after tomorrow some urgent business will interfere. By the time he thinks of it again, Mother will have finished the job.

When the potatoes are in full growth, he will say: "Look, how nicely they are doing! I'm the one who turned the earth."

Every now and then Mother breaks down. She lies in the twin bed on the right, so flat that her outline can hardly be seen under the blanket. She wants to rest, nothing but rest. With closed eyes she drifts down the river of sleep for days while the household continues without her. But the underlying order of things, the fabric of the family's life, disintegrates.

Though no one is bothering him, Father is unable to work. Puffing smoke, he dashes up and down the length of his study, finally knocks out his pipe and, with a bad conscience, looks in on her. "Are you asleep?"

As she opens her eyes with difficulty, he has a lot of good advice that occurred to him while doing his parish rounds: medicines, doctors, alternative practitioners, diets. . . . His voice has just a trace of impatience, a hardly noticeable insistence: Can't you do something about it? Can't you get over this?

Except for his teeth, occasional laryngitis, or a bout of diarrhea due to excitement, he is never ill. The whole family is allowed to participate in his toothaches. His coughs are orgies of moans and groans. He is anxious about her silence. She is bothered by his anxiety.

She gets back into harness much too soon. While the family breathes a sigh of relief, the uneasy interval of her absence recedes. Mother is back. She can be safely ignored.

In the congregation she is seen as the stern and forbidding, he as the kindly permissive one. The children know better. Requests that raise problems irritate him. He believes that a firm no is never out of place. Then they appeal to their mother. It is she who agonizes over the pros and cons. While she is struggling with her conscience, the children tiptoe around her and try to read her face to see which way the wind is blowing. But she does not give the slightest hint before having consulted with Father. In this family he has the final say, she the ultimate responsibility. Problems are *her* department.

Difficulties arise when he is "different." Like on Mondays— the minister's Sunday—when he comes home just a tiny bit tipsy after two glasses of Rhine wine: happy, talkative, full of good humor and tenderness. She sees none of it; sees only the glint in his eyes, hears only the touch of heaviness in his speech, freezes under the onslaught of bad childhood memories.

The little presents he carefully selected for her remain unnoticed on the corner of the table. She stares past him as he tells of his outing, soliciting her smile, which she will not grant him at any price.

By and by his good mood flickers and dies. On such evenings he withdraws early, while she continues to putter about the house for a long time, sighing so loudly that he would hear her even in the bedroom, had he not long since fallen asleep.

The forgiveness of sins is more of a problem for her than for him. Her conscience is as unforgiving as her memory. Even though she would like to believe that God has granted forgiveness, she does not feel it. The ease of the redeemed will not come over her. There is always a residue that cannot be willed away, worked off, or put behind. When discussing the Bible, she always defends Martha's ungrateful role of hard work and ceaseless striving against Mary's devout contemplation at the master's feet. She believes that in all "essential things" Father has always been ahead of her, but in the practical affairs of life he is at risk, and she must be constantly at pains to warn him of looming dangers, clear his path of rocks, although no calamity ever happens to him. And he tells her so: "Nothing is going to happen to me," or, "Better to be trusting and take a fall than to mistrust and be proven right."

She considers his lifestyle unhealthy. He does not "eat right"; does not get enough vitamins; eats no lettuce, no fresh fruit, and hardly any vegetables; eats too little—like a bird. "Without vitamins a person can't live," she says. He puts down his fork and knife, raises his shoulders, and turns up his palms in mock exasperation: "Am I alive or not?"

"Oh, Father!" she sighs.

On hot days he sits for hours on the south balcony, working hard, sizzling. "That's not normal," she says, "look at yourself in the mirror, your head is about to explode."

He works up a powerful thirst, drinking by the quart a brew made of tea and fruit juice, mixed with a slimy concoction of yeast for fermentation.

"All that liquid can't possibly be healthy," she says. She finds the "endless drinking" that goes on in this family uncanny. She is never thirsty. When she was little, she was scared to death when her brothers got drunk and beat each other up. Ever since she has considered thirst as something indecent. Anyone who drinks when thirsty "can't control his impulses, lets himself go."

She is the last to join the family gathered on summer evenings on the balcony. Exhausted from a frantic day, she rests both arms on the railing and watches the swallows flying their easy, elegant arcs. Should she have another life on earth, she would like to be a swallow.

"Don't you like to be with us?" Father asks.

She dislikes going on visits and having visitors. The least favorite guests are those who enter rooms without asking, occupy chairs, impose themselves, settle in, spread out, invade one's space, share confidences, get chummy, obnoxious, and annoying.

When she gives the children permission to attend a party, she does so with reservations. They must be the first ones to leave, at the latest "when the party is at its peak." Under no circumstances are they to be among the last when "things get out of hand" and "barriers are coming down." In general, they should "maintain distance," "be reserved," and not "lower themselves to the common level."

During menopause she develops a fear of people, hides in the house, and does not want to see anybody.

In the silence of her dark bedroom, black thoughts grow rampant, but she cannot talk about them: that she might become a burden to him, and that he—universally popular, welcome everywhere, spoiled by sympathy—might look for easier, happier relationships. He is unable to calm her fears. For her sake, he renounces having visitors even though he is used to different ways. The parsonage in St. Goar was a home with open doors. In Simmern there were friends and helpers. In Auel there are only parishioners, neighbors, admirers, and those who are beloved in Christ. No friends.

Only once, on the beach at Juist,[4] he met someone who almost became a friend, had he not been driven away by the devil of politics. And his departure "without a word" proved that it was not a real friendship after all.

Alone, dressed in a linen jacket, light trousers, and tennis shoes, Father sets out from the family's staked-out beach terrain and returns hours later in the company of another man. Mother, who is lying in a deck chair nearby, reading "The gray beach by the gray sea . . . ,"[5] feels slightly irritated as she looks up. Father waves, and the portly gentleman next to him doffs his straw hat: Herr Jacobi, a lawyer from Essen[6] and World War I veteran, is a nationalist and skeptical of the Republic.

During the evening stroll on the promenade the families become acquainted: Frau Jacobi, a teenage son, an almost grown daughter, who wears her black braids coiled and pinned over her ears.

From now on there are joint family activities — strolls along the promenade and nightcaps, of which Mother silently disapproves: "If the Jacobis aren't constantly on the go, they're not happy."

On a sultry, windless day the two gentlemen take a hike around the island. Although there is no cloud in the sky, Mother cautions as they depart: "This doesn't bode well!" In fact, a thunderstorm gathers in the afternoon. During the downpour mother and daughter are waiting at the hotel window, sighing at the thought that something might happen to Father: a cold, rheumatism, pneumonia . . . . Finally the men come walking up the road, barefoot, pants rolled up to their knees, tennis shoes tied together by the laces and thrown over their shoulders: Father sporting on his head a handkerchief tied in knots at the four corners, eyes sparkling in his copper red face; Herr Jacobi with his deformed, dripping straw hat, which he doffs with a dramatic gesture all the way to the ground whenever one of the guests who have sought shelter on the porch waves or laughs at them. In high spirits, they jump over puddles and overflowing ditches. Father wrings the water out of his socks and whirls them above his head.

Mother doesn't even turn around as he enters the room. With frozen mien she continues to stare out the window, but for once he won't let her spoil the fun. He grabs her, pulls her out of the chair, whirls her — who is stiff as a poker — around, tilts up her chin, and kisses her on the mouth.

Later they meet the Jacobis on the promenade, probably according to an earlier arrangement. Forming a large, loosely knit group, they walk along the quay, the two fathers, engaged in a lively conversation, in front; the ladies follow. Mother, in her only summer dress, is silent and feels overwhelmed by the elegant Frau Jacobi, who is volubly chaffing the men: "Kids, they're just like kids! You can't leave them out of sight for a minute!" Following at some distance are the "young folk," with Gerhard keeping close to the beautiful Jacobi girl, who is graciously letting him carry her cardigan.

The child has never seen her parents so relaxed and cheerful in the company of other people, so young, so lovely and light, the breeze playing with their clothes, the evening sun on their tanned faces—almost like other children's parents, almost like normal people.

Happily she runs ahead on the seawall, jumps, whirls around, tosses sand into the wind. When the others catch up with her, she throws herself at her father's chest and clasps him and Herr Jacobi in a tight embrace. "You're like kids, just like kids!" she says, echoing Frau Jacobi. "Now, don't be impertinent," Mother says, but Frau Jacobi only laughs. "It's vacation time," she says, "there's nothing wrong with getting carried away once in a while."

Mother declines sharing a nightcap with them during their last evening at the beach hotel. She has to put the child to bed.

She silently supervises the child washing her neck and brushing her teeth. Later on, she lies down on her bed but does not go to sleep; she tosses, sighs, coughs.

Sometime during the night Father returns. "A wonderful evening," he says. He hasn't had such good conversation for years. "Why didn't you come back?" he asks his wife. "Frau Jacobi was there till the end, an intelligent person and very amusing. It's good to have people you can talk to just person to person—other opinions, other interests, a fresh breeze. By the way . . . he hesitates, then goes on, "Herr Jacobi is a Jew; I would never have thought it." He quickly adds: "Of course, he's baptized; a better Christian and patriot than a lot of Germans. He's widely traveled, has seen the world with open eyes. There's much one can learn, broaden one's horizon. . . ." Yes, they did have a few drinks, a couple of glasses of wine, maybe three. For the first time Mother speaks up: You're not by any chance on a first-name basis with them, are you?"

"No," he says, "but why not?"

"What ever became of the Jacobis?" I ask Gerhard.

"Which Jacobis?" he asks.

"The ones we met on Juist, of course. Don't you remember?"

"Oh, those! I have no idea. Why?"

"After all, you had a crush on their daughter."

"Haven't you ever lost track of someone you had a crush on?"

"They were Jewish; did you know that?" My voice is sharp, full of apprehension. We are on dangerous ground.

We exchange a few more sentences: I didn't mean it that way. Neither did he. So everything is okay.

But it isn't okay. Once again we have entered a zone where explanations explain nothing.

10

"Republic" is a dirty word in the parsonage at Auel. It is related to other dirty words like monkey business, blatherskites, smart alecks, bootlickers, blockheads, weaklings, wheeler-dealers, naysayers, traitors, compromisers, appeasers, international riffraff, renegades . . . .

The "Reds" are at it again! The "black robes" are behind everything! Pack of brownshirts! The "Yids" have their finger in every pie! "Locarno"—sickening! The "Reichsbananer": black-red-mustard![1]

Father's voice expresses disgust. The same disgust he has for onions, which come to the dinner table covered by an upside-down bowl. Onions are the Jews' favorite fare!

Politics is one of those topics that turn your stomach, like sex, crime, money.

He is annoyed by the Republic.

If it were only a little less conspicuous, not so loud, blathery, obtrusive, vulgar, such a mass spectacle.

It lacks discretion, modesty, dignity.

They can't do anything without shouting: election campaigns, propaganda speeches, government turnovers, parliamentary debates, parades, demonstrations, street brawls. . . . He casts his ballot in a sour mood: I don't even know these people. Don't want to get to know them. Don't want to have anything to do with them. He couldn't care less about majority rule. The masses are an ignorant lot. What kind of people would let themselves be put into power only to be deposed again by the majority? Rabble, riffraff, cattle, pack, "the gutter" . . . Poor Germany, your fate is being determined in the streets! Turn off that box! he shouts, when politicians raise their voices on the radio that the family has bought recently. One of them, by the name of Hitler, shouts more loudly than the rest. He can't even speak correct German. An Austrian: that's all we need!

When they march down the street—no matter whether they are Reds or brownshirts or carry the black-red-gold flag—he says: "Close the window! There's a draft!"

Once, when the French were still occupying Auel, he left the house, looking back as usual to wave at Mother, who was anxiously signaling him from the window because she saw a French soldier coming down the narrow sidewalk. Father was supposed to step into the gutter and doff his hat, but he did not see the soldier and thought his wife was waving him good-bye.

As Father was waving, with his head turned, the soldier let him get close and then pushed him into the gutter with the butt of his rifle. He took such a bad fall that mother had to come out to help him get up.

From time to time he receives some older gentlemen, whose visits always cheer him up. They are dressed in civilian clothes, but their voices are unmistakably those of members of the imperial officers' corps. When they have dinner with the family, the children are to be seen but not heard. Father monopolizes the guests. Even Mother is excluded when he withdraws with them to his study. He gets some wine from the cellar and returns, not with the ordinary stuff drawn from the little cask sent each year from St. Goar, but with a bottle of the very best, reserved for special occasions. The unfamiliar aroma of exquisite cigars wafts ceremonially through the house.

Mother remarks on how unassuming and modest these gentlemen are. The highest-ranking among them, who has an aristocratic name, is, at the very least, a general; he arrives without a suitcase, carrying instead a cardboard box tied with twine. "That is true nobility," Mother says, "genuine distinction utterly unheedful of appearances."

They are the authors of the letters that are kept in an envelope marked "comrades in arms."

"My dear Pastor," a captain writes from the western front in 1918, "I plead with you to lend us your help on the home front. You, who are so well acquainted with war, must open the eyes of the poor, ignorant people. Make them aware of the humiliation, the oppression, the hunger and want they are suffering as long as they continue on their path of cowardly submission. Damn it: Germans are born to be free. We are always standing in the forefront, ready to fight. Why do they make us retreat? Whoever relies on that scoundrel Wilson is doomed to defeat. May all those traitors, compromisers, and so-called victors gag on their own poison."

Ten years later, a Herr von D—— writes from Pomerania: "By attacking Paragraph 218,[2] liberalism and Marxism are destroying the very roots of the Christian nationalist concept of the state. The parties of the political center refuse to make decisions. Hence, we Protestants are all the more duty-bound to hurry to the front, to fight against these contemporary evils, and to complete Luther's unfinished work."

So what did my father think of the Republic?

On this point, the family's collective memory is silent.

Once again I return to Auel, this time alone. It is winter; the rosebushes in Limbach's garden are protected by pine twigs, the flower beds carefully covered. At the time, the schoolteacher was still able to do the work himself; now he is confined to the house. "I hope he'll still be around to see the coming of spring," his daughter tells me in the hallway.

I find him sitting in the same chair, carefully dressed, but he has greater difficulties standing and is a little slower in getting up and walking around than the last time I saw him. I am expected. An open ring binder with documents about the conflict between church and state during the Nazi period is lying on the table.

We discuss the Christian-German movement, the forerunner of what later, under the Nazis, became the German Christian Faith movement.[3] In the twenties they still had a national-conservative agenda and made an effort to restore the monarchy; they were antidemocratic, opposed to the League of Nations, and against Stresemann's policy of peace.[4]

He has no doubt that my father sympathized with these people, the teacher tells me; yet it is out of the question that he actively participated in any propaganda or subversive activities against the Republic. There was not a word of that in his sermons—he can guarantee that much. Romans 13 kept him from doing that: "Let every soul be subject unto the higher powers." And, according to Schlatter, "higher powers" refers to "any actual and existing power" that "has been placed above us in God's order." A Christian must obey "all those who have been empowered to govern, regardless how such government is structured or defined." Since at that time the authority of the state resided in a republican form of government (God help us! your father would have said), every Christian had an obligation to be loyal to it. Certainly not to love it. Nobody could ask for that; even Jesus did not ask the Jews to love the Roman emperor when he commanded them to "render unto Caesar the things which are Caesar's."

The minister once said to the teacher: "Can you imagine that God would want to anoint any of those mediocre baldheads with the holy oil of authority?" He, the minister, could certainly not believe that. To him, the "right order" was hierarchical: a splendid head of state, chosen and anointed by God, and underneath him the people—all equal before God, yet "everyone in his proper calling, chosen for him by the Lord"—who were brave, honest, hard-working, obedient German people only insofar as they were part of such an order. Everything else was nothing but chaos, a shapeless mass, rabble.

My father did not fight against the Republic, the teacher says, because that would have meant to attack it, to get involved, to engage in brawls. He was merely disgusted. Disgust avoids things, looks away, refuses to touch, keeps the object of disgust at arm's length.

My father was quite skilled in keeping things at arm's length, he says, whether it was a matter of "dreary finances," "faceless bureaucracies," the Republic, or working with the young.

His concept of duty, as he understood it, was useful in helping him avert his eyes. For him, duty meant exercising the responsibilities of his office, tending his flock, laboring in his vineyard, keeping the peace, and wrestling for the salvation of souls. Here there was also room for love, which, ever since the "failure of the German people," had remained without an object—except for what remained with the Kaiser: loyalty, sadness, hope for his return, which never happened. Not even old Hindenburg, the president of the Reich, could make that miracle happen. Instead, he took an oath on the constitution—"a meaningless scrap of paper"—and publicly shook hands with that "proletarian" in front of the Garrison Church of Potsdam in 1933. He surely knew what he was doing, the hero of Tannenberg,[5] and even if he didn't, the "Lord of all history" knew, He who "administers justice beyond our knowledge and understanding." At any rate, there was no need for a mere country parson to understand it.

"Knowledge puffeth up, but charity edifieth," Paul writes to the Corinthians. He who is blind but has faith pleases the Lord better than Thomas, who could not believe in Christ without touching His wounds.

"It all depends on how you look at history," says the schoolteacher.

"If you believe in God's direct involvement in the historical process and you become aware of events that seem incompatible with God's will, you simply take the position that God is unfathomable. What else can you do?"

"But you can't simply tune out," I say. "He held a public office; he was dealing with living human beings."

"He was able to tune out because he drew a clear dividing line," the teacher says. "He divided man into what is 'essential' and what is 'external.' In his 'essential' identity man is one of God's children, a neighbor, a brother in Christ; in his 'external' identity he is a citizen, a member of a particular nation, class, party, and religious denomination—an object of social conditions. So he simply tuned out."

Put into practice, this was the way it worked: he objected to the "black robes," yet the arch-Catholic dean of Saint Servatius was an "ideal colleague" and a "man of thought and intelligence." The Jews poisoned the people, but Rabbi Selig of the synagogue at Auel was "a good soul."

He feared the Reds, but the Red Schmitz Gustav, who lived in Zange, was "a thoroughly decent fellow who had fallen on hard times through no fault of his own; one has to lend him a helping hand."

In 1933, when one of the brownshirts was elected mayor of Auel, the teacher warned him: "Reverend, you better beware of that man." He stared at him in total surprise: "Why, I know him personally; he's not a bad sort of fellow, not too bright, but he couldn't hurt a fly. We'll get along with him all right, don't worry; I'll have a little talk with him."

As it turned out, the mayor appears to have stuck up for him, because he escaped occasional interrogations unscathed. You've got to know how to talk to those people, he would say triumphantly. After all, the Nazis are people just like you and me; they don't mind a little straight talk. All it takes is to know how to deal with people and believe in their good qualities.

"What a fool!" I say. But then I stop, startled by the angry glance the teacher directs at me.

"Don't talk like that," he snaps. After a pause he continues, slightly embarrassed, "I was very fond of your father." "Like everyone who knew him," he adds.

He, too, knows about the incident with the soldier who pushed my father into the gutter. As for himself, he managed to deal with this problem more diplomatically. Knowing that many French soldiers used the same route that he took to school every day, he decided to take a detour via side streets and backyards. Though he had to leave home half an hour earlier, he spared himself the indignity of having to doff his hat. "Your father was a man without guile," he says. "He believed in goodness, truth, and beauty, even when there was no trace of them anywhere in sight."

11 During the third and last of my visits the schoolteacher talks about the struggle between church and state. The manner in which he studies me over his horn-rimmed glasses gives me to understand that a new situation has developed: no longer mere conversation or chatting about memories and exchanging ideas, but instruction, a sort of old-fashioned colloquium, in which one person does the talking, the other the listening. Questions are permitted, but no conclusion or critique.

Obediently, like a first-year student, I take out my notebook and pencil to take notes. He is evidently pleased. When I cannot keep up with him, he stops, watching as I write, until I look up.

His narrative goes back to the spring of 1934, no farther, because, as he says, my father did not become aware of church politics until that time; "in his limited way" he even took a political position. His limitations, the teacher explains, were defined by the special relationship between the German Evangelical church and the state. This relationship goes back to Luther's concept that worldly and spiritual power are joined in the person of the sovereign, a concept that in more recent years has reemerged as the Prussian "throne-and-altar" tradition.

When the worldly powers violate the law, the Lutheran Christian is only allowed to suffer "for Christ's sake"; he must not rebel or resist. (The fact that Luther, after 1530, proclaimed that "Christians, as citizens, had the duty to resist" has largely dropped out of the church's memory in the course of the centuries.)

Positivist church historians—whose voices are most loudly heard in the German Evangelical church at the end of the nineteenth and beginning of the twentieth century—conceive of the church as the servant of the German state and of the German people. God, the "Lord of all history," demands patriotism as "obedience toward His created order, which manifests itself in the people, the nation, and the fatherland"; "Protestantism and German identity are one"; "the Christian individual positions himself on the political right." To which Karl Barth, representing the theology of resistance and the tradition of Swiss democratic Calvinism, replies: "The church is in no manner the servant of humanity; neither is it the servant of the German people. It solely serves the word of God."

The positivists charge Barth with "subversion" and "ahistorical divisiveness." This conflict is older than the Third Reich.

In the Weimar Republic, 70–80 percent of the Protestant clergy are politically conservative nationalists; most of them belong to Hugenberg's German National People's party.[1] The rest is divided among the socialists, the democratic liberals, and those with a fundamental belief in Germany's manifest destiny. Even though the Weimar constitution puts an end to the established church at the national level, the treaties with the various churches at the state level insure a degree of state supervision that Hitler will be able to exploit in his effort to keep the church in line. His strategy: religious posturing at the outset ("positive Christianity"); a show of neutrality in all questions of church politics; intervention "for the sake of national and ecclesiastical peace" as soon as there are any signs of resistance; retreat into neutrality, compromises, and enticements as soon as some of his goals have been achieved.

Appeal by the German government to the German people, 1 February 1933: "May Almighty God take our labors into his merciful hands, enlighten our will, bless our understanding, and reward us with the trust of our people!" The Evangelical church rejoices at such "an auspicious beginning" (as well as the end of the unpopular Weimar state).

And again rejoicing at the results of the election of 5 March: an end to "party strife"; "annihilation of the Communists."

Proclamation of the Bavarian Church Council, 16 March 1933: "A state that once again lives and acts according to God's commandments may be assured not only of the church's applause but also of our joyous and active collaboration and support."

For years, the fiction is maintained that Hitler is somehow "personally" allied with the Protestants because, in contrast to the "Roman" church (as evidenced in the struggle between church and state, 1872–87), they have always considered themselves a national church. With his concept of "positive Christianity" he even seems to take the side of the orthodox, who defend scripture and faith against the liberals, in internal church wranglings. In the early years, even those who belong to the Pastors' Emergency League, including Niemöller and the Confessing church, fall prey to this deception. Their resistance is sparked not by political events—which even Barth believes to be unimportant and transitory phenomena—but by theological controversies that arise between them and the German Christian Faith movement, which, though it has adopted the goals of the National Socialist party, is never openly favored by Hitler. The official church likewise opposes the German Christians, but its resistance is short-lived because there are too many points of agreement: glorification of the nation, aversion to democracy, condemnation of Marxism. "Those who did not believe in Hitler's mission in 1933 were considered outlaws even by the members of the Confessing church," Barth says in a lecture he gives in Schaffhausen in 1936.

Within the church itself—and not as a result of external pressure—there is a growing desire for a stricter hierarchical organization, modeled after the National Socialist party: a "Reich" church. A three-man council proposes measures for restructuring the church, a step that Barth sees as "internally unnecessary and based solely on political enthusiasm and expediency; hence, a decision that, though taken within the church and by the church, is essentially nonecclesiastical."

Nevertheless, to the great surprise of the government, the first election for Reich bishop does not result in the appointment of Hitler's favorite, District Chaplain Ludwig Müller, but that of Pastor Bodelschwingh, the candidate of the young reformers.

For the first time, the Party drops its cover of neutrality by using its proven method of showing the "will of the people"—mass demonstrations of brownshirts, Hitler Youth, and factory cadres—and by airing its disapproval in the press and on the radio. The protests are sanctioned by Hitler's refusal to receive Bodelschwingh. The chief rationale is that "Bodelschwingh does not have the Führer's confidence." Hermann Göring, a friend of the German Christians, confers upon Minister of Culture Bernhard Rust complete authority over all Evangelical churches in Prussia. Rust, in turn, appoints a fellow Party member, August Jäger, as commissioner of the Prussian churches, with authority to take all necessary steps "for the sake of peace within the church": dissolution of all elected church agencies and appointment of specially authorized officials, who in turn will appoint new agencies. District Chaplain Müller occupies the building of the Council of Churches in Berlin with ss units, takes over the building of the Protestant Church Council "in the interest of the church and of the Gospel," and Jäger transfers to him authority over all the churches within the Old Prussian Unity church.[2]

All important positions within the church are filled by German Christians. Some of the leaders of regional churches refuse to cooperate; the Rhenish church does not refuse but accepts the newly authorized Dr. Krummacher "in order to prevent worse." For the first time, press releases contain references to the fateful division between the church's "external organization" and its "substance of faith," a dichotomy based on Luther's doctrine of the "two realms," which is one more handicap for the official church in mounting an effective resistance. The Confessing church does not accept the division yet to the very end remains ambivalent about the principle of political resistance. Hence, it fails to serve as a beacon either to the laity within the church or to outsiders.

After the church has been brought politically into line, the government retreats behind its cover of neutrality. It presents itself as "democratic" and schedules "free" church elections for 23 July 1933, though the National Socialist party puts its entire propaganda apparatus at the disposal of the German Christians. Brownshirt commandos disperse meetings of the opposition (at that time, the young reformers) despite their ardent declarations of loyalty. Due to all sorts of public and internal manipulations, the election results in a 75 percent vote for the German Christians.

The young reformers desist, dedicating themselves instead to a "theological-missionary reorientation." The remaining resisters around Niemöller declare the election illegal. Since they remain within the official church—including the Pastors' Emergency League and the Confessing church—the schism continues to be an internal matter to the end, and the struggle between church and state turns into an internal battle between those who are loyal to the state and the hated radicals. Again, without pressure from above and "in order to prevent worse," the Church Council of the Old Prussian Unity church confirms Ludwig Müller's appointment as regional bishop.

At the Tenth General Synod of the Old Prussian Unity church, 156 representatives of the German Christian Faith movement oppose 71 representatives calling themselves "Gospel and Church." The "Aryan paragraph" is passed by a two-thirds majority: a person can be a pastor only if "he is totally committed to the national state and the German Evangelical church and of Aryan descent." The regional church of Saxony spells it out even more bluntly: "Pastors who are unable to prove that they will commit themselves totally to the National Socialist state and the German Evangelical church may be retired from active service."

The Pastors' Emergency League is formed in opposition to the Aryan paragraph, which it considers a "breach of Christian commitment": in September 1933 it has thirteen hundred members; in December 1933, fifty-five hundred; in January 1934, ten thousand. Ludwig Müller is elected Reich bishop at the German Evangelical National Synod. He establishes a "Ministry of Spiritual Affairs" consisting entirely of German Christians—among them a Dr. Forsthoff, who has no qualms about "our church identifying itself completely with the state." He declares that any concept that postulates the interrelationship between the visible, earthly church and the invisible church, namely, the kingdom of heaven, would turn the church into a politically independent institution, that is, into an opponent of the totalitarian state. But Forsthoff cautions the church not to act according to the word of the Apostle that sets God's law above man's law. It should do so only "if the state denies the church the space and the freedom to accomplish its work. However, as long as the state does not interfere with the church, it would be irresponsible to sacrifice the church to an illusory concept and thereby drive it into political opposition—the only kind of opposition possible—to the state."

Although the opposition within the church rejects the division between the spiritual and the institutional church, they consider it "an extraordinarily difficult question to decide where the limits of the state are to be drawn, an issue that cannot be decided in general terms but must be examined in each particular case." This means that the decision is referred to each individual conscience, placing the Confessing church under the constant threat of internal division.

After the Party has emerged victorious and the German Christians have done their duty, Hitler drops them when a functionary of the German Christians in a speech delivered during a membership rally at the Berlin Sports Palace (12 November 1933) toots the horn of national socialism just a bit too loudly: "When we focus on those aspects of the Gospel that speak to our German hearts, we can proudly say that Christ's teachings reveal themselves to be clearly and radiantly in harmony with the principles of national socialism" (sustained applause). The final resolution (with only one dissenting vote) calls for applying the Aryan paragraph also to the laity and for cleansing the Gospel of anything un-German.

All of a sudden those who were all too eager to obey are out in the cold. Partly because of expected public outcries (including protests from the official church), partly because he doesn't want to be tied to any particular religious group, Hitler drops them and even consents to "temporarily suspend" the controversial Aryan paragraph. He does not interfere when Minister of the Interior Wilhelm Frick promises to dissolve the German Christians in return for Niemöller's putting an end to the Pastors' Emergency League. Niemöller ("we don't want to create martyrs") refuses.

The Faith movement falls apart. Its moderate members reconstitute themselves in a new organization renamed "Reich Movement of German Christians." The radical Thuringians secede. Once again Hitler has shown his "goodwill." Church leaders regain their courage and demand the dissolution of the Ministry of Spiritual Affairs. Reich Bishop Müller concedes, relinquishing his patronage of the Faith movement, but surreptitiously staffs the Ministry of Spiritual Affairs with "moderates," which leads to further protests. Suddenly he, too, finds himself isolated both from the Führer and from most of his supporters. In order to regain the government's goodwill, he bestows a special favor on Reich Youth Leader Baldur von Schirach: he signs an agreement incorporating the Evangelical Youth Organization into the Hitler Youth. The church leaders protest.

On 3 and 4 January 1934, representatives of the "Confessing" opposition within the church conduct the first of their now famous "free reformed synods" at Barmen-Gemarke.[3] In their declaration, formulated by Barth, national socialism is described as "a temporary political experiment conducted by man." They reject, on theological grounds, the state's claim to absolute and total power.

The official church reacts with horror to this "harsh, uncompromising attitude": only a Swiss Calvinist could deal so cruelly with the most sacred feelings of the German people. Hitler is still exercising restraint. Two factions within the government are squabbling with each other: Göring, Rust, and Goebbels favor the German Christians; Frick (supposedly with Hindenburg's support) seeks peace with and within the church. To mollify the opposition, he inserts a few conciliatory phrases into the treaty integrating the youth organizations of church and Party (membership is "encouraged" but "voluntary"). Reich Bishop Müller feels encouraged by the stronger Göring-Rust-Goebbels faction; under penalty of law, he prohibits any opposition to his leadership of the church (the so-called "muzzling edict"). He also succeeds in reactivating the Aryan paragraph. The Pastors' Emergency League demands Müller's resignation and withdraws its confidence in him by public proclamation from the pulpit. Müller dodges the issue and feints illness; he does not want to make a decision until an audience of church leaders with Hitler, which has been postponed until 25 January, has taken place.

The schoolteacher describes this audience as an instructive example of the failure of German political resistance whose significance reaches beyond that particular period in time and the Protestant church.

Göring has carefully prepared himself for the occasion by digging up and collecting politically incriminating material, including presumably treasonous contacts with foreign countries and subversive speeches and sermons delivered by pastors of the Emergency League. Niemöller himself plays into Göring's hands by telephoning one of his allies just hours before the audience with Hitler: "We have deployed our forces; we have sent a memorandum to the president of the Reich; we have pulled it off. Before he meets with the church leaders today, the chancellor will report to Hindenburg and will receive his extreme unction from him" (text of the recorded telephone conversation).

Göring reads the text aloud before the stunned church leaders have a chance to speak. Furious, Hitler jumps up, screaming "in holy wrath" (according to State Bishop Koch of Saxony) at the representatives of the church: "Do you think that with such shamelessly underhanded machinations you can drive a wedge between the president and me and thereby undermine the foundations of the Reich?"

Niemöller steps forward and takes responsibility for the content of the telephone conversation. He defends himself by pointing out the "difficult battle the Pastors' Emergency League has fought to maintain the church's spiritual integrity, a battle that was not fought against the Third Reich but on its very behalf." To which Hitler replies: "Let me worry about the Third Reich! You worry about your church!"

Hitler completely ignores the representations made by the church leaders; he does not take notice until Göring starts reading the police reports. In passionate tones he denounces the clergymen's ungratefulness. After all, it is he who saved the church from communism. He threatens to withhold government subventions. In the end he assumes a paternal role, admonishing the church leaders that "in the face of the looming political dangers they should sit down together with the Reich bishop in the spirit of Christian brotherhood."

"'It is not for my sake but for Germany's sake!' he said. And those who had the honor of being present at that historic hour were impressed with the seriousness with which the chancellor spoke of the situation of the German people. . . . How could we not be deeply moved?" (Church President Koch in a speech to the Confessing synod at Barmen, 1934.)

"Deeply moved," all of the church leaders, except Niemöller, capitulate. "Impressed by the momentousness of the hour," they pledge "unswerving loyalty to the Third Reich and to its Führer"; in the sharpest terms they denounce "all machinations of dissent aimed at the state, the people, and the movement"; and they unanimously support the Reich bishop whom they had come to depose. Müller makes a few minor concessions, which they do not demand in writing and which are never implemented.

The German Christians are triumphant: "This goes to show what a word from Hitler is able to accomplish. Their proclamation proves that their opposition to the Reich bishop was never—as has been alleged—based on fundamental principles of faith or doctrine" (from *Evangelium im Dritten Reich*, a Sunday newspaper of the German Christians).

Finally everything falls into place: the sheep have been separated from the goats, and the latter have been branded as public enemies so they can be easily selected for the concentration camps. The good folks of the church turn away in horror. They don't want to have anything to do with traitors.

"Your father," the teacher says, concluding his historical seminar, "also did not want to have anything to do with traitors."

12

In December 1933, shortly after the uproar at the Berlin Sports Palace, the members of Auel's Protestant congregation met in the grand hall of the Hotel Felder. Members of the Ladies Aid had prepared an enormous Advent wreath. Advent and Christmas carols were to be sung later in the program. Limbach, the schoolteacher, sat at the piano ready to provide the accompaniment. Long before the beginning of the meeting all chairs were taken. Word had gotten out that the minister would "let the cat out of the bag." Those who came late had to stand or go back home.

The minister did not like to use the lectern on the raised platform where the band usually performed. Today he preferred to stay below at his table and did not want to be up there, far from his congregation; he wanted to be among them because it was to be a "person-to-person conversation," not a sermon. He asked their indulgence to let him begin with an exposition of his own views on the controversial issues that were to be discussed; of course, he would consider them in the light of the Bible, since for him there was no other way to reflect on the ways of the world.

It turned out to be a kind of sermon after all, partly because he had selected a Bible verse as his topic: Jesus' words to his disciples before He was taken prisoner: "All ye shall be offended because of me this night."

Usually he starts out with an immediate leap into the specific situation described in the text, if possible by way of images that he fashions from contemporary descriptions of the Holy Land and from historical research. In this case it is the Lord's evening stroll with his disciples under the olive trees in the Garden of Gethsemane: a hushed group, whispering, looking around fearfully, listening to sounds under the pressure of the imminent catastrophe. The traitor has already been expelled, the last supper taken, the word of parting spoken. The Lord speaks in ominous prophecies. His voice, His skin, which they seek to touch, convey His fear of death. No heavenly host, no bolt of lightning, not even the heroic pathos of dying together. He coolly rejects Peter's protestations: All ye shall be offended because of me this night. . . .

At this point, the minister interjects a query: Offended because of Christ? Who is offended and why? First, the Pharisees and the scribes, because He upsets the system of their theology; second, the military rulers, because He stirs up the people; third, the oppressed people themselves, because Jesus does not present Himself as a revolutionary or a savior from bondage; fourth, and last, the disciples, because He refuses to use the power and glory with which He has been invested. How does Jesus react to this? Although the offense is still in the future ("Ye *shall* be offended"), He does not suggest how it can be avoided, nor does He ask them not to take offense. He does not say a single word suggesting that whatever will be offensive to them is, at bottom, not offensive at all, but God's gracious will, whose ultimate purpose is always beneficent. He simply asserts, as firmly as if He were stating a fact taking place in the present or the past: Ye shall be offended. . . .

The minister briefly summarizes the rest of the story: fear and trembling; the sleeping disciples; the clanging of armor and weapons behind the wall; conspiratorial whispering: Whomsoever I shall kiss, that same is He!

A brief pause for thinking and feeling about what has been said, then the leap into the present: today's Christian community has, on the one hand, the advantage over the disciples because it knows about Easter and Pentecost; on the other hand, it is at a disadvantage since it lacks Christ's living presence that would bind the community together in a common purpose: to be the followers of Christ.

Hence, today's Christian community is just as much affected by the Lord's dark prophecy, the message of this story, as were the disciples: being offended by Christ or by His followers is neither accidental nor avoidable; it is not a defect that can somehow and at some time be remedied; nor is it simply a temporary phenomenon or a failure on the part of the disciples. It is, rather, a fundamental attribute of Christian life in this world, from which God has not spared His Son and from which He will not spare His congregation. Hence, even today's Christians have no other choice but to live with this offense.

Then the minister turns to his audience, looking from one to the other and giving his voice that special, personal tone as if he were sitting face to face with them explaining God's rule as it manifests itself in their individual lives. (Just as in church, the noise level—coughing, sniffling, rustling of clothes—must have suddenly subsided in the ballroom of the Hotel Felder so that the clatter of trays in the pass-through and the shouting of orders from the kitchen could be heard. . . .)

"Let's talk about ourselves," he says. "Let us try to understand those among us who, caught up in the general enthusiasm for this new beginning among the German people, wish also to give a new form to their faith—more radiant, prouder, more imposing, closer to those ideals that, after years of tired resignation, are finally being honored again. In their love for their Führer, they are eager to embrace their Savior too.

"But suddenly they realize that He does not fit into this embrace, and they are offended by the unfitness of our Lord: that He was born of a Jewish mother; that He was sent first and foremost to be the messiah of the Jews; that He has come not to reject but to fulfill the Old Testament, the story of the people of Israel and its leaders; that, instead of praising man's power and greatness, He speaks of sin and repentance, of the eye of the needle at the entrance to the kingdom of heaven, of the strength of the weak, the poverty of riches, the blessedness of the lowly and rejected. They would like nothing better than to tear off His beggar's garment and clothe Him in purple, set a helmet or crown on His head in place of the crown of thorns, put a proud horse between His thighs instead of a wretched ass, and send Him off, a shining hero, into battle against the people's enemies. But He will not permit it! Such mummery belongs to the Tempter, whom He refused in the desert: Get thee behind me, Satan!"

Again he pauses, breathing, with his eyes closed, to gather his strength; then he rises to his full height and speaks, at first softly, then gradually more loudly, energetically, even angrily: "If we look at the meeting of the German Christian Faith movement at the Sports Palace in the light that God's word sheds into our dark world, we experience, despite our horror at the excesses of human impudence, a sense of relief—relief that the cat is finally out of the bag! On that occasion a certain Herr Krause (he spits out the name with utmost contempt) spoke of doing away with the Old Testament because it contains 'Jewish quid pro quo morality' and 'stories about cattle traders and pimps.' This theological upstart called for a revision of the New Testament with its 'distorted and superstitious accounts by the Apostles' and for a complete excision of Saint Paul's 'scapegoat theology and inferiority doctrine.' It is a relief, also, because finally this Herr Krause helps us to see that the so-called Faith movement is taking giant steps away from our Savior, that it deserts, betrays, denies Him—and all because of the offense that is inevitably a part of Him and of us who are trying to be his followers."

His voice trails off, he braces himself with both hands on the table and leans far forward, speaking once again in a more private tone: He, the pastor himself, has experienced that offense, and it has been painful because he is by nature sensitive; it hurts him to cause annoyance and displeasure on both sides, as has lately been the case. "Some are angry with me for a certain reticence vis-à-vis the new political order; others think I am not focusing strictly and exclusively enough on preserving the rituals of the church. Surely there are some gentlemen who, every Sunday morning as well as here today, are angry that they have to listen to my words and write them down, while they would much rather be at home in bed or drinking beer." With that, squinting so that his small eyes become mere slits, he fixes his eyes on a man dressed in an overcoat who is sitting next to the exit at the far end of the hall and busily scribbling in his notebook. Alerted by the commotion around him, the man looks up, meets the minister's silent gaze, clears his throat, starts shuffling nervously, tucks away pencil and notebook, and slips out through the door with lowered head.

While the minister's smile spreads from row to row, warming up his audience, he embarks upon the conclusion of his speech.

It is, he continues, certainly unpleasant if not dangerous to give offense. Hence it is of such great importance for the members of this congregation to remain firmly united, so as to support and strengthen each other. This is the reason why he has called the meeting; not to scold, as some of them may have assumed, but to plead with them from the bottom of his heart: Let us stand together! Let us call out to those who, without being aware of it, may have gone astray: Come and return to the fold! Stay with the Lord, who does not spare us offense, but who also gives us the strength to endure and overcome it. Even though we are not going to slaughter the proverbial lamb, we shall celebrate together and partake in a festive Christmas communion with the Lord, who bids us to His table: Come, all is prepared!

With these words he quickly left the hall, briefly placing his hand on the teacher's shoulder as he passed him, seeking his eye, and smiling at him as if to say: Are we finally in agreement? And that's what we were, says the schoolteacher; for one evening we were comrades in arms, almost friends. . . .

When he returned and asked for an opposing presentation—"Now it is your turn!"—nobody raised his hand. It was not a matter of disgruntlement or resistance among those who were gathered, the teacher says, but, on the contrary, an excess of agreement. He afterward talked to various people, including those who had gone over to the German Christians under the influence of the former vicar. Although they did not remember exactly what their pastor had said, they were all under the impression that there was nothing to add: he had spoken to their deepest concerns, solved their problems, and decided for them.

The minister suggested that they all sing a hymn together: first, four verses from "Raise high the gate . . . ," and then, by popular demand, the Reformation song, "A mighty fortress is our God."

During the first verse, the door leading to the hallway crashed open, and three brownshirted storm troopers stepped into the hall, among them the mayor, whom the minister considered a somewhat simple-minded but "basically decent" fellow. Heads turned and whispered words mixed with the singing, which gradually tapered off and, except for the piano and the pastor's voice, finally ceased altogether. The minister got up and flashed a friendly smile across the room to the mayor, who was still standing near the door with a somewhat sheepish expression. "And now," the minister called out, "in conclusion let us sing the third verse of the hymn we just began." With a thundering voice he led off: "And though this world, with devils filled, should threaten to undo us . . ." The piano joined in, then the congregation, more defiantly, more urgently, more joyously with every word that followed:

> We will not fear, for God hath willed
> His truth to triumph through us:
> The Prince of Darkness grim,
> We tremble not for him;
> His rage we can endure,
> For lo! his doom is sure,
> One little word shall fell him.

They sang so loudly that their voices drowned out the piano, and it was all the teacher could do to hold them together and to keep the happily rising voices in the key of C major. When he finally looked up from his hymnal, the uniformed men had disappeared, and the door had closed behind them.

During the short time that remained until Christmas, the elders who had joined the Faith movement dropped their membership, and the renegades within the congregation followed suit. The communion celebration on Christmas Day continued beyond the noon hour even though no one was served wine from a personal cup. Several times the sexton had to go with his basket down into the cellar of the parish house to get more wine because the supply in the vestry kept running out.

On the way home from the gathering at the hotel, a quick beer under his belt and his head full of the catacomb-sound of the hymn they had sung, the teacher visualized the minister smothering with his good-natured benevolence not just the little German Christian propagandists of Auel but the big government and Party functionaries. The minister was, of course, no fighter like Niemöller, no theological thinker like Barth, no organizer like Provost Grüber,[1] but in the struggle between church and state his "gift" for convincing people— by assuming their goodness or their good intentions—to do good might have proved to be useful. "You have to respect him for that," he mumbled to himself on his lonely way home. "Let him have faith in the basic goodness of Hitler and his cohorts, as long we keep him on our side." He had to laugh to himself at the thought of the minister in a magician's robe pulling white doves of innocence and rabbits of goodwill out of the pockets of surprised Party big shots. He was lucky that he didn't meet any of his students along the way; they would have thought he was drunk.

The teacher says that from that moment on he waited for a signal from the minister, some sign that he was one of them and ready to work with them. But there was nothing: no suggestion to have a conversation, no argument, no rebuke for underground activities.

But then it happened, six months later, when the minister at a meeting of the elders took his council members by surprise with the incredible assertion that until this very day— when some "well-meaning" anonymous person put the copy of a circular issued at Barmen-Gemarke into his hands—he had been unaware of the existence of a Confessing congregation in Auel, unaware of secret meetings, unaware of trips to neighboring communities to attend religious services. Even though he was constantly making the rounds of his congregation, knew everything about everyone, had his finger on every pulse, he claimed that he did not know anything about these goings-on.

That put an end to the teacher's hoping and waiting. Now the time had come to tell him the truth and to force him to make a decision. And while the schoolteacher is saying that, I remember the meeting of the elders he may be referring to: the one of which my mother used to say that it was the beginning of the end, the beginning of the torment that crushed our father and finally killed him.

13

As usual, the meeting of the elders took place in the meeting room of the parish, a narrow, high room, filled with the cold, stale smell of the church and the cold light of bulbs under flat porcelain shades hanging on long strings from the ceiling. All of the elders were already gathered around the long table underneath the cross mounted on the wall when the minister entered, just a little late, which was not his habit. Tucked under his arm was one of those longish, dark-stained wooden plaques inscribed with an admonitory saying that used to be common in pious households of another era. As silence descended, he put it, text down, in front of his place at the head of the table.

"I brought something for you," he said. "It comes from my parents' house, and I want to tell you a story that goes with it." Although he must not have been in the mood for joking, he gave a humorous account of the time when he was a young substitute preacher in Düsseldorf-Rath and finally "got to do a little preaching." On the Saturday before his first Sunday sermon, plagued by stage fright, he got on the train to St. Goar to try out his sermon on his father and mother. His parents sat far back in the dusky light under the organ loft of the church, while he, standing high and lonely in the pulpit, began to speak. He was bothered by the empty pews, their glossy surfaces, the distorted echoes of his own voice, which seemed pompous and vacuous to him, ill suited to penetrate the ears and hearts of his listeners. Discouraged, he continued to read from his draft until his father admonished him, by way of a suggestive cough, not to cling to either the script or the balustrade and to let his voice be filled and carried by the meaning of the words. At last the current swept him along. In his imagination he saw the pews filled with attentive listeners. He even dared to make some gestures, which the wide sleeves of his robe made look grand and dramatic.

On the way home his father offered some well-meaning criticism. His mother remained silent. At last, when he urged her to speak up, she said: Something is missing! She was unable to say what. She would think about it. At the beginning of the following week, a package was delivered to the parsonage in Düsseldorf-Rath. "Here it is," he said, turning the wooden plaque face up so the elders could read the pyrographic inscription: MORE LOVE.

He asked the elders to keep these words in their minds and hearts while he would proceed with what he had come to say. He had brought along a hammer in his briefcase—a little, silvery thing, more like a toy—as well as nails, which he bent one after the other as he tried to hammer them into the wall just below the cross. As he was looking around helplessly, annoyed because his symbolic gesture had failed, several of the elders jumped up to assist him. The head elder went up to the sexton's apartment to get some more nails and a proper hammer. When he returned and managed to hang the plaque with a few forceful strokes, the worst had already been said: there was a clandestine congregation behind his, the minister's, back.

"Have I not always dealt with you forthrightly and openly?" he asked, as the elders sat with their eyes cast down. "Have I ever given you a reason to believe that my work was not guided by Scripture and faith? Have we not always cooperated in holding the congregation together and leading them on the path following Christ? Now all of a sudden you agitate for dissent, divide the flock, conduct Bible readings in public houses and private apartments, drive to other communities and congregations for religious services, issue secret membership cards, and communicate by secret letters." He pulled an envelope from his coat pocket and held it up. "You follow directions from a church leadership that is not mine. You divert offerings, which is a loss to our congregation. You call yourselves a Confessing congregation as if you owned the confession of faith of this Evangelical church. My very own vicar, with whom I meet and discuss matters every morning, collaborates with you without saying a single word to me, and so does my colleague, the prison chaplain. The young lady vicar, who takes her meals in my house, solicits new members for the separatists during Bible class. A student of theology, whom I myself confirmed and encouraged to go into the ministry, acts as your secret courier — or "missionary," as you are pleased to call him like someone sent on a foreign mission, as if you were dealing with heathens instead of your own sisters and brothers within the Old Prussian Unity church!

"What arrogance! What monstrous, unchristian presumptuousness!" ("As if it were a personal matter between him and us, an affair of the heart," the teacher says. "As if he were resolving a domestic squabble by talking things out. As if disagreements would simply melt away by demonstrating MORE LOVE. But he might have succeeded, even in this meeting as in so many other meetings, gatherings, and services, had it not been for an evil presence, an adversary, a sower of discord. I would have been happy to leave this part to someone else, but no one wanted to take it on.")

"Do you really consider yourselves wiser and stronger in faith than our board of governors and the superintendent general?" the minister asked, without, however, getting an answer, except for a derisive sound when referring to the superintendent general. To which he reacted with some asperity: "Even if I am not in agreement with him in all matters, he and I are most deeply united in the conviction that our church can survive this time of serious challenge only if it remains unified and refuses to be divided."

He paused, but since there was no response, he continued, more at ease: "I do not presume to call into doubt the goodwill of my colleague Niemöller, but sometimes I have the impression that his recklessness does more harm than good. A pulpit is not a submarine!"

He sensed that they appreciated his humor and flashed a winning smile, which some of the elders reciprocated; not, however, the teacher: he had opened his ring binder and was searching among his papers.

The minister watched him with raised eyebrows; the corners of his mouth twitched, telling the audience without words what he was thinking: What a nit-picker and pedant, what a hairsplitter and faultfinder, always looking for a fly in the ointment; he never commits himself wholeheartedly to anything! The teacher felt that the general amusement was at his expense; he seemed tense as he got up and—as if confirming what the minister had suggested with a wink to his audience—started to speak in a dry monotone and without verve, choosing his words slowly and carefully, pausing time and again to reflect, laboriously pulling sheet after sheet from the rings of his binder, and passing them around.

("One had to be so careful," he says to me. "For heaven's sake not a word against the Führer, against the government, against the Party! There were Party members among the elders. The head elder, a member of our Confessing congregation, was a storm trooper, completely convinced that the Führer was a friend of the church; he claimed he had never heard of harassments, raids, and arrests. I didn't try to change his mind but was happy when he alerted us to impending raids.")

So with all due caution, his eyes fixed on his documents, the teacher gave an account of the development and secret nature of the Confessing congregations within the church. As he talked, he sensed the boredom that the minister conveyed to the others by his posture and facial expression. Like someone getting ready for a long, boring session, the minister leaned back in his chair, crossed his legs, let his eyes wander to the view outside the window, played with his pencil, and barely glanced at the papers that were being circulated before handing them on: nothing in there that could possibly interest him; when would this man finally stop so the heart could speak again, the voice of the father and good shepherd?

In order to stir up the languid atmosphere, the teacher rose and paced up and down the narrow aisle between the table and the wall, as he did in school, speaking with barely noticeable irony of "the great event that brought the Evangelical church into line with the new political order."

Unfortunately he did not attend the meeting of 27 June 1933, at Koblenz; but he did make it to the one at the Cologne fairgrounds on 5 July. He and his wife and some friends took the train, but even though they had arrived early, they could barely squeeze in between the masses of uniformed storm troopers, ss men, Hitler Youth, and members of the Steel Helmet organization.[1] They all seemed to have suddenly got religion. A storm trooper band played ear-shattering music, and Pastor Oberheyd, dressed in the uniform of an ss officer, spoke about a new kind of "manly" ministry. The superintendent general offered his fraternal greetings to the leaders of all the organizations. He was brief, since he had made his most important point already at Koblenz: his willingness to cooperate with the government's authorized representative.

But the audience did not show any genuine enthusiasm until the representative for the Rhineland, Dr. Krummacher, began to talk about the new church.

I made a few notes of what he said, the teacher continued, returning to his binder. He pulled out a sheet and read with a straight face:

"With the beginning of the new political order on 30 January 1933, the old tradition that has brought many blessings to our people shall be revived, namely, church and state shall no longer exist merely side by side, but march forward in unison. The state, as the man, has been courting the church, the woman. But since 30 January we have often noticed that the church has acted rather coy in her relations to the state. So we thought we should become a bit more insistent, and the result of this more insistent wooing is the state commissioner. However, I am sure no harm is intended; it's an act of pure love. . . ."

The down-to-earth language of the state commissioner was widely applauded, the teacher continued. There was only one brief interruption. A girl's voice shouted, "Lies!" The security guards immediately stepped in. She finally left voluntarily—a high-school student!

138

While the teacher was reading, he noticed, glancing over the edge of the paper, that the minister kept crossing and recrossing his legs and sighing impatiently. He used the brief pause during which the teacher refiled a sheet of paper to interject lightly that all of this might be true, but that pressing duties had prevented him from attending the rally—not exactly to his everlasting regret, he added with a wink. For this reason he was not as well informed as the teacher, but he did seem to remember that the government's action of bringing the church under its political control was not accepted without some opposing voices. In fact, didn't the president of the Reich personally intervene? And hadn't his intervention resulted in the cancellation of all suspensions and the recall of the state commissioner and his appointees, including Dr. Krummacher?

The teacher let out a bitter laugh, revealing, for a moment, his agitation, but he immediately got hold of himself and continued with his annoyingly monotonous presentation. The minister did not interrupt again until the narrative reached its temporary conclusion with the founding of the Pastors' Emergency League in September. Then he got up to give his reply, thanking the teacher for his detailed account and assuring him of his understanding: surely his colleagues of the Emergency League were moved by serious considerations of conscience; he had no doubt about that whatsoever, and he did not object to their asking themselves hard questions and struggling for answers; what he did object to was what all this was leading to—a schism within the church. There are two ways of thinking, each appropriate in its own time, he said: rational thinking, which divides, splits, separates, dissects, and—just for the sake of precision—cuts at the root of life, and thinking that comes from the heart, that lovingly embraces and nurtures life by strengthening what is good and hindering what is evil not from without but from within, through the gifts God had bestowed upon us: commitment to our fellow men, preaching God's own word, and, above all, prayer.

"Hasn't our own congregation been privileged to learn just recently how this second way of thinking and speaking is able to vanquish the evil forces of divisiveness?" he said, referring to his triumphant performance in the grand hall of the Hotel Felder. "Is that not reason enough to continue on the path of unity that has been so evidently blessed by God?"

His eyes moved from one person to the next, finally resting on the teacher, who stared straight ahead with an expressionless face and did not respond to his silent plea. With the mere suggestion of a sigh and a shake of his head the minister turned his eyes away from him and continued in an optimistic vein: "We do not stand alone in our decision. Throughout the church those who have a true insight into the problems have turned their backs on the German Christian Faith movement. I am asking you now to examine your conscience to find how we can best serve peace: Is it by working together within the church, which is struggling to achieve a reconciliation of opposing forces and does not exclude anyone who is of goodwill, or is it by insisting on a narrow literal-mindedness that is bound to lead to division?"

The elders were relieved. They were pleased that they did not have to examine their consciences right then and there under the minister's eyes but could do so in the privacy of their homes. Some of them, ready to leave, surreptitiously looked around for their overcoats, when the teacher got up once more and said: "I'm not done yet."

Stubbornly and without making an effort to establish rapport, he waited till they had heaved their collective sigh of exasperation and proceeded to enumerate issues that would still have to be discussed: the "Aryan paragraph," the "youth agreement," the "muzzling edict," and the arrests. Obviously getting impatient now, the minister interrupted him again and again.

"The Aryan paragraph has long been abolished," he declared. The teacher disagreed, citing the dates from memory: introduced on 5 September 1933; suspended 16 December; reactivated 3 January 1934.

"I must have missed that," the minister said, obviously annoyed, adding that, of course, he was opposed to it. Yet he could understand the new government's negative attitude toward the Jewish domination of the press, the stock exchange, and the theater. As everyone knows, he is, has always been, and is proud to be a German nationalist. How could he ever forget what the Jewish press did to the Kaiser during and in the years following the war? "These wounds have not yet healed. But that's beside the point. This paragraph must and will be abolished. The way it is being applied shows that even today it is no longer being taken seriously. All of the eleven ministers in our regional church who would be affected by it have been exempted."

"It is a matter of principle," the teacher said.

"Principle . . . principle," the minister sighed, shrugging his shoulders.

He interrupted a second time during the description of the audience with the Führer on 25 January and forced the teacher, who had good reasons for wanting to keep it short, to read the transcription of the disastrous Niemöller telephone conversation. He did not bother to comment on it but simply echoed in a reproachful tone: "Deployed our forces . . . pulled it off . . . received his extreme unction from the president . . . What kind of talk is this?" He turned to the elders: "Doesn't that sound like rebellion, like a coup? Wasn't Hitler justified in feeling betrayed? Didn't he have reason to assume that the Evangelical church was hatching a plot against him?"

"My friends!" He leaned over the table, trying once again to focus their attention on himself by looking intently at each of them. Having succeeded, he continued: "For fourteen years we have demonstrated our loyalty to all sorts of regimes—the Reds, the black robes, and others—no matter how difficult it was for us at times. Are we going to stab this government in the back, just because of a few growing pains—the first government that has explicitly committed itself to a positive Christianity? Are we to overlook everything that is positive and cling only to the negative, instead of showing patience and goodwill, which the government has repeatedly demonstrated toward us? In recent times our church has given an extremely poor account of itself, partly because of the excesses of the German Christians, partly because of the hardened position taken by the Pastors' Emergency League. Is it any wonder, then, that the state has tried to impose its order? Rather than squabble among ourselves and indulge in pointing a finger, does it not behoove us to reestablish unity within our church, thereby proving to the public that there is no need for state intervention?"

With these words, the minister sat down quickly and held his head in his hands as if he did not wish to see the effect of his words, as if he already knew while speaking that this time there would be no agreement among them. The silence that solidified after the sound of his voice had trailed off caused the teacher to feel something like physical pain.

He had never seen the minister so lonely and had never been so conscious of the fact that harmony, agreement, and sympathy constituted the element in which the minister had moved during his entire life. Now all of a sudden he was expected to learn to move in an altogether different element: in conflict, opposition, loneliness. . . .

Furtive glances crept across the table, touched his hand, which held the Bible, and his bowed head. One elder, mumbling an excuse, slipped out and did not return. No one had the courage to end the silence with a kind word or two. In the end, that responsibility fell upon the minister himself.

He struggled to his feet under the burden that the unspoken decision had placed on him and uttered, without raising his eyes, the plea that the disciples addressed to their unknown companion on the road to Emmaus: "Abide with us; for it is toward evening, and the day is far spent. . . ."

"That was the point at which we had to go our separate ways," the schoolteacher says. He shuts the ring binder, leans back, and looking into his memory with closed eyes, draws for me a picture of that separation:

One after another the elders step into the circle of the street light in front of the parish house. The minister is last; he stops at the foot of the stairs and looks from one face to another: "Do we really wish to part like this?"

Once again he awaits their answer; once again they remain silent.

He sighs, steps up to the head elder, shakes hands with him, then with the others, managing to say a few personal words: best regards to the wives; good wishes for a sick child. "God willing, next week we shall meet under a happier star!"

Relieved, they all say, "Good night." Some press his hand with special fervor and warmth as if they wanted to apologize wordlessly for the worries they have caused him. Then they quickly hurry off, all except for the teacher.

As the sexton locks the parish house from the inside, they too turn to walk away, but they turn in a common direction even though the shortest way home would already separate them here. The teacher would turn left around the corner of the parish house, past the old mill, and across the little bridge spanning the millrace; the minister would turn right, along Tierbungert, around the corner at Alsberg, and into the street leading to the railroad station.

Without comment, however, they choose a route in between, one that permits them to stay together for a while, perhaps to talk.

They walk behind the yard of the school for young ladies: the minister upright, leaning his closely cropped head slightly backward as if he were studying the stars; the teacher bent forward, a gaunt figure with short torso and long, bony limbs, a shock of black, tousled hair falling onto his lowered forehead.

As they approach the corner where the minister finally must turn to the right and the teacher to the left, they both slow their steps and wait again. The minister finally puts an end to the silent contest and speaks first: "What you are doing here violates all authority!"

"Yes," the teacher says.

"I cannot do it!" the minister says, shaking his head at first gently, then more and more vigorously. As he does so, he quickens his step and crosses diagonally over to the other side of the street, walking straight ahead—practically in line with the teacher but separated from him by the width of the street—up to the corner, where they have to part at right angles.

The teacher proceeds haltingly on his way. Now he turns around once more and watches the minister crossing over to the illuminated Alsberg side, still shaking his head as if to say: I cannot do it!

For the first time he looked old to him, the schoolteacher says; he had the back, the shoulders, the gait of an old man. On 9 February of that year, 1934, he had turned fifty-nine. . . .

As incredible as it may seem, they never again talked about these things, although they still met as before to prepare services and make arrangements for special church holidays. It was "all business," the teacher says, and the irritation that always lurked behind a mask of friendly tolerance expressed itself only in the old controversy about the use of music in Sunday services: the minister wanted it to be mere background to gospel and sermon, while the teacher saw it as a force in developing a sense of community, the congregation's only opportunity to express itself actively by voice or instrument vis-à-vis the minister's monologue.

In the sermons of those years there was, on the one hand, much talk of modesty and of deep faith and trust on the other; of fulfilling the small, seemingly unimportant duties that God has placed before us; and of proving ourselves good Christians within the family, toward our neighbors, and in our assigned places on earth.

Why deal with problems that are beyond the grasp of God's humble children? Why worry about vague and distant problems, when so many opportunities for doing good are near at hand? Do the right thing and leave the rest to God. He will provide.

There was only one brief and muted dispute between them. It was sparked by the meager proceeds of a collection for the benefit of foreign missions, which were being counted in the vestry. (The elders, who held the plates at the church exit, are building little towers of silver, brass, and copper on the vestry table, counting out numbers with lowered heads and half-muffled voices. The child would like to help, but children are not allowed to handle money: money is dirty and may be touched only if they thoroughly scrub their hands afterward, for which the vestry has no provision.)

"No bills," says the elder who, together with the teacher, is doing the counting. "I'm not surprised," says the minister, "what with all the other collections that are being conducted in this congregation."

The teacher knew full well—and after some hesitation came out and said so—that this remark was aimed at the collections of the Confessing congregations for the benefit of pastors of the Emergency League who had been suspended or arrested.

If the church ousted its most courageous witnesses, the congregations had to step in and help out, he said. But "most courageous witnesses" did not sit well with the minister; perhaps "courageous," but "witnesses"? Was the teacher so sure that these clergymen had truly borne witness for Christ and had suffered for His sake? Or did they suffer because they adhered to outdated principles and forms, like Pastor Schneider of Dickenschied, who suffered for his Calvinist practice of public confession and banishment? If their witnessing for Christ had been the sole cause of their troubles, one would have to suppose that teaching God's word and performing Christian labors of love were restricted in this Third Reich. "But that surely is not true, Herr Limbach, it is simply not the case," he said with a pleading tone, which revealed to the teacher that the minister was not just addressing him, but was also speaking to himself, to his own conscience, which, despite his deep trust in God, remained unquiet.

"No one has ever tried to stop me from proclaiming Holy Scripture or my faith, from doing my work, from stating my opinion—no Party member, no storm trooper, no SS man. Not a single time—and you know I am speaking the truth—not one single time have I preached differently from the way I normally preach because of the presence of a Party undercover agent. And when I was being interrogated, I never retreated an inch from the words I had spoken. Yet I have never been suspended or arrested. No one has forbidden me to speak or hindered me in following Christ in word and deed, because He did not call for revolt against the Roman rulers but preached on behalf of peace: Blessed are the peacemakers, for they shall be called the children of God! Blessed are the meek, for they shall inherit the earth!

"If I or any of my flock were ever to be barred from this path of following Christ, I would resist. I am no coward, Herr Limbach! I would go to jail and in my cell raise my voice in hymns, like my brother Schneider."

"Would you go to a concentration camp?" the teacher asked.

The noise of children could be heard from the adjacent room. The minister took a step toward the door. "Concentration camps!" he said contemptuously. "Have you, too, become a victim of that gutter gossip that has been pouring from the same witches' cauldron that brewed those lies about German crimes during the occupation of Belgium? These people never cease to befoul our poor fatherland. Until I personally see one of these—as you choose to call them—concentration camps, I don't believe a single word of it."

"How can you see if you don't look?" the teacher asked. But the minister was already at the door, tore it open, and thundered at the top of his voice into the church: "Children, can't you be quiet? You are in the house of the Lord!" He bumped into the woman who was at the point of entering to remind him that the children's service was about to begin. "I'm coming," he said to her and, over his shoulder to the teacher, "We'll take this up another time!"

There never was another time.

From the vestry, the teacher could hear the minister's words reverberating through the church: instead of the hymn announced on the blackboard, he wanted them to sing another. He gave out the number in the hymnal, and the teacher, who had often enough been the church organist, immediately knew which hymn was meant: "Keep us, Lord, by Thy word!"

He quickly completed his accounts and was already on the stairs leading to the churchyard when the children were still singing the third verse of "United in Thought." He felt sick with sadness thinking that this poor Christianity was unable to stand united although it prayed so fervently to the Holy Spirit for unity. He became angrier and angrier at the authors of the Bible, who left their readers dangling between "Let every soul be subject unto the higher powers" and "We ought to obey God rather than men." Despite his annoyance at this short- or farsighted minister, he felt a sad kind of solidarity with him, who—just like he himself—sang and prayed for guidance but did not receive a clear answer. Why didn't the Apostles express themselves just a bit more precisely?

"What if you had not left?" I asked, a little more emphatically than I had intended, angry at this sagacious teacher, this know-it-all, who, from the high ground of his wisdom, had watched my father tapping around in the dark. "If you had waited for him for just the half hour that it took to get through the children's service! If you had intercepted him in the churchyard in spite of the unpleasantness of the situation! If you had been willing to put your embarrassment aside and said to him: You don't know anything, Reverend; your ignorance is verging on criminality! Let me tell you the truth about Pastor Schneider in the Black Bunker of Buchenwald. How they beat his naked rump with sticks; how they hang him by his twisted arms from the window sash; how he still keeps shouting through the window at each execution: Murderers! Thieves! Adulterers! Servants of the devil! Herr Limbach, you had received your information from Barmen-Gemarke! You knew from the beginning what was going on."

"Not from the beginning," he interrupted me harshly. "At the beginning no one knew. But from the very beginning my own attitude was different: I was not disposed to trust them, did not give them 'the benefit of the doubt'; I mistrusted them, was cautious and circumspect. Not because I am by nature distrustful, as your father always assumed, and which never ceased to amuse him, but because I come from a different social class where trust is a luxury and an impediment. Have you ever asked yourself why progressive workers always talk about class conflict, whereas the entrepreneurial middle class can never get beyond the idea that "we all sink or swim together"? The world looks different when seen from the bottom up because you see it through different eyes; and you don't acquire those different eyes deliberately but through experiences—unpleasant, ugly, painful experiences—that cannot be explained. At least they cannot be explained to people like your father, for whom that unpleasant way of seeing never was a necessity. Have you never, in the parsonage at Auel, heard them talk of "the simple people," their "straitened circumstances," the "foolish grudge of the village schoolteacher against the academic elite"—all the more unfounded and incomprehensible to them because "one is so considerate of them"? But there was a time when the schoolteacher was something of a houseboy in the local church and parsonage, an all-purpose maidservant. Things have changed in the meantime, but attitudes don't change that fast. On occasion, the bitterness of generations of village schoolteachers wells up against a certain kind of Christian education and Christian bourgeoisie with its guileless certainty of its chosen and secure place in God's order. It was in just such a guileless and secure manner that Noah in his ark floated past those who had drowned or were drowning. But one day God called: Get out of that crate, Noah! Then they all had to get out. There are people who, to this day, have not heard that call. . . ."

He had gotten up while he was talking and was breathing quickly as he trotted back and forth with crooked, wobbly knees.

"My father was a humble man," I said. "No arrogance, no barriers dividing him from his fellow man. Anyone could talk to him."

The teacher wheeled around. "Really, anyone?" he barked at me, his eyes now really flashing with anger, just as my mother used to say. "So why did you not talk to him, if it was so easy? You were not too young to notice some of those things and to ask him about them? Why did you not ask him what he planned to do when Hitler's henchmen came to drag Herr Heilmann, little Hanna's father, from his sickbed, where he lay with a serious liver ailment? You knew all about that.

I know that you knew! The child was your classmate. That day was her birthday. You had been invited."

"Hanna Heilmann . . . I don't even know her," I said; "I never heard that name." And as I said these words a membrane ruptured in my head and a face appeared in my memory: bright, blueberry eyes; a shock of dark, bobbed hair; bangs over her eyebrows, cut straight; small, red stones in her pierced ears: "Are you coming to my birthday party?"

"Whatever gave her that idea," I say to my mother. "I never invited her to my birthday." But my mother says, "Go ahead and go. It is not the child's fault. And why don't you look among your books if there is one that looks like new. You can take it as a present."

But Hanna is absent from school on her birthday. "She's probably sick," our teacher says; and Hilde Krämer, sitting behind me, whispers in my ear: "She isn't sick! They came to get her father last night—he's a Yid." I breathe a sigh of relief: "Then we don't have to go to her birthday party. It stinks in their house."

"He was impossible to talk to," the teacher said, and he suddenly held in his hand the yellow envelope I had seen during my first visit. He tossed it on the table in front of me so I could see my father's address at the old parsonage in Auel and the uncanceled stamp. "This is what I wanted to send him," he said, "but I couldn't bring myself to mail it. Perhaps it will give you an idea why . . ." He dropped into his chair and closed his eyes. He never took notice of my hasty departure.

I opened the envelope in the waiting room of the railroad station in Auel. It contained a collection of documents and handwritten notes relating to a murder and the subsequent trial that took place in February 1933. This is what had happened:

During the night of 14–15 February 1933, a group of SS thugs attacks the local labor union hall, smashes a glass case, and tears out the posted papers. They are clippings from the

Rheinzeitung containing information about the involvement of business and industry in Hitler's rise to power. Shots are fired from the windows of the union hall and from the street. One of the ss men remains lying on the pavement, shot through the head.

Because the wounded man is a Protestant, the minister is called to the scene. He arrives before the doctor and realizes that it is too late to administer the last communion. He kneels down by the body and prays the Lord's Prayer. Meanwhile the police have arrived. The labor unionists, among them a relative of the schoolteacher Limbach, are being arrested. The minister recognizes him as he is being led away and calls out plaintively: "Dear God, both of them members of my congregation"—"both" referring to the murderer and the victim.

At the trial, the dead man's cap—the most important evidence for the defense—cannot be introduced because it has disappeared. The ss comrades' sworn testimony contradicts the expert's opinion that the shot was fired from behind. The men who fired the shots from the labor union hall are put behind bars at the local jail.

The parents of the accused desperately try to find a courageous lawyer who is willing to take on such a delicate case. Finally they locate one who dares to refer in court to Reds as "German men": "As German men, they had a right to defend themselves." The judge admonishes him. The request for an autopsy is denied. The fact that a disinterested eyewitness—an elderly spinster who saw the shooting spree from her window and wanted to testify, was beaten up on the street in broad daylight, and now no longer wishes to appear as a witness—has no impact on the court.

No other witnesses are willing to come forward, including the minister and the doctor, who arrived shortly after him.

Years later, a brawl breaks out between different Nazi groups at a local carnival. The police arrest a member of the Hitler Youth who, drunk as he is, spills some secret information: he heard that the victim's cap had been removed by his comrades. And that his comrades had given false testimony because the shot had accidentally come from their own ranks and hit him from behind, a fact that should have been evident—from the nature of the wound and the hole in the cap—to anyone knowledgeable about wounds from his war experience.

The whole matter is handled quietly in a session of the court from which the public is barred. The ss comrades are given a friendly warning; the prisoners are set free without apology or compensation for damages. Instead of hush money, they are given jobs in a distant factory.

Attached to these documents is a short letter from the teacher, requesting "His Reverence" to answer one question: "Why did you remain silent?"

The child no longer wants to be called "the child." Her pronouncement, made from her place at the head of the family dinner table, framed by her mother on the left and her father on the right, is met by laughter from her brothers and sisters.

"If you really want to be a grown-up, some things will have to change," the father says.

"Well, in that case perhaps better not!" the child says.

She does not hold her father's hand anymore, no longer needs a footstool to look out of the window. Her mornings are no longer spent in her father's study but in school. When she returns home early, she slinks past the kitchen and up the stairs to the door of the study, which is now also closed to her as well as to the older children. She clears her throat, coughs, moves the loose door handle, listens for a sign that she may enter, but her father is so engrossed in his work that he does not take notice. Sometimes she makes a fresh remark; then he brushes the back of his hand over her mouth: "Hush your mouth!" When she gets tiresome, he says, "Go with God, but go!"

He likes to comment on what is pure and clear about the child: her pure voice, the pure tone of her violin, her pure forehead and clear eyes. He points out to visitors that she is still "a mere child," a little rascal, a wild fawn, a tomboy who might as well have been a boy. When she rocks back and forth in the very top of the fir tree, he laughingly admonishes her from the balcony: "Not so wild!" Then she rocks even harder. She knows it pleases him. He is also pleased with her accomplishments in school, including the teachers' complaints about her back talk and sassiness. But there is an aspect of her growing-up that he disapproves of; it is never mentioned, not even hinted at or alluded to—only that constant cool ray of disapprobation aimed at the same secret spot that apparently delights neither him nor God. Something that should not be!

If thy right eye offend thee, pluck it out, and cast it from thee.

15

But how do you do that? How can you get hold of its wet slipperiness in its socket?

It is not meant to be taken literally but metaphorically, he says; bad thoughts should be weeded out with God's help.

But what if He does not offer any help? What if the bad thoughts grow even more rampant with every effort to tear them out; what if they make a thicket, a snake's nest, a forbidden chamber that the innocent child is not allowed to enter?

She does not ask, but thinks about these questions, hides with her thoughts behind the bush like Adam and Eve, is ashamed and afraid. In bed, she pulls her knees up to her chin so as not to get drawn into it. In the cellar, she sings at the top of her voice, keeping her eyes firmly on the open door as she retrieves a bottle or jar of preserves. Coiled snakes attach themselves to her feet as she trembles and stumbles back toward daylight.

"You need not be afraid, God is with you!"

But the child knows that down there, where it is dark and damp and slimy, there is no God!

After a while she comes to terms with the split: she presents to the parents the clear, babbling brook of her daylight life; in her lower depths, which devour ever larger portions of the world, she remains impenetrable and silent. Never a question about the difference between boys and girls, why she bleeds, where children come from, and what the dogs are doing in the street. For years she has been reading the unabbreviated Bible and never asked about circumcision, King Solomon's concubines, Abraham's maidservant, Noah's nakedness, or the sins of "the woman of great sins." She never says a word about the things her sister whispers from one bed to another, or about what she sees on the toilet walls at school and in *Der Stürmer*,[1] which is displayed in a glass case in the market square.

"Promise me that you won't read that dirty rag!"

"Why not?"

"Because I say so! That's enough!"

At this time the nightmares return: giving away the implements of Holy Communion; watching the flashing metal blade descend on Father's head; encountering the enormous black cats with their glowing red eyes as large as saucers.

When father and child pass each other in the house, they sometimes stop and say, "Do you remember—the two of us?" Then they repeat it once more, loudly, stamping their feet on "two" as they used to do, but it no longer sounds right.

When she goes to bed, the child finds her name spelled in alphabet cookies on her pillow. Ruefully she collects and hides them in the farthest corner of her bedside table drawer. She no longer likes alphabet cookies.

At night they still play sixty-six on the edge of her bed, and with every announcement of twenty or forty they shout in triumph or despair. Neither admits that they are bored silly.

They do not want to hurt each other.

In her confirmation lessons the child learns what Luther meant when he said in the first sentence of his commentary on the Ten Commandments: "Thou shalt fear and love the Lord!" The same children who used to run up to the minister with a happy smile during the children's service now cast down their eyes in fear. He makes them line up in paired rows in front of the parish house, the boys on the right, the girls on the left. "Stand up straight!" he says to the boys; "Stop chattering!" to the girls. Then: "Forward, march!" Without a word they clatter upstairs to the classroom. When he gets to the lectern, they have to be standing at attention in front of their chairs. Whoever falls out of line is sharply reprimanded, especially the daughter, who is supposed to set an example. Answers have to be given "like the crack of a whip": the names of the Prophets, the books of the Bible, the Apostles, the Ten Commandments, the seven supplications of the Lord's Prayer with commentary. One of the children, a redheaded boy named Pechmann, always starts sweating profusely, cannot get a word out when the minister calls on him, stands there blushing and opening his mouth, his heavy tongue moving about aimlessly; he rocks back and forth, clinging to the back of the chair in front of him.

"Can't you at least stand up straight?" the minister asks, disgust in his voice.

Pechmann can't stand up straight. Nor can he "straighten out" his mouth, which, in the minister's opinion displays a "cunning smirk." The boys grin; the girls giggle: tough-luck Pechmann![2]

"But he did memorize the psalm!" the child says on the way home. "He knew it by heart; I heard him myself."

"So you say. Hic Rhodos hic salta!"[3] he says.

He does not like it when people get mixed up in things that do not concern them. Mind your own business.

"You take care of memorizing your verses, and I take care of the teaching, agreed?"

"Agreed," the child says and shakes the proffered hand.

"That's my girl!"

He loves children, but not teenagers. At the dinner table he complains that, as a boy, he never was as obnoxious and obstinate, as silly and pushy, as forward, ill mannered, bumbling, underhanded, and spoiled as today's young people. This notorious puberty that everybody is talking about nowadays never was a problem for him, and his father would not have put up with it. "It's a different generation that is being brought up in these brownshirt camps and institutions. Let the younger people wrestle with those problems." So he leaves the girls' group in the hands of the deaconess and the boys' club to whoever happens to be the vicar. When the vicar complains about the lack of discipline, the minister says: "I can see that you didn't do any military service. Those who have learned to obey know how to command."

Is it possible that a great and wise man like my father is afraid of teenagers?

After the child gets beyond the shrill sounds of the beginner's stage, she is allowed to play Handel's Largo on the violin in church. During evening rehearsals, a student accompanies her on the organ, which seems to float like a lighted ship above the darkness of the church below. The echoing acoustics expand the sounds of the violin, conjuring up presumptuous dreams. Down there in the empty pews they will be sitting and listening with devoutly bent shoulders and bowed heads. Just as her father all by himself is preaching to them from the pulpit, so the child will be playing to them all by herself from the height of the organ loft, and as long as she will be playing, he, too, will have to listen to her in silence.

Once, in the middle of a rehearsal, the lights go off, and the solid chords of Handel's harmonies give way to threads of halftones spun by high-pitched flutes, like some snake charmer's tune without harmonious order, without tension or resolution, beginning or ending. Like a spider's filament it envelopes the child and pulls her up to the organ, which is hardly audible above the clanging of her stumbling steps on the stairs; up to the organ bench, where the organist continues to spin his thread with one hand and, with the other, enfolds her neck and draws her toward him, thrusting his tongue into the mouth she had opened to scream; thrusting deeper and deeper, while the child falls backward under the weight of his body, her head hitting the organ bench, while violin and bow fall from her grasp, making a horrible sound: the broken violin that will never sound again, the child that will never be a child again! Flooded by upwellings from below, she holds still until light enters under her lids: the rectangle of the door opening to the stairs, and then the sound of echoing steps, which may have been present earlier but only now reaches her ear.

Holding her hastily packed-up violin, she runs down the circles of the spiral stairs, meets her father in the foyer, hopes and fears in her spinning head that finally there will be an end to that split and to secrecy; she waits for the tremendous unleashing of the storm that will whirl together darkness and light and pluck out forever all that is offensive, so that once again she can be a dear child, a pure heart pleasing to God.

"You played beautifully," the father says, stroking her bristling hair. "Why did you stop so suddenly?"

"The lights went out," she says, hesitates, and again waits for a moment. If his eyes were to give the slightest hint of suspicion, she might try to tell the truth; but they are showing only love and trust, offered without caution or reservation, without the shadow of a doubt, without the slightest spark of comprehension. It is the warm, bright look of blindness, and the idea that learning the truth would force him to change and to suffer pain makes her feel such unbearable pity for him that lying to him seems an act of kindness.

"Probably a blown fuse," the child says and adds needlessly: she dropped her violin in the dark, that's why she is in such a state of shock. "Everything will be all right," he says, and, indeed, when she opens the case at home and inspects the violin from all sides, she cannot discover a crack or even a scratch — except that, when she is playing, it seems to her that the sound is different, not exactly flatter or harder, just different.

The Bible passage selected for her at her confirmation reads: Blessed are the pure in heart, for they shall obtain mercy. She kneels down on the red velvet cushion, feels her father's hand burning her hair and scalp, and bursts into tears: not, as the mother later explains, because she is so deeply moved by being admitted into the community of the faithful, but because of the unutterable pain she feels for not being pure of heart, for lying to her father, for never seeing the Lord, neither in life nor in death.

A brisk new teacher visits each class at the girls' high school, asking those who have not yet joined the Hitler Youth to stand up. A few do — each time there are fewer — and they are asked why not.

The daughter replies, as she was told to do at home: "My father told me not to!"

"Why?" the questioner asks.

"I don't know. You'll have to ask my father."

Afterward he gives a little speech, while those who have not yet joined remain standing. He explains how gratifying it is to be part of the community of the people and how harmful it is in every respect to stand on the sidelines when a people joins together in a tremendous new enterprise.

Then they are allowed to sit down again.

Standing up while the majority remains seated does not bother the daughter. In fact, she would prefer to have the heroic part of being the only one. She has accepted the part of standing out as an individual and not to feel the worse but the better for it. But here she is standing with others who are not part of her clique, girls who are looked down on by both the clique and the teachers. The clique consists of the daughters of the leading families, those who set the standard, in both academic performance and general cheekiness. The others tag along. (Looking through old class pictures a few years later, she has already forgotten the names of most of them.)

During the noonday meal, she asks her father why she is not allowed to join the Hitler Youth. "They don't do anything bad," she says. "They sing folk songs and read aloud from the old heroic legends. They play cops and robbers in the old munitions factory."

He thinks she is ungrateful: "Don't we sing enough at home? Isn't there a large yard to play in and an abundance of books?"

"But . . . ," she says.

"But me no buts," he replies. "And now let's drop this tiresome topic."

This is the way in which the daughter learns about "tiresome topics"; she will never forget them, never be able to speak about money, politics, crime, or sex without hesitating in front of this barrier, without breaking it down too aggressively with a "sharp tongue," "unfeminine harshness," "a relentless openness."

There is also a rule against disparaging other people, but the family negotiates this problem by using euphemisms that suggest the negative as a nuance of the positive: He is a nice fellow ... He surely is trying very hard ... They must be decent, hard-working people ... It's surely not her fault ... He does have some good qualities. ...

These introductory or concluding clauses are linked to the actual judgment by words like "but" or "otherwise" (. . . but she does have lovely eyes; . . . otherwise he's quite a decent sort). The judgment itself is also expressed in code: She isn't exactly the most beautiful (handiest, most pleasant, cleverest) woman . . . not completely convincing . . . not a very pleasant type . . . not particularly charming . . . not overly blessed with intelligence; . . . one has seen better manners, heard more compelling speakers, entertained more interesting guests. . . .

In a fit of irony directed at itself, the family has invented a standard closing sentence for negative judgments: "What really counts is purity of the soul." It never fails to elicit laughter.

After the introduction of National Youth Day, the daughter coaxes permission out of her mother to go to the meetings now and then, or, as Father would put it, "to put in an appearance." She is welcomed with hellos and "At last!" and is allowed to accompany folk songs on the accordion, read aloud during "fireside evenings," and recite poetry on festive occasions.

After a while she gets into trouble because she is not wearing the standard brown uniform jacket. Like her father, she despises its "pukey" color and appears in an olive green velvet jacket, which sticks out in parades. The section leader asks her to step forward: "Why aren't you wearing a uniform jacket?"

"My parents won't buy me one."

"Why not?"

"You have to ask my father."

During parades she should either wear a standard uniform or not show up at all.

She does not show up. Since the olive green jacket is unacceptable, she takes advantage of the generally lax atmosphere in Auel (which, according to Mother, is the reason why neither good nor bad things ever really happen there) and quietly drifts away from the National Youth Organization. In a pinch, she resorts to the violin. Since her performance in uniform (but without standard jacket) of Beethoven's Romance in F major in front of Elly Ney,[4] she is considered a "young talent" and has been asked to be available for special occasions.

"With Beethoven you can never go wrong," the father says.

"As long as you people get a special deal," says the schoolteacher's son, who still has not joined the Hitler Youth, "you with your monkey jacket and violin and your father with his robe and pulpit, you don't care what's happening and you let them do with you whatever they want."

"What?" the daughter wants to know. "What are they doing?"

"Born stupid, and learned nothing!" he snorts.

"I'm going to tell my father; he'll come after you," she screams.

"You'll never tell him," he says.

"Don't you want to see Hitler?" she asks her father.

"Hitler?" he says, pausing as if he could not connect the name with anyone he knew, then he remembers: "Oh, him! . . . Perhaps not. . . ."

"Don't you like him?" the daughter asks.

"He has never been introduced to me."

A crowd is waiting on the Rhine promenade in St. Goar. Hitler is supposed to have already passed through Oberwesel.[5] Everybody is pushing and shoving to be there and as far up front as possible. The terrace of the hotel is deserted except for the parents and the daughter; they are still seated, folding their napkins with incredible slowness and inserting them in the paper envelopes that are marked with their names.

"May I be excused?" the daughter asks.

"Well, if you must."

She presses forward between shoving hips and shoulders and sweating armpits and has already reached the second row from the front, when they start screaming, her voice blending with and carried along by the general "Here he comes!" and "Heil!" Between the head and the shoulder of the person in front of her she catches a glimpse of black metal, white motoring caps . . . gone!

Dejected, she slinks back to the hotel. She finds her father alone on the terrace. She is ashamed for not having stayed with him and having joined the crowd down in the street, walking the wide and level street of the multitude, which leads to perdition, rather than the steep and narrow path leading to salvation.

"So what did you get out of it?" Father asks.

"I saw the Führer," she lies, blushing; but most likely he does not notice because he is looking at the boat passing by out on the river.

"So?" is all he says.

An aunt with Nazi sentiments, who comes for a visit once a year, tries to win Father over to Hitler. She herself was at first skeptical because of his lower-class origin. But that changed instantly when they met face to face. Those divine eyes wrought an inescapable spell. It came over her like a revelation: He is the one! Why should we await another?

"You are getting old, Reinhold," she says. "You are losing your enthusiasm. Outdated prejudices keep you from recognizing the divine spark in this man. Did Jesus not also come from the lower classes? Wasn't his father a simple carpenter?" She herself, now well into her sixties, has been rejuvenated by her love for the Führer.

"That may well be," he says. "I guess I'd rather stay old."

For his sixtieth birthday the schoolteacher gives him *Mein Kampf*.[6]

"What am I supposed to do with that?" he asks.

"Read it!" says the teacher.

"Sometimes I just don't understand you," he says. "Will you be very angry with me if I ask you to take this book back with you? I don't want that stuff lying around in my house."

In the end the daughter has to abandon her monkey jacket and put on the earth brown uniform of the National Labor Service camp Ahrhütte-Eifel rather than the pukey brown one of the Hitler Youth. Her father's influence does not extend this far.

Her parents come for a visit on a weekend on which she has been denied furlough privileges. For a few hours, the daughter is allowed to walk with them. She cries without interruption into one of her father's large, white handkerchiefs: "I can't stand it anymore! Do something, Father! Get me out of here!"

"What a beautiful view," Father says, as they sit down on an open hilltop. "Back there, I suppose, is where the Rhine runs." She has never seen her father sitting on the bare ground, only on chairs, benches, or at most on a tree trunk. On the rough, flat soil he somehow seems lost, does not know what to do with his legs, moves them from one side to the other, stretches them out, pulls them up, squats, kneels, gets up, and takes a few steps, hands clasped behind his back.

"He is not well," Mother whispers. "Don't burden him with these things."

On the way to the railroad station, the daughter holds back her tears, but as he leans out of the window of the compartment, they burst forth again. Once again he hands her his soaked handkerchief. That is all he can do for her.

After a tearful night, she decides to present herself as a solo entertainer. On special occasions she gives a whining rendition of the *Niederländisches Dankgebet*[7] on her violin, accented by the sounds of an accordion, in addition to providing background music for KP and folk dances. She saves her tears for the nights, when she buries her face in the soiled handkerchief, which barely retains the fading scent of cologne.

16

He likes to think about retirement. On Mondays—clergymen's Sunday—he gets a small taste of it. Shortly before noon he hastily leaves the house, his eyes lowered so as not to see anyone or be spoken to, waits at the stop of the trolley to Bonn till everyone is aboard, and only then chooses the car that holds no one he knows.

Once the trolley has crossed the bridge over the Rhine, he breathes more easily. Swinging his cane, he strolls through the streets, with no one bothering him, buys a bag of rolls, takes his time enjoying the view from the cannons on the old city wall overlooking the river and from Arndt Gardens, savors his slow descent down the stairs to the Rhine promenade, chats with some fishermen, studies the time tables of the Cologne-Düsseldorf excursion steamers, and sends greetings to St. Goar with one of the ships chugging upstream. He spends a quiet evening in the senior gentlemen's lounge of the Association for Reading and Recreation, but before going there takes a glass of wine at Streng's Wine Tavern on the Mauspfad.

That is where the daughter finds him on her way back from swimming practice: always sitting in the same dimly lit place between the wood-paneled walls, behind a glass of Rhine wine, which the old waiter has served him without waiting for an order, a chaotic mass of bread and crumbs on the table in front of him, washing down a piece with each sip.

Delighted, he looks at his daughter, embracing her still shivering limbs in his warmth: "There you are at last!" He blows on her wet hair, rubs her bluish hands, orders a hot dish or drink. "My youngest," he says to the waiter; "she gives us nothing but pleasure."

The looks on the faces of the single gentlemen, sitting by themselves in quiet contemplation at some of the other tables, suggest that they are pleased with what they behold: father and daughter—how charming! Conscious of their approbation, they both lean even more closely toward each other, chat even more intimately, snuggle down in the gentlemen's anonymous benevolence like chickens in warm hollows of sand. Mother, who would admonish them—don't make such a spectacle of yourselves!—is absent.

That is how they would like to spend their evenings once he is in retirement, which he plans to spend here in Bonn, in one of the quiet streets near the Venusberg, where elderly gentlemen greet each other, doffing their hats: How do you do, Your Honor? How are you, Professor? Please give my regards to your wife.

On sunny days he will be down at the Rhine early in the morning to watch the boats and water levels. Occasionally he may take a ride to Königswinter or Unkel[1] for a hike on the hilltop trail along the river. Of course, he will do a little work; he doesn't want to give up working altogether: substitute preaching; visits to the sick and lonely; on cold winter days, trips to the university library to read all the books he has not had time to read in forty years of active service; some research in theology, where much new work has been done in recent years. The daily grind has made his intellectual life a hand-to-mouth affair, but things will be different once he has retired. Perhaps he will decide to write a doctoral dissertation. As for brains and the ability to learn, he'll match those anytime against the younger folks, and that smart little Miss Vicar is going to be surprised. . . .

He was, after all, a bit miffed that she charged him with holding theological views that did not go beyond Schlatter's teaching. Nowadays, she said, that's no longer acceptable. At the family dinner table, to which the vicar is invited whenever she conducts Bible studies in Auel, she talks about a Pastor Hesse, who also had grown up in the tradition of Protestant German nationalism and studied with Schlatter, faithfully accepting his concepts of "the natural society arising from the family and the people" and "God's active work in history." But during a conversation he had on the train with Karl Barth in 1933 this man's eyes had been opened to the dangers of "natural theology," which denies such irreconcilable dichotomies as creation/redemption, nature/divine grace, the spirit of nationalism/the principles of the gospel by inserting an equalizing "and" within each pair. "Pastor Hesse has drawn the necessary conclusions from this conversation," she says, "and so would you, sincere and upright Christian that you are, if you were only willing to confront the theological issues!"

"Of course," he says, swallowing his annoyance at her blunt challenge. "I would, if Barth's theology did not contain so much that is hard and heartless and that always makes me think of Saint Paul's words to the Corinthians: Though I speak with the tongues of men and of angels, and have not charity, I am become as sounding brass, or a clanging cymbal."

In the course of the conversation it becomes clear that the minister, despite his daily grind and lack of time, has come to know something of Barth's dialectical theology, albeit mostly those parts justifying his criticism that it lacks a comforting warmth: he speaks of a cold distance between God and man, of a "glacial rift," a "polar region," a "zone of devastation." God is the "totally other," who cannot be known by man, neither in history, nor in nature, nor in man's devout consciousness. No matter whether man does good deeds or is a sinner, the nature of his actions is always human, hence different from God, hence evil. No chance of getting closer to Him by means of faith, obedience, or pious deeds. Nothing but a one-way street that leads from up above to down below: "Dominus dixit," for Barth, is not a staff to lean on, nor a guiding, helping father's hand, but a "warning signal," a "fire alarm"; it is not meant to console, but to "shatter," "undermine," "cause anxiety." And those who are seeking comfort from the Savior or the Good Shepherd in their anxiety and distress will find Him described in Barth's theology as an "eschatological event" and a "bomb crater of God's unknown reality."

Yes, the minister too is opposed to an exaggerated intimacy with God and to blurring the line between worldly and spiritual matters. However, he considers it nothing less than unchristian self-righteousness that Barth tosses all the religious thinkers of the past into "the garbage can of the eigh-

teenth and nineteenth centuries." Should all that work have
been nothing but a waste of time: all that pious Life-of-Jesus
scholarship,[2] all that hope that a historically documented Jesus could be fused with the Christ of our faith into an un-
assailable human-divine reality? Barth makes short shrift of
generations of religious scholarship: "There has never been a
Christ outside the realm of faith," he asserts, and "any striving for certainty, whether it be based on religious feelings or
on historical research, is an act of treason against Christ."
Tearing down and destroying were Barth's forte, but what
did he offer in its place? Faith defined as "respect for the
divine incognito," "halting in fear and trembling before God,"
"stoic endurance in negation"; at any rate, "no solid ground
to stand on, no order providing a clear framework, no air in
which one can breathe—a position in midair, without any
foothold." No, thanks! is all the minister can say: he prefers
the theological garbage can, where he finds himself in the best
company.

"It's easy for you to talk that way," he says. "You are not
in charge of a congregation. You don't stand in the pulpit
every Sunday having to dispense the bread of life in such a
way that people can eat and digest it. Jesus was far more
compassionate toward humanity than your Karl Barth. He
offered them parables and miracles and real bread, real fishes,
real wine. He healed the sick and raised the dead in front of
their eyes, and He did not disown Thomas when he asked to
place his fingers in Jesus' wounds to dispel his doubts. Your
Barth may be a wise and faithful man, but it is written: 'And
though I have the gift of prophecy, and understand all mys-
teries, and all knowledge; and though I have all faith, so that
I could remove mountains, and have not charity, I am nothing.'"

Under this barrage of words, the vicar has grown silent,
lowering her head with its pale knot of hair deeper over her
plate, because now he takes on the Confessing synod, the
quarrels over the ecclesiastical committees established by

167

Reich Minister Kerrl,[3] and the question whether cooperation or resistance is called for.

"The whole thing smacks of divisionism," he says. "Barth with his theological intolerance started it all. How is the state to respect a church that not only is divided into many factions but in which opposing camps within these factions are fighting each other to the point of schism? Where is the laity to go for guidance if these gentlemen, who seem to have a corner on faith and confession, offer so little by way of God's grace and peace on earth? It seems as if the horrors of the Inquisition itself had suddenly taken hold of our dear Evangelical church." Finally the vicar bursts out in anger. Her voice is shrill, her lips are damp. Her arteries swell along her skinny neck. The more she defends her cause, the more imperturbable the minister seems to become; he can now allow himself to smile again and to keep silent until she is finished, conscious of his victory over this "zealous bluestocking" who is "not exactly graced with either beauty or charm."

As for the role of women, he admits that Saint Paul's commandment "Let your women keep silence in the churches!" is not quite in tune with modern times, but if the ladies insist on opening their mouths, they should at least be sure to speak soft words of praise, approbation, and encouragement. If opposition is unavoidable, it should be presented without a sharp tongue, preferably in the form of questions. Feminine enthusiasm for a cause or idea is detrimental not only to their charming demeanor and melodious voice but to the issue or idea at hand, no matter how praiseworthy it may be.

Without paying any further attention to the vicar, he leans over to his daughter with a roguish smile and whispers: "An umbrella would be appreciated!" He is convinced that spittle flies from the mouths of argumentative women, that they speak with "foaming mouths."

That takes care of Miss Vicar and her arguments.

One winter evening, after the daughter has gone to bed but is still reading under her blanket with a flashlight (Bulwer-

Lytton's *The Last Days of Pompeii*), a late visitor arrives. He has announced himself by a phone call, which prompts Father to request that the family leave the room: the late visitor wishes to speak with him in private! When the doorbell rings, he opens the door himself and takes the guest upstairs; their animated torrent of words suddenly runs dry. Silently they enter the study. The connecting door to the daughter's bedroom, which is as usual a crack open, is firmly closed.

A muted conversation begins, in the course of which Father jumps up and repeatedly paces the length of the room. Whenever he approaches the door, the daughter catches a few words. She cannot make out any of the visitor's comments, but his mumbling voice, interrupted by anxious breathing, conveys a sense of fear and threat that gives her goose bumps all the way up her back to her scalp.

"You must be mistaken," Father says. "There's a lot of talk. You mustn't take it personally."

The daughter slips out of bed, bends down to look through the keyhole, and sees a piece of fringed table cloth and a signet ring on a hand holding a cigar, trembling slightly next to the Hindenburg ashtray. Then Father's body blocks the view through the keyhole. "Maybe others," he says, "but surely not you, a much-decorated veteran!"

The visitor's voice continues in a long monotone, which Father interrupts vehemently: "No, I simply can't believe that! It would be . . ."

A drawn-out "Shhhh!" from the visitor makes him lower his voice. Father sits down again and speaks softly. When he leans forward, his shocked, incredulous face appears in the keyhole.

Her feet are getting cold and she creeps back into bed, sleeps a little, but wakes up with a start at the sound of scraping on the other side of the door. For the first time she hears the visitor speak without making an effort to tone down his voice. She has heard this voice before. But where? When?

"Perhaps you will think about our conversation," says the visitor; "if it won't be too late by then!"

Father responds with a loud and hearty invitation to spend the night: "It's the dead of night, you can't . . ."

"Yes, I can," says the visitor. "There are taxis at the railroad station."

"Well, if you must," Father says. "But you have to promise me that if anything like that happens to you—anything at all—you will let me know! Call me or stop by. I will do whatever I can. But I just cannot believe it. . . ," he continues in a conversational tone meant to calm his visitor.

He is probably grasping the visitor's hand or shoulder in a gesture of warm friendship as they go downstairs. She cannot make out the words, but the tone of his voice suggests something like: let's sleep on this . . . haste makes waste . . . things look different in broad daylight. . . .

Through a crack in the curtain, the daughter spies her father accompanying a small, portly man to the gate of the front yard. He grasps his hands and shakes them long and vigorously so that the visitor's arms swing from his shoulders like the limbs of a rag doll. Although they are standing under a street light, the man's face remains obscured by the broad brim of his hat.

With quick, small steps, like a wind-up toy, he walks off in the direction of the railroad station, turns around once more at the corner to look back at Father, who has remained standing at the garden gate, raises his hand partway so as to form an angle at the elbow, and moves his hand stiffly back and forth at eye level. Something in that gesture evokes a dim recollection—the color of sand, the warmth of sunshine. Isn't that the way Herr Jacobi waved to them from the pier on the Island of Juist at the end of their summer vacation?

During those years, the daughter is often sick: bad bouts of the flu, late eruptions of childhood diseases, pleurisy. In between her feverish dreams she overhears her parents' conversations; she will never know whether the anxiety she heard in their voices was real or part of her dreams.

170

"I'm at the end of my rope," Father says. "I am emptied out, burned out, preached out. It is not a matter of God's word. That remains vital and to the point, continues to hit the mark, here and now. It is my fault—I am a poor laborer in the vineyard, a salt that has lost its savor." Then he is silent, and she knows that he is weeping, though she cannot hear a sound or a word from the other room. Nothing but anxious silence.

What are her parents doing in that silence? Are they sitting and staring at each other? Are they holding hands? Is he standing at the window, while she is anxiously studying his back? The daughter has never seen her father weep. She has seen him "moved," with light veils of moisture covering his eyes, which he quickly dissipates by winks and smiles. But never any tears.

Then she hears him read aloud. Images unfold in her mind. Later she finds them again in David's psalms:

"I am poured out like water. . . .

"My heart is like wax; it is melted in the midst of my bowels. . . .

"My strength is dried up like a potsherd. . . ."

Mother interrupts him: "They that wait upon the Lord shall renew their strength. . . ."

But what if the waiting continues too long? "It is not that I have lost my faith," he says. "But it feels different than it used to. It is no longer a source of strength but a burden. It moves neither mountains nor hearts. When, in the last few years, have I moved anything or anyone?"

Mother disagrees: "There have been movements, small ones, personal ones. You mustn't expect miracles!"

"Why not?" he says. "Why shouldn't one expect miracles?"

Auel is not a good place for miracles, she says; it is a slow and sticky town, hard to move. "How about looking for another assignment? A new start, a new congregation? You have always enjoyed new beginnings."

"It isn't worth it anymore," he replies. In the next room, the daughter's tears are streaming down her temples into her pillow because everything is so sad; the whole house is permeated by sadness like a cold fog. She heaves a deep, loud sigh, hoping that her parents will hear her, come in, enfold her in their arms, comfort her so that everything will be as it used to be: a weak child, strong parents, a safe home. . . . But they do not come; the tears stop running. She hears her mother's voice in the next room: "Though I walk through the valley of the shadow of death, I will fear no evil: for Thou art with me."

Father's letter to Herr Jacobi comes back, marked "Addressee moved; no forwarding address." He calls their pastor and learns that the Jacobi family emigrated "abroad." "I just can't understand it," he says to Mother. "Without saying a word! We were such good friends, and I told him that he could, at any time, . . ."

"It may be for the best," Mother says.

"What do you mean by that?" he almost shouts at her.

"Shhh! Don't wake up the child!"

It is happening! Nobody knows what, but the longer the wait, the greater the suspense. If it were only to happen now!

"Be quiet," Mother says. "Don't commit a sin!"

For the time being, soldiers are arriving. The old post office is crammed with troops and horses. Military maneuvers in the woods beyond Zeitstraße. Requisitions for rooms in the parsonage keep changing: officers in the guest room, orderlies in the attic. The children are admonished to keep their distance, to be polite but reserved. Officers no longer represent the social elite as they used to. A lot of them are nothing but upstarts. So far, so good: most of them have been well brought up and are respectful of their landlord's status and authority.

But then there is one who is entirely different, a careerist veterinarian and super-Nazi without manners, who shouts "Heil Hitler!" in the house at the top of his voice and complains that the minister answers with a simple "Good morning"; he gets plastered night after night, can't find the keyhole, and tramps noisily up the stairs, cursing rudely, mostly about the clergy. Ministers are nothing but "preachers." They are finished, as far as he is concerned. If he were the Führer, he'd send every one of them to the western front to have them dig trenches. That would be the end of all clerical coddling!

Mother turns a cold shoulder when she meets him on the stairs. The daughter hides wet sponges and dead mice in his bed. But Father sticks to his "Good morning, Doctor!"

"You simply don't hear what you don't want to hear!" Mother chides him. It doesn't bother him. If that fellow really has something to say, he'll be ready to listen. So far all he has done is grunt. Is that a reason for Father to learn the language of the pigsty?

One evening something happens that comes to be known in the family's memory as the "miracle of the boots." It begins by someone kicking open the door of the study. Father, looking with raised eyebrows over the edge of his book, notices the pigheaded doctor invading the family circle. With slurred speech he asks for the bootjack so he can get these damn, filthy boots off his feet. "Damn it, that boy of mine is nowhere to be found! Whenever you need those fellows they're gone. But he's gonna get it this time!"

Leaning against the door post, he tries to lift one of his fat legs to yank off his boot, loses his balance, hops around, and stumbles into the nearby rocking chair, which tips over backward as he lands in it with his full weight.

"Does one have to tolerate this?" Mother says.

Under her icy look of contempt the veterinarian kicks his legs like a helpless bug trying to get up and struggles to get on his feet, but cannot make it. Finally he falls back like a sack, spreading his legs and filthy boots over the sides of the chair.

"Do you wish to spend the night here?" Father asks, winking at his daughter, who is rolling on the sofa, almost choking with suppressed laughter. Father closes his book, places it carefully on the table, and lightly steps up to the rocking chair.

"Don't!" Mother says.

He bends down, grabs one of the kicking legs by the foot, and expertly yanks off both boots, pulling the heel with one hand and pushing back the toe with the other. He slightly turns up his nose in mock disgust: "A good foot bath wouldn't do any harm!" Then, with a smile, he extends both hands to the dumbfounded man.

(It is that smile that comes to the daughter's mind a year later, when she is reading Schiller's essay "On Grace and Dignity": "If those who are powerful desire to gain affection, their superiority must be tempered by grace. . . . We demand grace of him who obliges, dignity of the person obliged: the former, in order to rid himself of the offensive advantage that he has over the other, should transform his disinterested actions into affective actions by tempering them with affection so he appears to be the one who gains the most.")

With a short, quick jerk, Father pulls the veterinarian to his feet, gives him a slight shove in the direction of the door, and says: "All right, young man, it's time to say good night!" With a stupefied look in his bloodshot eyes, the doctor crawls away in his stocking feet. "Now wash your hands!" the mother says as soon as the door closes behind him. "Why should I?" he replies, lightly clapping his hands a few times before holding them up. Not a speck of dirt adheres to them. His dry skin is never dirty, never greasy. He does not need to wash to be clean.

"Don't you find this disgusting?" she says.

In the course of the night, the veterinarian undergoes a miraculous change. That is how he puts it when he appears in the study the next morning with a bouquet of flowers to offer a formal apology.

Never again will he utter the word "preacher"; and, he suggests, the minister's gentle kindness has convinced him that maybe there is after all something to be said for the Christian faith.

To Mother's disgust and the children's mocking derision, he now tags along with the family, Sunday after Sunday, to attend church; even Father is not "exactly thrilled." "But you can't choose among them. The spirit moves whomever it chooses. Even drunk veterinarians have immortal souls."

Shortly before moving, the family has one more grand celebration—a final climax, a farewell to four different childhoods, to the house, the town, the office, and to twenty years of peace: Dorothea's wedding.

It is a special event when a pastor's child enters into marriage, the minister says in his wedding service, barely able to control his emotions.

The wedding dinner is served at home. Floral decorations from the garden; menu and place cards written by hand. The oldest uncle says grace in a sonorous voice.

Large napkins are bunched up in stiff collars. Delicious gravy drips from heavy beards. The aunts are dressed in black and dark blue with filigreed lace trimming; they hold protective hands over their plates. Of all that is offered, they prefer to take just a taste—a bite, a spoonful, a leaf, a smidgen. They manage to nibble for hours at the puny servings on their plates and to sip from the drop or two in their glasses, pursed lips barely touching the rims when toasts are raised during the after-dinner speeches.

Dessert is followed by homemade verses and sing-alongs. The lyrics are passed out on sheets, with familiar melodies marked in parenthesis: "There lies a crown . . ."; "Three fellows went across the Rhine . . ."; "My sorrow, I know not its meaning . . ."

Father quietly keeps to himself. When the gentlemen go into the parlor to smoke, he disappears and does not return. The daughter catches a few muffled remarks as she is passing around the cigar box: Reinhold is no longer the lively, radiant man of infectious good humor that he used to be, the center of every festive occasion. He now appears to be all but extinguished. . . .

One of the uncles claims to have heard about a mysterious rash, not really serious but persistent. The doctor has taken a tissue sample from Reinhold's arm and sent it in for analysis. "God grant that it may turn out to be nothing serious. After all, he is the youngest. . . ." For a second the daughter thinks she caught a gloating note in their talk; she hastens to suppress her suspicion, but a knot remains in her solar plexus, shortening her breath and speeding up her heart. Why isn't he coming back? What keeps him so long? She leaves the room discreetly, goes upstairs to the study, puts her hand on the door handle, does not hear anything, no breathing, no steps—a deathly stillness, while downstairs Hermann starts playing "The Happy Farmer" on the piano.

Between the tinkling of the piano and the frightening silence she is confronted with the image of her ungodly childhood dreams: her dead father stretched out under the blue blanket; hawk's profile with sunken eyes and dropped chin; a row of yellow teeth between parted lips.

Dear God! she prays without hope. Dear father! Dear God! She feels nothing, no pain, no sorrow; nothing but horror slowly rising like black, icy water.

Finally Hermann stops playing. Sparse applause.

The daughter tears open the door and dashes toward her father, who is standing at the window, his back turned to her; she clasps him in her arms, and lies: "They're asking for you. What's keeping you? Without you it won't be any fun!"

Glancing down, she notices the gauze bandage on his left arm. "What's that?"

He pulls down his shirt sleeve and fastens the button.

"I'll be there soon," he says. "You must take my place."

"Is anything the matter with you?"

"Nothing at all. Run along. Go with God, but go!"

He does not come until evening. When his baritone joins in the singing, the guests are relieved. He alone manages to give it the right blend: festive emotion, Rhenish good cheer, and soulfulness.

"Evening comes to greet us," they sing. "The fountain by the gateway . . ."; "The moon is rising slowly . . ."

The daughter accompanies them on the accordion. With a keen sense for changes in atmosphere, she gradually moves on to more patriotic songs: "This lovely land and time of year . . ."; "Morning glow . . ."; "A rock too hard for comfort . . ."; "I once had a faithful comrade . . ."

Finally, by popular request, the national anthem.

A mighty wave of emotion sweeps the family out of their chairs and into each other's arms in a silent embrace.

"Now would be the time for the trumpeter to blow," says one of the aunts, lifting her finger as if she could actually hear him and the echo from the rock of the Lorelei; as if it were the Rhine that ran past the house instead of Wilhelmstraße, which has been renamed Claus Clemens Straße; as if it were Grandfather, instead of his youngest son, who is now raising his glass without a word. But everyone knows for whom and for what this final sip is taken.

"Do you know Rilke's 'Cornet'?" the daughter whispers in the ear of her dinner partner, an armored-infantry soldier. "'Riding, riding, riding . . .'"[1] He does not remember, but as far as riding goes, the cavalry is definitely a thing of the past. It's all tanks now!

On the day of the move to Bonn, Father is relocated to the house of some relatives. At home he would just be in the way. It might also be too hard on him.

His illness is not mentioned. Mother knows something but doesn't say a word, and nobody asks her. The doctor appears rarely and does little more than renew prescriptions and engage in cheerful chitchat. Afterwards, Mother accompanies him to the front door. They have long, muffled conversations in the hallway.

The rash on his forearm disappears, but now the glands in his armpits and groin begin to swell. Elongated knobby protrusions show up in front of his ears, changing the shape of his face. The hawklike urgency of his profile subsides. His features look somehow shrunk and leveled in the broader surface of the face. Gray tones dull the copper color of his skin.

For a while he still does some preaching in an outlying church, as he and his successor had agreed. Upon request, he also officiates at special functions, mostly funerals. But when he notices that his successor resents such requests, he finds excuses and gradually withdraws his services.

Visitors from Auel always put him in a state of happy excitement, which evaporates quickly once he hears the bad news they bring. The congregation split into two camps after his departure. Two rival pastors are vying for their souls. Fist fights have broken out over the use of the parish house.

After those visits he has sleepless nights.

"They are going to kill him with this!" Mother says. In the hallway she asks visitors to spare him. Fewer and fewer of them stop by. He continues to wait but does not ask any questions.

He is allowed to eat anything he wants but has no appetite. Still, he dutifully eats whatever Mother places in front of him, trying to suppress his nausea. The jacket he puts on for this occasion hangs loosely from his shrunken frame. Without complaint he even swallows the pills she places with a glass of water next to his plate.

Although the doctor has given him permission to get up and go out, he spends most of his time lying on the couch in the dining room, whose furniture is arranged just as it was

18

in Auel, although in a smaller space. Mother supplies him with books and turns on the radio at the appropriate times for him to listen to the news and bulletins from the front. Open books are lying upside down next to his face, which is turned toward the ceiling, eyes open. More and more frequently he forgets to move the pins that mark the advance of the German troops on the map. Sometimes he holds up a hand mirror and at length contemplates his changed face.

When the daughter comes for weekend visits, he buttons up his shirt and puts on a tie. He gets up to greet her, but as soon as she turns away he lies down again. She covers up her fright by playing the part of the cheerily voluble nurse: "Come on, let's get up! We'll go for a walk! A daily stroll down to the Rhine—you promised. Promises made should be promises kept. Each new day bids us our promises to pay!"

"Not right now," he says, looking embarrassed and guilty, "perhaps later, tomorrow; yes, perhaps tomorrow. . . ."

At that point she has to leave the room. She cannot endure watching him lying there and doing nothing. She is annoyed with him for not fighting back, not getting angry, not kicking out the doctor with his pills and drops, for no longer wanting to be the impatient, unreasonable, indestructible, on-top-of-everything father he used to be. "What is it? What's the problem? Are you in pain?"

No, he doesn't actually have any pain; he is just tired, tired to death.

In early October 1940 the veterans of his regiment celebrate a reunion in Königswinter in honor of the eightieth birthday of their former commander, that same "true aristocrat" who, in the years after 1918, had traveled with his belongings in a cardboard box tied with twine. Initially, Father sent his excuses due to poor health, but just a few days before the scheduled event he suddenly feels better.

His eyes under the bushy, gray eyebrows seem livelier. On the patch of lawn squeezed in among the houses, he exercises his legs, weakened from so much lying down, and waves in passing at Mother in the window above: things are looking up!

She does not trust him and voices her misgivings, which he dismisses with a touch of his former impatience. Shrugging her shoulders, she leaves the room while he tells the organizer on the telephone that his participation is possible though not yet certain.

In the morning of the day in question he gets up early and eagerly, asks for a white shirt and dark suit, and has the ribbons of his two Iron Crosses fastened in his buttonhole.

With humorous exaggeration, he says that he feels on top of the world and quite capable of taking the Honnef trolley to Königswinter and back. But Mother would prefer to have the daughter accompany him. She prevails against protests from both sides. The daughter, of course, does not reveal the true reason for her lack of enthusiasm: a secret date in the Gronau.[1] (Keeping things to herself has long become a habit; the break is complete and the conscience dulled by consideration. Why trouble them? They have enough to bear.)

Naturally, she gives in—still the dear child, the obedient daughter. Unlike other daughters, she has never given her parents any trouble. To pass the time, she takes along Ernst Jünger's *Auf den Marmorklippen*[2] and starts reading in it as soon as she sits across from her father in the trolley, ignoring all his manifestations of happy impatience and anticipation, until he cannot hold back any longer and puts his hand across the page: "Look, how beautiful!"

In the light of the rising sun the river flows through transparent veils of autumn mists that are half hiding the pale, smoky blue outline of the Siebengebirge. . . .

The manager, dressed in tails, shows them to a partitioned section of the glassed-in patio overlooking the Rhine. As they enter, the gentlemen, gathered in small groups, turn around to greet them with a rising chorus of welcoming voices. A short man with a military bearing walks up to Father with outspread arms, grasping him by the shoulders: "What a delight to see you, Reverend! You look splendid, completely unchanged!" In point of fact, his cheeks have that old copper tone again and the knobs in front of his ears are hardly noticeable. Perhaps things aren't quite so bad, the daughter thinks, as he moves with light, energetic steps from group to group, shaking hands, slapping shoulders, remembering everyone's name instantly. So swift and successful is his plunge into the living past that he fails to notice that the daughter remains outside the wall of yesterday's voices, words, gestures, and postures that encloses him. She moves surreptitiously toward the door in order to hide in one of the easy chairs in the foyer to continue reading *Marmorklippen*, its lofty words that are so far above the humdrum of daily life:

> *. . . the realization that a measured order is eternally embedded in the chance and confusion of this world. As we climb, we approach the secret that lies hidden in the dust. With every step we take in the mountains, the horizon of chance recedes, and when we reach the summit we are everywhere surrounded by the perfect ring that weds us to eternity. . . .*

As she tries to reach for the door handle behind her back, the short, military gentleman, whose birthday is being celebrated, intervenes. Under no circumstances will he let her take French leave. "You are very much needed, not just as a feast for the eyes of these superannuated gentlemen. There is someone else who feels like an outsider." With that, he points to a young man who is standing by the window with his back turned, holding a glass. "My grandson," he says, "and my driver for the day. Keep him company, or he will want to escape too."

He turns around on his heel and shouts in a high, penetrating voice that makes their heads snap around: "Gentlemen, dinner is served."

He then marches up to the head of the table. Father has to sit at his right and the daughter at the lower end next to the grandson, who introduces himself as a lieutenant on home leave. With a quick, furtive glance she determines that he is not suitable for a flirt: a heavyset, soft body that doesn't quite fit into the evidently custom-tailored uniform; a large head with a disproportionately high, arched forehead; greasy, yet dull, thinning hair that is too long and badly trimmed above the collar. Without making an effort at further conversation, he devours his appetizer. His grandfather tries to catch his eye with a look of disapproval across the length of the table, but he remains tucked in under his forehead like a turtle under its shell.

"What an oaf!" she thinks.

Not until the third course does he raise his eyes from his plate and slowly focus them on her. Strange eyes, she notices; too light, bright blue, set deep in the shadow of the forehead. Does she still attend high school, he wants to know.

No, she graduated last spring, having skipped one year like all of her classmates; she is now doing her time in the National Labor Service. His brief, pointless laughter sounds like an Aha! separated by a puff of air. His breath suggests that he has had more to drink than the wine with which he refills his glass every time the bottle comes his way.

"So you must be very proud to be able to serve the fatherland at least with a spade," he says. She snaps back at him: "What do you mean, a spade?" But he meant his remark to be taken figuratively: physical labor rather than military service.

Somehow she feels as if he is mocking her, even though he speaks seriously, with a soft voice that excludes the others and establishes an inappropriate intimacy between them. What is he up to? she thinks, counseling herself to be cautious; but she immediately violates her own advice by countering vehemently but in a low voice, thereby inadvertently confirming the inappropriate intimacy: She isn't proud at all! Camp life among the brownshirts really makes her puke! She actually says "puke," an expression she is not permitted to use at home or among grown-ups; and she would not have used it now if something had not clicked between them: his look, his voice, and her pent-up anger of many months at the demands for conformity, the pressures, and the refusal to let her have special privileges. It will be the best day of her life when she can finally take off her uniform, her cap, and all the tin insignia, throw them in a corner, and finally begin her studies—music! She wants to be a famous violinist. At this point she remembers to be cautious and quickly interjects that she does not object in principle to doing her turn in the National Labor Service, at least as far as farm work is concerned. Working on a farm is the least objectionable part of it. What is truly unbearable is camp life and having to wear a uniform. She has always deeply resented uniforms.

"Your father seems to have liked wearing them," he says.

"It's different for men."

"Are you sure?" he says, pouring himself another glass without noticing that hers is empty. No longer caught in his look, she estimates how many glasses he has emptied just in the course of this dinner—not sipping and tasting like the elderly gentlemen but greedily gulping, with that jerk of the hand used for tossing down shots of hard liquor.

"Never get involved with men who are drunk; they are unpredictable," Mother has said.

Across the width of the table, a major with graying hair, but still in active service, engages the lieutenant in a discussion about the Poland campaign: A victorious advance like this must surely be an extraordinary experience for a young officer who so far has had to prove his valor in drills on the barracks grounds. He asks several short, direct military questions. The lieutenant tries to answer them in the same short and direct way but cannot manage, gets tangled up, and leaves unfinished sentences hanging in midair, his heavy tongue searching for words. When the major attempts a few lame jokes to help him out, the lieutenant falls into a silly giggle, which causes general embarrassment. His grandfather again launches disapproving looks but again fails to meet his grandson's eyes.

The daughter plans to disappear right after the coffee. For the time being, she turns her back on the lieutenant and concentrates on the conversation at the upper end of the table. It concerns her father, the former volunteer chaplain, who apparently was the cause of much amusement at headquarters. His modest protests notwithstanding, he has to listen to the inevitable company wit telling a few "priceless stories," among them the one about the Christmas service in 1914. Just back from the trenches, the company had been ordered to line up in the square in front of the church and to march behind the chaplain into the church to hear the service. The chaplain had just pushed open the portal, when the local priest came sailing across the square with flying black robes, followed by a few old crones also dressed in black "like a flock of crows." The narrator, who was a young captain at the time, noticed right away that *Monsieur le Curé* was out to teach the chaplain a lesson. But the chaplain began to chat in his usual naive way with his opposite number, notwithstanding his less than admirable French — those classicists, as we all know, don't waste their time on a living language that might be of some use. The chaplain always carried a dictionary in his pocket, which he now proceeded to fish out. He did his best to explain to the curé that they had had a long-standing "agrément" to use the church for their Christmas service, thinking that "agreement" had the same meaning as the French "agrément." The curé, who could not make heads or tails of all this palaver — he had never understood a word of German, let alone spoken one, the knucklehead! — marched right past the chaplain, positioned himself squarely in the open church door, let his crones enter one by one, and shut the door with a bang from within.

"So there stands our beloved Reverend, a closed church door in his face and at his back a company of either grinning or grumbling soldiers, and somebody," says the narrator, "well, guess who, had to step on — pardon me! — step in. So I talk to him like to a — pardon my language — stubborn ass:

You can't do this to these people who've been in the mud till yesterday; they can't stand there and wait till some . . ." ("Now, please, I must insist . . . ," the minister interrupts) ". . . all right, then, till this blackrobe is done reading his mass."

The chaplain had to agree. He would be the last one to neglect the welfare of soldiers in battle. But should he here in front of the church, or worse, inside, start a fight—a falling-out between Christians who had come together to celebrate the birth of our Lord? "You cannot ask me to go that far, Captain! I'd rather have everyone return to quarters!" "That would suit them just fine," says the captain. "Did we win on the battlefield only to be overpowered in church? Let me take care of this, Reverend!"—"You should have seen him," the narrator says, pointing to the minister, who sits without looking up, pushing the remains of the meal on his plate into a little pile, "how he came at me: 'You take care of your company, Captain, I'll take care of my church. Right now, I'm in charge!'"

With his tail between his legs (in a manner of speaking, of course) he returned to his place in the company, while the chaplain bent down to listen to the sounds from within the church, as if waiting for something. Then he gave his orders to move in, but to do so quietly: no talk and no racket.

The old crones had just taken communion and stopped dead in their tracks, like thunderstruck cows, while the soldiers edged their way into the pews, avoiding those where the black purses and prayer books had been left behind.

"Come on, Granny," one of the soldiers said, "we don't bite!" The chaplain, having taken a seat in the first row just in front of the still chanting curé, turned around and put his finger to his lips.

As soon as the curé had finished, the chaplain got up, stood next to him, and announced the opening chorale: "Praise, all ye Christians, God our Lord. . . ." He cast a sideways glance at the curé, which was intended to convey that "all ye Christians" indeed meant everybody, including the curé and the old crones, who were just then retrieving their purses and prayer books.

The curé did not return his glance. Even as he retreated with dignity surrounded by the soldiers' booming song, he looked neither right nor left and went the length of his church, followed by his crones, as if it contained nothing but air and incense. However, a week later, when the troops were moving out, he told the translator that as long as there had to be any "Krauts" in the village, he would have preferred to keep this unit and its chaplain. With these fellows, at least you knew what you had; with somebody else, there was no telling.

At this point the narrator concludes his story and is rewarded with hearty laughter. The guest of honor finds that this charming story represents the wide range of the German national character—toughness and discipline, but also generosity and feeling; manly courage in battle and a deep longing for peace.

No one, except for the lieutenant, laughs at these solemn words; he apparently has no clue about when to end the joking and when to start being serious. After several outbursts of hysterical giggles, he now also wants to tell a story. Ignoring his grandfather's discreet warning cough, he begins quite innocuously with the familiar scheme of "what's the difference between . . ."

The governor general of occupied Poland, Dr. Hans Frank, was recently asked by a reporter whether he knew the difference between the protectorate in Czechoslovakia and the governor generalship in Poland. As usual, Dr. Frank came back as quick as a shot: "In Prague, to teach the people a lesson, they displayed large red posters announcing that seven Czechs had been executed that day. So I tell myself: if I were to hang up a poster for every seven Poles that had been shot, all of Poland's forests could not produce enough paper. . . ."

The lieutenant's voice, heavy with drink, has become less and less distinct toward the end of the story, but the gentlemen must have caught a good part of it, because as soon as he finishes, a grim and suffocating silence descends. The scraping sound of a chair being pushed back does not so much interrupt the silence as accentuate its intolerable weight. Nobody turns his head, and the guests seated at the other side of the table lower their heads as the guest of honor walks behind their chairs up to his grandson and digs his hand with the signet ring so firmly into his shoulder that the white knuckles stand out.

The shoulder slumps forward. The hand pulls it up again. Pushing himself up with his fists planted on the edge of the table, the lieutenant gets up and straightens himself.

At the outermost edge of everyone's attention a whisper can be heard: "What is it, Reverend? Are you not feeling well?"

The daughter just barely sees her father leaving the table, and there is something in his step and the way he holds his shoulders and neck that makes her follow him. But she is not fast enough: as she gets out into the foyer, she catches a glimpse of him closing the door of the men's room behind him.

She waits a while in front of the door, but then some of the gentlemen arrive, and she is embarrassed to stand around in front of the men's room. She retreats to the window side of the foyer, parts the curtains, and notices the guest of honor and his grandson passing by on the Rhine promenade, quickly, silently, the older man a few steps ahead. Though the grandson is much taller and larger, he looks from above like a limp sack being dragged behind.

Just then her father and another gentleman come out of the men's room. As he passes her, he waves: "We'll be leaving soon!"

She takes refuge behind her book in one of the easy chairs. In the pure air of the *Marmorklippen* she soon feels better:

. . . and we were gladdened by the knowledge that destruction among the elements is not the end but an illusion that wafts like wisps of surface fog that must fall

prey to the sun. And we perceived that if we lived in those cells that could not be destroyed, we would step from each phase of destruction through wide-open portals into ever more festive and radiant chambers.

Instead of taking the trolley back to Bonn, they ride in the car of their host, who will under no circumstances allow Father to expose himself to more stress. It has not occurred to the minister that the lieutenant will do the driving, and he must have inadvertently given some sign of concern or anxiety, because the host hastens to assure him that his grandson is a totally reliable driver. Lowering his voice, he adds that the wine served with the dinner must have been unusually strong. "These young people nowadays can't hold their liquor. But everything is under control now!"

Actually, the lieutenant seems to be a new man: cold shower, neatly brushed hair, jacket straightened and buttoned. As he opens and holds the door of the car, he unnecessarily clicks his heels. They drive in silence, Father sitting in his corner with closed eyes. The lieutenant's round back suggests submissiveness. There is no hint of rebelliousness or any suggestion of asking her to enter into a secret alliance with him. The daughter is just a touch disappointed, as if an expectation, an unspoken promise, had remained unfulfilled. She tries to convince herself that she really did not much care for him from the very start. She peeks over his shoulder at his wrist watch: not even 6:00 P.M.! If all goes well, she can still meet her date in the Gronau. High time to think of some plausible excuse: girlfriend, house concert, lecture — anything "essential" has always worked before.

Suddenly Father starts talking, and his voice betrays that, despite his closed eyes, he has neither slept nor rested.

"Lieutenant, is there any basis in reality to what you just said?"

He does not express himself more precisely, but there is no need for it. They know immediately what he is referring to. The daughter is a little annoyed: so he must have heard it after all! She breathes more easily when the lieutenant answers, without turning his head: someone has told him the story. Whether it has a basis in reality is beyond his knowledge.

"In that case, how can you spread such poison?" Father asks, his voice trembling with agitation. "Aren't you ashamed of yourself? Don't you have any moral conscience at all?"

The lieutenant does not answer, but when the daughter, following a silent command, looks in the mirror, she sees his bright eyes focused on her, again asking her to enter into a secret alliance with him and sending a message she does not want to receive. She quickly turns to her father and pats his hand: "Don't get excited!"

"Don't worry," he says softly; and then, more harshly to the driver: "Please drop us off after you pass the bridge! I want to walk home. The fresh air will be good for me after this . . . this foul stench!"

"But, Father!" she exclaims in horror, "you can't . . ." Just at that point they are crossing the bridge. The lieutenant eases the car to the center, turns left after the exit for Bonn, and heads for the river, as if he knew that her father did not want to walk anywhere else. He stops under the ramp, gets out, tears open the rear door.

"You're quite welcome, Reverend," he says and has already walked back around the car, when it occurs to Father that he never even shook hands with him. Now he is sorry, after all. The young man will have to return to the front and, who knows, perhaps encounter death. "God be with you!" he shouts after him.

That was the last time I went for a walk with my father. I see the two figures approaching out of the darkness under the bridge ramp, but not so close that I could (or would want to) begin to say "I" to the girl dressed in a pleated skirt, a white blouse, white knee socks, and walking shoes, her hair done up in a faddish wave. She subtly urges her father on as they walk among the crowd of evening strollers catching a breath of air after work and before supper: the mist of the river, the smell of tar, the smoke of the tugboats pulling long lines of barges—the empty ones high above the water, the loaded ones deep down to the gunwales in the undulating broth. At the very end is the dinghy that reminds her father of his childhood, when the boys used to swim up to the line of barges slowly churning their way upriver. The closer you got, the swifter the barges rushed past; the trick was to jump up from the water just at the right moment, to grab the dinghy, and to climb into it for a free ride, so later you could enjoy an easy swim downriver. Once he cut his hand on a jagged piece of metal lining; blood streaming down his arm, he held it up so that his father, sitting in his study, could see the blood; but he mistook it for a friendly greeting and merrily waved back. His father's failure to see that his youngest son was seriously injured unreasonably offended him at the time. "Are you listening at all?"

"Of course," she says, her ears still ringing with yesterday's sound of the anchor bells and the barge chains rattling in the dusk, as she and her boyfriend ducked down in the sandy hollow behind the breakwater when the ship's crew rumbled into the dinghy and rowed toward the river bank. "Don't worry," he said, "they can't see us."

Thus, as they walk close to each other, awkwardly trying to stay in step, their thoughts fly swiftly in opposite directions toward private, personal images, which they keep to themselves. In the deserted space between them fright remains like a stumbling block, which they do not touch but carefully avoid with every step they take. Again and again it gets in their way and must be negotiated anew, more difficult with each effort because every thought, every conversation, no matter how light and remote at first, exerts a gravitational pull toward it. Yet a secret fear acts as a counterforce, so that in spite of talking and moving forward together they fail to make progress but remain in a dazed suspension, which they blame on each other.

"You are not listening at all!" he says; and she: "We'll never get home this way!" And he: "Don't pull so hard!" leaning more heavily on her arm. Finally he stops just as the chimes of the church in Beuel[1] strike six o'clock and her date—if he is on time—is beginning to wait for her in the Gronau.

"Should I call a taxi?" she asks, but he won't hear of it. He just wants to sit down on a bench to catch his breath; there is plenty of time, and Mother is not expecting them yet. They can talk for a while; there are so few opportunities now that the daughter is gone all the time. The weekends go by so fast; they are almost getting to be strangers.

Again she gives in, boiling with impatience. Then they sit under trimmed trees, between flower beds that are filled with the little blue asters of this autumn season. Reddish mist above the river. On this side the sun has already disappeared, but on the opposite bank, up and down the hillsides, window panes flash—red bundles of rays from the windows of the Hotel Petersberg.

"Do you suppose we will ever go there again—the two of us?" he asks. If she could only remain silent now instead of rubbing his hand in a pretense of concern ("Your hands are cold! You'll catch something!"); if she could just drop this damn cheerful bedside manner; if she could stop thinking about her date, which she won't be able to keep anyway, and forget about the clock on the steeple of the church in Beuel and her latent restlessness; if for once she really were to pay attention—instead of nicely inclining her head and letting words drop inside her only to have them vanish down there together with undertones and warning signals that she keeps ignoring—this could have turned into a conversation between two human beings. As it is, her politely dutiful comments produce nothing but a solitary monologue, a call into the void.

He asks if she had a pleasant time, probably referring to the lieutenant and his story. What does she think of it? But she does not answer him, saying instead, "It was all right." He does not insist and says that he did not really enjoy himself. Years ago he would have had a better time of it. "But that's probably because of my illness. It makes me look at things in a different light. For instance, that story about the French curé. In reality it wasn't like that at all."

"How was it?" she asks without really wanting to know. He notices and continues talking, skipping about like someone in a swamp jumping quickly from tussock to tussock as the ground gives under his weight. He talks about fatigue and sleep and explains that his pattern of sleep has changed. There used to be these short transitions while falling asleep and waking up, which rarely lasted longer than it took to say the evening or morning prayer; in between there was deep sleep, perhaps dreams, which he could never remember the next morning. It is different now, possibly because he rests too much and does not get enough exercise, as Mother always says. Now all of his sleep is like those transitions, but he cannot fill it with prayer. His thoughts are not working properly either; he is simply getting old, and the worn-out little cogs fail to mesh. It can happen that a thought snaps in midcourse, simply disappears, falls into a bottomless abyss. Then he quickly reaches back to grab hold of the thought at a point where it was still solid and clear, but the abyss grabs it faster and swallows it with hide and hair before he can catch any part of it. And so it goes on, a kind of feeding frenzy. As soon as he turns toward a thought, it drops out of sight; and it seems to him as if everything, absolutely everything, was gradually falling into the abyss. He cannot understand why he does not notice it during the day: one simply sets one foot before the other, speaks one word after another, without realizing at all that there is no bottom to anything. But when it happens to him at night, he has to get out of bed—quietly, so that Mother will not hear him. Then he goes into the dining room and sits in the stiff Worpswede chair[2] until he feels solid ground beneath him again and can see the firm shapes of the furniture in the light the street lamp casts through the window. Then he can think again, but on the way back to bed it starts all over again. Once he fell down in front of the bedroom door even though he had already taken hold of the door handle. It scared Mother half to death, so now she hardly dares to go to sleep. Poor Mother! she takes everything so hard. We have to take good care of her.

In between these comments he mentions the past, but without calling it the past. He gets mixed up in time, as if the temporal sequence of his life had become a circle, a stagnant pool separated from the river. He speaks of his father, who was never sick. In the wintertime he cut a hole in the ice near the riverbank, jumped in, and never caught any of the illnesses his wife prophesied as she rubbed him down with the big bath towel. But he died quickly, with barely enough time to make his peace with God, and already. . . .

He thinks of Limbach, the schoolteacher, who once said, "You never learned to be afraid, Reverend."

"What should I be afraid of?" he asked him in return; and the teacher nodded thoughtfully: "That's just what I mean. You have never known what fear is. But then you never set out to seek it either."

"I never set out?" Father said with a laugh. "I who have been everywhere, while you tended your garden during summer vacations? Don't forget, I was a soldier during the war, three years in the trenches." But that was probably not what the teacher had meant.

A little later, Limbach started talking again about the prodigal son's brother, who dutifully stayed at home, while the other sat by his swine and husks and felt so forsaken in the end that he renounced his freedom or adulthood or whatever he may have been seeking and ran headlong back to his father.

"So, what is it you are trying to say?" Father asked.

"What I mean is that if the brother who stayed home were to feel afraid—where would he go?" the teacher replied. Then he left, casting one of those furtive glances over his shoulder that Mother did not like. He had a way of expressing himself cryptically. Presumably that was one of the reasons why they never really became friends, which Father now finds regrettable. He believes that he now understands the teacher better than he used to, even what he said about fear. . . .

She is still sitting with her head inclined in a pose of Christian devotion, listening and yet not hearing that her father is on the verge of learning about fear, and that he is calling for someone to accompany him into the darkness. In her thoughts she has already run away to the Gronau (is the boy still there? how long will he wait?), and returns only for a moment when she hears the word "forsaken." It sets off a bell in her head, perhaps the bad conscience with which she grew up, and she clicks her tongue in reproach: "How can you speak of feeling forsaken?" Then she begins to rattle off the names of all the people who are or used to be close to him. Not all that many, it occurs to her as she is talking, and none could be called close friends, although there are all sorts of people who admire and respect him, who are loyal or grateful to him. Every time she pauses in calling the roll of names, he says, "Oh yes," as if that person had just come to mind. Only when she mentions Herr Jacobi does he say nothing and turns his head away. Her enumeration becomes even more breathless, and when no new name occurs to her, she mentions the children, two sons, two daughters, Mother—we all love you so much! Again he responds with an "Oh yes," and resumes his talk about being forsaken as if the whole list of names had failed to convince him. It is what Jesus felt when he said to his disciples in Gethsemane: "Could ye not watch with me one hour?" and then again on the cross when He cried out: "My God, my God, why hast thou forsaken me?" He has preached about these words from his pulpit a thousand times, he says, and experienced all sorts of emotions, even to the point of tears, but he has probably never really felt forsaken. His head has always been too full of the work he did with people and all the good he planned to do. Yet, being able to feel forsaken and to communicate this feeling would probably have been more important than anything else; it would have provided the right background, against which the light of the resurrection could have risen in all its glory. Not that he would presume to be able now to preach better, more poignantly, more movingly if he ever had another chance at it. On the contrary, the insights he has gained in the meantime can for the most part not be expressed in words. It might happen, were he to stand in the pulpit again, that he would be unable to utter a single word, as it has sometimes happened to him in his dreams but never while he was actually preaching.

She does not know how to respond; he too remains silent and no longer objects to her calling a taxi. She installs him in the rear seat of the black Mercedes, and when he moves over to make room for her she mumbles something about "following on foot," slams the door, and runs off so as not to have to see his eyes through the rear window. At first she takes long leaps, then kicks up her heels in a childlike canter. ("She runs like a horse, that child," Mother used to say; "when will she ever learn to behave like an adult?" And then he would say: "Never mind, she is still a child.") This entire family, united in wholesomeness and caring love for each other, has run away from this new, quiet father, who is distancing himself discreetly behind closed eyes. Instead of seeing him for what he was, they clung—with the best of intentions—to the carefree, indestructible, always-on-top-of-the-world father who did not exist anymore but who had to play the part for better or for worse to keep up their spirits, to retain their love, to please them without consideration for himself. During his last night in the hospital, he tipped over a glass of raspberry juice in his bed, soaking the sheets, but he did not ring for help because, he felt, the poor nurses needed some rest too. All night he lay with a feverish thirst in the wet stickiness, and the next morning the Catholic sisters said they had never had such an undemanding, considerate patient; if only all of them were like him.

Early in December of that last winter, the daughter came home late one night. As she tiptoed through the dining room in her stocking feet, she came upon her father sitting in his Worpswede chair in the dark. Alarmed, she called out: "Are you still here?" And he replied: "Not much longer!" She did not know any better than to explain in breathless detail why she was so late—even though he had not asked for an explanation—and to kiss him good night quickly but with special affection, which made her feel particularly caring and loving. Just as the whole family felt permanently caring and loving during that nearly twelve-month period of his illness, and out of sheer love and caring affection let him depart alone and forsaken.

The first time this dawned on her—his eyes were following her through the rear window of the Mercedes—was when she submitted the obituary to the *Generalanzeiger* in Bonn: "Our beloved husband and father . . ." And his eyes kept following her—like the church bell that followed the wayward child with a terrible clanging and calling[3]—as she pedaled her bicycle with the clattering chain up the Kaiserplatz and along the Hofgarten, wanting to reach home but unable to do so because she was irresistibly urged forward, past the house on Lennéstraße, left on Arndtstraße down to the Rhine, past the bench where she had sat with her father, to the Gronau, where now there was no boyfriend waiting, where no one at all was walking on this 1 January 1941, down the towpath in the fog of this gray, damp winter day on the Rhine, till the tires got stuck in the sand, and then on foot over the wet stones of the breakwater to the fog-shrouded end.

20 The schoolteacher has died. The announcement arrived as I was about to take another trip to Auel to finish our conversation. Now I have no one to help me with this work. No one will check the images emanating from my overheated memory. Imprisoned in my study, which is overcrowded with the past, with stacks of manuscripts, with piles of crumpled sheets of paper, I try in vain to get some perspective on my subject. The ark is still sealed. Its images haunt my mind even as I sleep. I see the child, her violin under her arm, returning from church with her father, her hand tucked into the pocket of his overcoat—a clear, cold day. A man approaches them from Bahnhofstraße. Father also notices him, stops short, and turns as if trying to avoid him by crossing to the other side of the street. Then he changes his mind, walks faster, setting a new, nervous pace. While walking, he lets go of the child's arm and holds out both hands toward the man, who studies him with distant, cold eyes and walks past him, almost touching the proffered hand.

I meant to ask the teacher whether the man might have been his relative, the "Red" agitator at the union hall; whether he despised my father so much that he would not shake hands with him; whether he, the teacher, also secretly despised my father; whether he had said all those good and nice things about him only out of kindness and consideration, the same kindness and consideration that prevented him from opening my father's eyes.

All this work would, then, have been for nothing. I would never have left my father's study, never seen the truth.

In the dead of night I go in search of someone, some other human being. When I spot the light from Thomas's desk lamp shining through the rural darkness like a beacon, I am close to tears. I cut myself a switch for protection against the dogs, who roam unleashed at night, and I walk across the fields to the neighboring farmhouse.

"I must talk to you," I say.

He pushes his papers off to the side and gets glasses and a bottle of wine.

"It's about the incident at the union hall," I say. "I have to find out what the teacher thought about it, but I can't ask him anymore."

"I guess he himself didn't know what to think," Thomas says. "Otherwise, why would he have given you the letter with the unanswered question?" He, Thomas, just can't take this whole matter very seriously. "A lot of people at that time behaved despicably. So did your father. Why shouldn't he? Just because he's your father?"

"Please try to understand," I tell him. "Because he is my father I can't look at it as just another despicable incident. This is either *his* story and I can really make him out in it or everything I have done so far is nothing but subjective nonsense.

"I had meant to ask the teacher to put his question differently," I say. "Not: why did he remain silent? but: why did he fail to see? If he were to put the question that way, I might try to give an answer, the only one I am able to see. I might have asked him: Could it have been like this? Is the minister you see the same person as the father I remember? But the teacher is dead. There is no other unbiased witness left. From now on I can speak about my father only in the subjunctive: if he had been the way I see him, then this story would have to be told in such and such a way."

"Try it!" Thomas says.

"If you try to be objective."

"I'm not a witness," he replies.

"You could attest to my trying to tell the truth." He leans back in his chair, indicating that he is getting ready to listen for a while. We have not had a good talk for a long time. Something has come between us that now has to be addressed. With a weary sigh, I focus once more on the incident at the union hall.

My father would have been roused from sleep in the middle of this particular night of February 1933. Still half asleep, he would have dressed and, with the messenger waiting at the door, taken the pouch with the implements for administering communion. On the way to the scene of the incident he would have found out as much as he could from the messenger: there had been a shootout between the Reds and the brownshirts. Someone was hit, possibly killed—a Nazi. If my father had been the person whom I now see, he would have been convinced even before he arrived at the scene that one of the Reds must have fired the shot in question. Not only because a brownshirt had been shot. There was yet another reason for his snap judgment, namely, that everything had already been decided long before he actually looked at the specific case or analyzed it in detail: Red equals blood, murder, violence. Red equals evil: as deeply rooted in prior knowledge as the premise of his theology. Not that he was particularly fond of the Nazis' preference for brown. He used to call it a "crap color" and associated it with unpleasant sensations: pushy, proletarian, disgusting, loud, extreme— but at least extremism from the Right. But, from his perspective, right was not simply a particular side of an object having many sides; it was the good and solid middle, the spiritual foundation, where all good, respectable, decent folks came together to take up arms against the Reds. It's a familiar story. One does not need to consider the past to see it happening.

As for the brownshirts, a man like my father could at least entertain the hope that underneath that ugly surface one might discover a good and decent core—if nothing else, the possibility of goodness and decency, which made it one's duty to wait, to give it a chance, not to throw out the baby with the bath water. It was altogether different with the Reds. With them, there was no distinction between surface and core. Red was Red all the way through, as dangerous as a spark in a haystack. Patient waiting was entirely out of place; one had to stamp it out, crush and extinguish it.

Hence, the question who fired the shot and hit the mark would have already been settled in my father's mind when he bent over the wounded man. It would have been settled instantly because it was of no consequence to him. After all, he was one of those people who, throughout their lives, concern themselves with what is essential, and his special brand of the essential was invisible: men's souls and God's realm. He had the vague look of an impractical person who has not learned to test the visible world for its texture, usefulness, purpose, and coherence. As he looked down at the wounded man, he had but one intention, could think of only one question, the one question that seemed essential to him: Is the man alive? Can he still make his peace with God? Or is he dead? Does his soul require pastoral intercession? In this matter, his observation was sharp and keen, his examination thoroughly competent: he found that the man was dead. It was time to help an erring soul through prayer.

If this is what my father was like, he would immediately kneel beside the man, without looking either right or left, and begin to pray. He would close his eyes and look inside himself, where he would be alone with his God in the realm of prayer. It is entirely conceivable that the same man who, outwardly, knelt pitifully and helplessly in the dirt of the street by the dead body felt strong in an inner realm, where prayer could shake the earth and faith could move mountains in service to the Lord, who would provide.

He would have been deeply shocked only at the moment of seeing the other man, the alleged murderer. His only reliably attested exclamation, "Dear God, both of them members of my congregation!" sheds some light on the context in which he saw both murderer and victim: my church, my flock, souls who are in my care and for whom I am responsible. The horror of seeing them in the role of murderer and victim would have weighed on his conscience in a manner that he had learned and practiced all his life: to seek out sin and guilt first within himself. To ask: Lord, where have I been remiss? He is a worthless shepherd who remains with his flock, instead of going after the sheep that is lost until he finds it and laying it on his shoulders to carry it back to the fold. Racked by such pangs of conscience, he would never have thought to question whether the man who had been arrested was actually the murderer. Completely dumbfounded, he would have followed this unfortunate member of his congregation with his eyes until he disappeared into the paddy wagon, incapable of seeing any connections, let alone thinking about them. Even if he had picked up the newspaper page that was perhaps still lying among the broken glass of the display case, even if he had read the article marked in red pencil that gave an account of how German industrial corporations were supporting Hitler's party, he would not have seen the light. He would have failed to comprehend why the Reds had chosen to put this particular paper on display, and why the brownshirts were so eager to tear it down. If there had been room for any other thought in his distraught mind, it would have concerned the dead man's family and his own duty to notify and comfort them before any unauthorized person got ahead of him. I can see him picking up his communion pouch and walking away with bowed head, his thoughts completely turned inward: Repent, for the kingdom of heaven is near!

It is possible that he had second thoughts as the trial was being conducted and a number of suspicious things occurred: the disappearance of the man's cap; the eyewitness being assaulted in the street. But what could he have testified to, since he had not seen anything specific, nothing that he could have sworn to? He would have been incapable of lying, not even "in the name of justice." What stood in the way was his conscience and his commitment to speak the absolute truth, which did not include the obligation to have accurate perception.

I even consider it possible that he never knew about any of this. Who would have had the heart to bother him with those unpleasant things? Even the teacher, who had a personal stake in all of this, did not open his mouth and did not mail the letter asking that terrible question, not even after the mistake had been found and the erroneous verdict reversed. I see a tacit agreement between him and his congregation. He was the kind of man they wanted him to be: cheerful in the

Lord, above the sordidness of the world, secure and fearless in the ark of his faith. Such a man could be a comfort to them, and no one expected more from him—neither Herr Jacobi, nor Schmitz Gustav, nor the Nazi mayor who protected him from his fellow Party members: Don't worry about him, he is old, he won't last much longer, he is such a kind and pleasant man!

That is what frightens me in the story of my father's life: this special kind of loneliness that does not have the appearance of loneliness because it is crowded with well-meaning people, except that the lonely one is incapable of reaching out to them other than by bending down from above, like Saint Martin on his horse bending down to the poor beggar. One may call it by many different names: being benevolent, lending a helping hand, dispensing gifts, providing counsel, comfort, instruction, or even service; but what is on top remains on top, and what is below remains below; and he who happens to be on top can never be the one who is being helped, counseled, comforted, instructed, or served, even if he is in great need, because this rigid constellation does not permit a reciprocal relationship. No matter how strong the bonds of love, there is no glimmer of what is called solidarity. No misery is miserable enough to bring down the rider from the high horse of his humble pride.

This may be the special kind of loneliness in which a person—in spite of the most careful daily scrutiny of God's word and commandment—could become guilty without being aware of it, because the perception of certain sins assumes a knowledge that comes from seeing, hearing, and understanding, not from dialogues in the private realm. Camilo Torres[1] had to study sociology in addition to theology to be able to understand the plight of his people and to act accordingly. The church was not at all pleased. It has always considered the sins of curiosity more sinful than the sins of willful ignorance, just as it has always looked more favorably upon those who seek what is essential in the realm of the invisible and dismiss the visible world as irrelevant.

"This particular kind of loneliness would have been my reply to the question Why did my father not see anything? if the teacher had asked it, or if you were to put it to me," I say to Thomas, waiting for a word or sign from him that I have succeeded in making myself understood. For a while he sits without moving with his back turned, staring at the black window pane.

"You don't believe me," I say.

"There are so many stories like this one," he says. "They have the ring of truth and are told by people one likes and respects. Every one of these stories minutely examines a tiny piece of guilt until one understands it in human terms and almost sympathizes with it. Just look at these people: human beings like you and me, every one of them a mixture of good and bad qualities—who isn't? And far off in the distance, almost in a different world, the incomprehensible magnitude of guilt lies in a mire of cowardice and meanness, as alien as a meteor dropped from another star. But it didn't just drop down on us; it was man-made, fashioned not by one person or a few but by many, almost by all. I simply ask myself: whatever happened to it in your engaging, sympathetic stories? Where is it hidden, in which fold of the cloak that you have spread so carefully over everything?"

"That's how it is with biased witnesses," I say. "Guilt attaches so closely to them that it never appears to them undiluted but only in murky involutions that cannot be neatly separated. The more precise they try to make the cut, the closer they get to themselves, the more deeply and painfully they cut into their own flesh, the more difficult the separation becomes, not only between good and evil, but also between themselves and the perpetrators of the past. Hence, in the end, they cannot continue the process of analysis without analyzing themselves, paying particular attention to all that seems unessential and is therefore being ignored and pushed to the periphery of consciousness by other priorities. For it is precisely there, in the realm of the unessential, that a leak, a secret aperture, may exist, imperceptibly admitting guilt.

"That's my problem," I say, and then we sit silently for a while, with our thoughts reaching out to the other, hoping to achieve understanding that lies beyond words. But the little room has become so oppressive from too much cigarette smoke and breathing, too many thoughts and hopes that we jump up at the same moment, take our jackets off the hook, and tear open the window: fresh air!

That same night we walked for three hours, following the winding river all the way to the electric power plant and back again. It was ridiculous how much we looked alike—long, ambling steps, hunched shoulders, stooped backs, hands buried in pockets, heads thrown back, seemingly looking straight ahead but really not focusing on anything or only on what was inside. We walked without talking, but neither of us felt a need for words or was embarrassed by the silence; we never noticed that we were silent. It was as if everything was running smoothly between us—on separate tracks, but not in opposite directions or at cross-purposes—at just the right distance to be aware of the other's separate identity, yet sufficiently close to signal to each other occasionally: Watch that root! . . . Hold my jacket! . . . Look, it's getting light already!

When we were almost home and could already see the house—the smoking chimney, the sunlight reflected in the window panes—I was finally able to talk about my father's death without the guilty conscience that beset all those who had been with him at Saint John's Hospital. Mother felt guilty because she had given in to the nurses and left him alone during his last night; Gerhard, because he had not had his final discussion concerning ultimate issues of faith; I, because of my impatience and false cheerfulness.

He alone took it lightly, as if the blood that ran from his mouth and nose after the hemorrhage had swept away all fatigue and anxiety. He had no pain, never had any. Now they were bringing champagne to stimulate his heart—those starched and armored nuns, who only the day before had moved through his room with frozen mien, were beginning to melt underneath their armor. That much he still managed to accomplish toward the end—such a modest person, such a good, unassuming, considerate patient. . . .

"Drinking champagne all by myself? Absolutely not!" he says and does not give in until glasses have been brought and filled, and everybody, even the attendant, is standing ready to make them ring. "And where is the cleaning woman?" While drinking, he touches the sprouting whiskers around his mouth—an unpleasant sight! He does not wish to come before his Lord like this. If Gerhard wouldn't mind running home quickly to get the razor . . . "But only if you really don't mind!"

While Gerhard is running through the desolate streets to make sure he will be back in time, Father gradually slips away. He is unaware of his wheezing and burbling breath, only notices our terrified faces, and shakes his head with a surprised, bemused expression:

What is the matter with you? Those are nothing but external symptoms!

1. Throughout this text the term "Protestant" refers to the Evangelical church in Germany without differentiating between its Lutheran and Reformed (Calvinistic) branches. According to information provided by the author, Rehmann's father identified more with Reformed than with Lutheran Protestantism although his background was in the Old Prussian Unity church (see chapter 11, note 2).

2. Barbara Kosta, *Recasting Autobiography: Women's Counterfictions in Contemporary German Literature and Film* (Ithaca NY: Cornell University Press, 1994), 92, 95. See also Michael Schneider, "Fathers and Sons, Retrospectively: The Damaged Relationship between Two Generations," trans. Jamie Owen Daniel, *New German Critique* 31 (1984): 3–51.

CHAPTER 1

1. A low mountain range on the east side of the Rhine, about fifteen miles south of Bonn (*see* chapter 2, note 2).

2. Martin Niemöller (1892–1984) began speaking out against Hitler and the Nazis as a young Protestant pastor in Berlin. Within his own denomination, he attacked the German Christian Faith movement, which believed in the unity of national socialism and Christianity, and he became a leading force in the Confessing church, which was founded at the Synod of Barmen in 1934 to oppose the Nazis' policy of making the German Evangelical church conform to their racial, social, and political doctrines. Niemöller was arrested in 1937 and remained in concentration camps from 1938 until his liberation by the Allies in 1945.

3. The Moravian Brethren (also United Brethren or Herrnhuters) are an evangelical Christian community dating back to the fifteenth century. Taking the Bible as a guide to faith and morals, they emphasize personal conduct rather than religious doctrine. One of their major colonies was in Herrnhut, near Dresden.

4. Reich President Paul von Hindenburg appointed Hitler chancellor on 30 January 1933.

5. The *Ermächtigungsgesetz* of 23 March 1933 solidified Hitler's position by providing him with dictatorial powers barely two months after being appointed chancellor.

CHAPTER 2

1. Part of the western section of the Rhenish Schiefergebirge, the Hunsrück is a range of hills and low mountains between Trier and the Luxembourg border to the west and the Rhine to the east.

2. The range of hills and low mountains on both sides of the middle section of the Rhine, extending approximately from the Ruhr to the Main and from the western border of Germany to a line connecting Dortmund and Frankfurt. The Hunsrück and Eifel constitute its western part, the Taunus, Westerwald, Siebengebirge, Bergisches Land, and Sauerland its eastern section.

3. Keßler appears to have been an obscure pastor appointed to the Prussian or German royal court. Paul von Lettow-Vorbeck (1870–1964) was a general primarily active in German East Africa during World War I. Elard von Oldenburg-Januschau (1855–1937), a Prussian Junker, was a conservative nationalist politician with close ties to Hindenburg.

4. Fritz Reuter (1810–74), in this largely autobiographical book (translated with various English titles), describes the life of the farmers and of the petty bourgeoisie of Mecklenburg (the area bounded to the north by the Baltic Sea) as well as his personal experiences in a realistic, humorous, and socially critical manner.

5. The Baedeker guidebooks, originally prepared and published by Karl Baedeker (1801–59), have provided information for many generations of travelers. *Kladderadatsch*, a Berlin weekly magazine of political satire, was published for nearly a century (1848–1944).

CHAPTER 3

1. Following the end of World War I, the Treaty of Versailles (1919) stipulated that Alsace and Lorraine be restored to France, the Saarland be placed under French administration for fifteen years, the Rhineland be occupied by the Allies for fifteen years, and the right bank of the Rhine be permanently demilitarized. Hence, the popular slogan among Germans during the 1920s and early 1930s: "The Rhine—Germany's river, not her border!" The colors of the flag of the new Germany (Weimar Republic) were red, black, and gold, arranged horizontally; the Belgian flag has the

same colors, but arranged vertically. Both the Dutch and the French flags have the colors blue, white, and red.

2. Then a province of Prussia, Westphalia is an area in northwest Germany primarily significant for the Ruhr coal and steel industry; its capital is the old university town of Münster.

CHAPTER 4

1. The epithet "Gray Eminence" refers to Friedrich von Holstein, a counselor in the German foreign office from 1878 until 1906. Although he was largely unknown outside government circles, he exerted a powerful influence on German foreign policy while operating behind the scenes. He was an opponent of Bismarck's Russian policy.

2. Friedrich Naumann (1860–1919), a Protestant pastor, renounced the ministry to enter politics, first as a member and leader of the Progressive party and later (after 1918) as founder of the German Democratic party. Adolf Stoecker, known for his virulent antisemitism, was chaplain at the court of Wilhelm II. The *Kreuzzeitung* (Newspaper of the Cross) was the organ of the ultraconservative Christian nationalists.

CHAPTER 5

1. In 1918, at the end of World War I, Wilhelm II fled to the Dutch town of Doorn where he lived in retirement.

2. In his younger years, before he became King of Prussia in 1861, Wilhelm I was often referred to as the *Kartätschenprinz*, partly because of his often stated opinion that the revolutionaries of 1848 should be summarily disposed of by the use of grapeshot, and partly because he commanded the Prussian troops in their brutal suppression of revolutionary movements in southern Germany.

3. *Zange* is the German word for "pliers," hence an appropriate term for an area where the working class lives.

4. The great hero of Norwegian legend.

5. The violet stripes and ribbon on the German uniform indicated that its wearer was a member of the clergy. A "southwester," in this context, does not refer to the better-known foul-weather hat used by sailors, but to the headgear common among German co-

lonial troops in the former South-West Africa (Namibia) and subsequently adopted by some regular German military units.

CHAPTER 6

1. Martin Kähler (1835–1912), a Protestant theologian at the universities of Halle and Bonn, advanced the concept of the "historical Christ," whose primary role was to awaken Christian faith. Adolf Schlatter (1852–1938) taught Protestant theology mostly at the University of Tübingen; his voluminous writings, though not ignoring historical issues altogether, did not probe the relationship between faith and history.

2. Karl Barth (1886–1968), a Swiss theologian, expounded what has come to be known as dialectical theology. His eminence as a twentieth-century theologian is based on his voluminous writings, including *Der Römerbrief* (1918; translated as *The Epistle to the Romans*). Barth was an early opponent of Hitler and the Nazi movement.

3. Christoph Friedrich Blumhardt (1842–1919), the son of Johann Christoph Blumhardt (1805–80), succeeded his father as the leader of a Pietistic revival center in Bad Boll. Increasingly in conflict with the church, he gave up the ministry in 1899 and became a member of the Social Democratic party; he was instrumental in the foundation of Christian socialism.

4. During the Franco-Prussian War, the German forces won a decisive victory over the French at Sedan on 1 September 1870. In Wilhelmine Germany, the battle was annually commemorated by patriotic festivities.

5. Adolf von Harnack (1851–1930), a Protestant theologian, was critical of nineteenth-century bourgeois liberalism and focused on theology in its relation to the social problems of his time.

CHAPTER 7

1. Bad Kreuznach is approximately twenty miles southeast of Simmern, the location of the minister's first pastorate.

2. Paul Tillich (1886–1965), a Protestant German theologian, emigrated to the United States in 1933, after having been dismissed from his professorship of philosophy at the University of Frankfurt because of his opposition to the Nazis.

CHAPTER 8

1. This verse from the hymn "Befiel du deine Wege" by Paul Gerhardt (1607–76) is here given in a translation by Frances Elizabeth Cox, as it appears in *Hymns from the German* (1864) with the title "The Trusting Heart."

CHAPTER 9

1. Goethe's novel *Die Wahlverwandtschaften* (1809) deals with the tragic conflict between private desire and social morality. It has been translated as *Elective Affinities*. In the several volumes of prose narratives by the Austrian writer Adalbert Stifter (1805–68) there is none with the title *Rosenhaus*.
2. Peter Cornelius (1824–74), *Weihnachtslieder,* opus 8.
3. "Victoriously we vanquish France, dying like a brave hero," is the opening line of one of the many military-patriotic songs of the Franco-Prussian War. By the time of the Weimar Republic, aggressively anti-French sentiments were no longer permissible, so the girls substitute their own words.
4. One of the East Frisian Islands, which belong to Germany but are situated off the Dutch coast in the North Sea; they are favorite summer resorts.
5. The opening line of a poem by Theodor Storm (1817–88).
6. A major industrial city of the Ruhr; hence from the same area where the mother grew up.

CHAPTER 10

1. The Locarno Pact, signed by Germany and several other European nations in 1925, was expected to usher in an era of international peace and goodwill. In 1936 Hitler denounced the so-called spirit of Locarno and remilitarized the Rhineland. "Reichsbananer" is the father's contemptuous double reference to both the "Reichsbanner" (Banner of the Reich), an organization of the Social Democratic party, and the flag of the Weimar Republic.
2. Paragraph 218 of the German criminal code essentially made abortions illegal, except under very special conditions.

3. The German Christian Faith movement (or German Christians) within the Protestant church was established in May 1932 by the Nazis. They were dedicated to aligning the church with the ideology and political goals of national socialism, combatting freethinkers, socialists, communists, and pacifists.

4. Gustav Stresemann (1878–1929), founder of the conservative German People's party, pursued a policy of reconciliation with Germany's former enemies both as chancellor (1923) and as foreign minister (1923–29).

5. In the battle of Tannenberg, 27–30 August 1914, the German forces won a significant victory over the Russians, taking ninety thousand prisoners.

CHAPTER 11

1. Alfred Hugenberg (1865–1951), a major financier and formerly the head of the Krupp steel manufacturing firm, became Party chairman in 1928 and a member of Hitler's first cabinet in 1933.

2. In 1817, the king of Prussia, Friedrich Wilhelm III, ordered the unification of the two most important branches of Protestantism in Germany, the Lutheran and the Reformed church, forming the *Altpreußische Union* (Old Prussian Unity church). The royal decree was valid in all Prussian provinces, including the Rhineland.

3. A part of the city of Wuppertal in North Rhine-Westphalia.

CHAPTER 12

1. Heinrich Grüber (1891–1975), a mid-level church administrator, founded the Agency to Aid Racially Persecuted Protestants in 1937 and, as its administrator, was put into concentration camps at Sachsenhausen and Dachau (1940–43).

CHAPTER 13

1. *Stahlhelm* (Steel Helmet) was originally a World War I veterans organization founded in 1918. In the 1920s it grew into a large paramilitary political group supporting rearmament. In 1934 it was absorbed into the National Socialist party organization.

CHAPTER 15

1. *Der Stürmer* (The Storm Trooper) was a virulently antisemitic weekly edited by Julius Streicher, who was executed in Nuremberg in 1946. The paper printed obscene and racially abusive cartoons by "Fips," which were designed to be posted on bulletin boards and in display cases.

2. Pechmann's name in German literally means "man of misfortune."

3. "Here is Rhodes, take a jump here!" is a common saying, which first appeared in Aesop's fables and refers to a man who is bragging about an extraordinary jump he made at Rhodes. The remark is attributed to one of his listeners, who wants him to give a practical demonstration of his prowess.

4. Elly Ney (1882–1968) was at one time Germany's most famous concert pianist, admired for her romantic interpretations, especially of Beethoven.

5. Oberwesel is the next town upriver from St. Goar.

6. Hitler dictated *Mein Kampf* (My Struggle) while he was in prison following the beer-hall putsch of 1923. It became the key document of his antisemitic views and his politics of power and world domination.

7. The German title for the "Nederlandtsche Gedenck-clanck" by the seventeenth-century composer Adrianus Valerius. The best-known English version is "We gather together to ask the Lord's blessing."

CHAPTER 16

1. Königswinter is a few miles upriver from Bonn on the east side of the Rhine; Unkel is several more miles upriver from Königswinter.

2. David Friedrich Strauss (1808–74), a German theologian, published *Das Leben Jesu* (1835), which was translated into English as *The Life of Jesus* (1846) by George Eliot. Strauss applied the "myth theory" to the life of Jesus, treating the Gospel like a historical work and denying all supernatural elements.

3. Hanns Kerrl was the head of the Ministry for Church Affairs, established in 1935. His previous appointment had put him in charge of problems of space allocation having to do with Ger-

many's rapid militarization. Thus, in his new position, he was humorously referred to as Minister of Space and Eternity.

CHAPTER 17

1. Rainer Maria Rilke (1875–1926), *Die Weise von Liebe und Tod des Cornets Christoph Rilke* (1899; "Song of the Love and Death of the Standard-Bearer Christoph Rilke"), a youthful prose poem that begins: "Riding, riding, riding, through the day, through the night, through the day."

CHAPTER 18

1. A park-like expanse of grass and trees on the Rhine within the city of Bonn.
2. *Auf den Marmorklippen* (1939) is a story by Ernst Jünger (b. 1895) that has often been read as a literary attack on national socialism.

CHAPTER 19

1. Beuel is a small town directly across the Rhine from Bonn.
2. Worpswede, an artist's colony fifteen miles north of Bremen, is well known for the painters, writers, and designers who have worked there since 1889.
3. Goethe's poem *Die Wandelnde Glocke* (1813; "The Wandering Bell") tells the story of a wayward child who, instead of going to church on Sundays, walks into the fields. One day the bell comes down from the steeple and catches and threatens to cover the child; horrified, the child runs into the church and from that day on never fails to attend the service.

CHAPTER 20

1. Camilo Torres (1929–66) was a Colombian priest and social revolutionary.

Ruth Rehmann was born in Siegburg, near Bonn, in 1922, the daughter of a Protestant minister. Today she lives in Trostberg, a small rural town between Munich and the Bavarian Alps. She was a founding member of *Gruppe 47*, a loose association of German writers established shortly after World War II, whose goal was the revival of a politically conscious and free German literature of high artistic quality after more than a decade of political and intellectual tyranny. Besides having written a number of radio plays and essays, she is the author of many short stories and novels: *Illusionen* (1959; trans. *Saturday to Monday* [1961]), *Die Leute im Tal* (1968), *Paare* (1978), *Abschied von der Meisterklasse* (1985), *Die Schwaigerin* (1987), and *Unterwegs in fremden Träumen* (1993), a historical-autobiographical study of the reunification of Germany in 1990–91 in relation to the First—and for forty-five years the last—All-German Writers Congress that took place in undivided Berlin in 1947. (An excerpt from *Traveling in Alien Dreams* appeared in an English translation in *Dimension*[2] 1.3 [1994]: 470–95.) Rehmann's most recent collection of short stories, *Bootsfahrt mit Damen* (1995), focuses on the theme of aging. An earlier story, "Hausbesichtigung," was published in an English translation as "House Inspection"; it appeared in *Dimension*[2] 2.2 (1995): 226–45. The entry for Rehmann in the standard reference work for contemporary German literature, *Kritisches Lexikon zur deutschsprachigen Gegenwartsliteratur* (1978–), reads in part: "Alert to the important questions of postwar Germany—dealing with the Nazi past and finding moral and political directions—she soon developed a sensitivity to the problems that began to develop in the young Federal Republic. Her stories and novels deal with the loneliness of human beings who lose their ability to communicate verbally and emotionally as they are helplessly enmeshed in modern bureaucracies and defunct traditions."

In the European Women Writers series

Artemisia
By Anna Banti
Translated by
Shirley D'Ardia Caracciolo

*Bitter Healing: German
Women Writers, 1700–1830
An Anthology*
Edited by Jeannine Blackwell
and Susanne Zantop

The Maravillas District
By Rosa Chacel
Translated by d. a. démers

Memoirs of Leticia Valle
By Rosa Chacel
Translated by Carol Maier

The Book of Promethea
By Hélène Cixous
Translated by Betsy Wing

*The Terrible but Unfinished
Story of Norodom Sihanouk,
King of Cambodia*
By Hélène Cixous
Translated by Juliet Flower
MacCannell, Judith Pike,
and Lollie Groth

Maria Zef
By Paola Drigo
Translated by Blossom
Steinberg Kirschenbaum

Woman to Woman
By Marguerite Duras and
Xavière Gauthier
Translated by
Katharine A. Jensen

*Hitchhiking
Twelve German Tales*
By Gabriele Eckart
Translated by Wayne Kvam

The Tongue Snatchers
By Claudine Herrmann
Translated by Nancy Kline

Mother Death
By Jeanne Hyvrard
Translated by Laurie Edson

The House of Childhood
By Marie Luise Kaschnitz
Translated by Anni Whissen

*The Panther Woman: Five Tales
from the Cassette Recorder*
By Sarah Kirsch
Translated by Marion Faber

Concert
By Else Lasker-Schüler
Translated by Jean M. Snook

Slander
By Linda Lê
Translated by Esther Allen

*Daughters of Eve
Women's Writing from the
German Democratic Republic*
Translated and edited
by Nancy Lukens
and Dorothy Rosenberg

Celebration in the Northwest
By Ana María Matute
Translated by Phoebe Ann Porter

*On Our Own Behalf
Women's Tales from Catalonia*
Edited by
Kathleen McNerney

Absent Love: A Chronicle
By Rosa Montero
Translated by Cristina de la
Torre and Diana Glad